DARKLY

DARKLY

HELEN HARDT

Entangled Publishing, LLC
10940 S Parker Rd
Suite 327
Parker, CO 80134
rights@entangledpublishing.com

Amara is an imprint of Entangled Publishing, LLC.

Edited by Liz Pelletier
Cover design by Bree Archer
Cover photography by elnariz/Deposit Photos
cagkansayin/Getty Images

Manufactured in the United States of America

First Edition May 2021

For all the Braden Black fans who clamored for his POV!

Content Warning

Darkly is a super-sexy romance that includes a dominating hero, scenes that depict bondage, kink, and the use of toys, alcoholism and abuse in a character's back story, and massive amounts of alcohol consumption.

Chapter One

Addison Ames hates coffee.

I don't think about Addison Ames much anymore, but sometimes the past inevitably collides with the present—like when I check my Instagram, which also doesn't happen often.

I have no idea how many followers—other than it's in the millions—I have on my Instagram, which is run by my social media team for the most part. Me? I don't have time for social media, but the team insists I post every couple of days, and that it has to come from me, to make it personal.

I'm not sure why anyone gives a damn what I'm doing, but apparently Boston's Blue Collar Billionaire is everyone's business.

I'm a private person by nature, so posing in front of a camera and a team of photographers isn't on my to-do list, either, but I complied, resulting in a spread in *GQ* magazine that I'd prefer to forget. Apparently it matters what I look like in skivvies.

Apparently it matters to a lot of people.

And so does social media.

So no matter how much I hate it, I post on Instagram once a week. My phone is set up to remind me, so when it buzzes this morning with the dreaded admonition, I pull up my account.

And I see Addison Ames's fake smile as she holds up a cup of some hipster drink from a new place called Bean There Done That.

Hanging out at the new Bean There Done That coffee shop in downtown Boston. The cinnamon mocha latte is to die for! @beantheredonethat #sponsored #coffeeisdope #coffeeaddict #coffee #latte #beantheredonethat

Coffee is dope? Really?

She reviles the stuff. I should know. We have a…history.

That history I try not to dwell on.

Normally I ignore her, but for some reason, the post triggers me. Maybe it's because I just got off a heated phone call with a supplier overseas. Maybe it's because I haven't had sex since Aretha and I parted ways. Maybe it's because I haven't visited my club in New York for a while.

Or maybe I'm just sick and tired of all the fakeness in the world, and I detest my part in it.

Addie already has hundreds of comments and thousands of likes for a post that only went live fifteen minutes ago.

You rock, Addison! #luvyourface

Love me some cinnamon mocha latte! Love your lip gloss. What's the brand?

Bean There is the greatest! #whoneedsstarbucks You and I both love cinnamon mocha lattes!

Love you, @realaddisonames!

More and more of the same.

Before I even realize it consciously, I'm typing a comment. I push Send.

Nice try, @realaddisonames. Coffee makes you puke. I should know. #youreafake

I instantly regret it, because snideness isn't my style. The past is the past, and to be honest, part of me admires Addison Ames. She's making a cushy living as an Instagram influencer with millions of followers. She's a hotel heiress, but she's not living off Daddy's money. Or maybe she is, but she's at least contributing to her own expenses.

Yeah, I should delete the comment. I swipe my finger over it, and the red trash can appears. I hover then, my thoughts hurling back through time...

I don't delete it.

I'll never forget her part in what ultimately happened all those years ago, so all admiration aside, I can't let her off the hook. Not this time. I just won't lower myself to her level again.

Not ever.

I shove my phone into my pocket without posting on my own account and gather some documents for my scheduled meeting with Legal. The earlier phone call with the supplier has put a kink in one of our larger contracts, and I'm not looking forward to informing my attorneys.

I whisk by my assistant, Claire. "No disturbances during this meeting," I tell her. "Please let Reception know."

"Sure thing, Mr. Black."

I walk briskly to Conference Room Two.

My brother, Ben, and three of our lawyers are seated.

Already, the headache is clawing its way across my skull.

. . .

A grueling two hours later, I head back to my office.

"Any calls?" I ask Claire.

She hands me a few message slips. I'm kind of old school. I like written messages. Voicemail is fine for personal use, but for work, I want a paper trail. Nothing gets lost in the shuffle—or erased—on my watch. I learned that lesson the hard way long ago.

I leaf through the messages.

"There was one problem, though," Claire says.

I raise my eyebrows and meet her gaze. "What's that?"

"Cindy down at Reception got a call from Addison Ames."

I frown. I guess I should have seen that coming. Why didn't she just delete my comment and move on? "What happened?"

"Apparently she demanded to leave you a voice message. Cindy was a little shaken."

Shaken? Anyone working for me can't be easily shaken. I make sure of it. Which means Addie was being extra bitchy.

"I'll take care of it," I say. "Thanks, Claire."

I close the door to my office, sit down at my desk, and call down to Reception.

"Yes, Mr. Black," a receptionist answers, slightly out of breath.

"Cindy?"

"Yes, this is Cindy. What can I do for you, Mr. Black?"

"I understand you intercepted a call from Addison Ames."

"I did. She demanded to speak to you. I explained you were in a meeting, but—"

"It's okay, Cindy. I know how she can be. I assume the call was recorded."

"Of course. All our calls are."

"Find me the relevant call. I want to hear it."

"I assure you I was very professional," Cindy says, her voice cracking slightly.

"I'm sure you were. Don't worry about this. You're not at fault, Cindy. Just get me the recording."

"Right away."

A few minutes later, the recording lands in my inbox.

"Black, Inc."

"Good afternoon. This is Skye Manning from Addison Ames's office. I'm calling for Braden Black."

I can't help noticing that Skye Manning has a seductively hypnotic voice.

"Mr. Black is in a meeting. I'll have to take a message."

"Addison Ames. The number is—"

"Tell them to connect you to his voicemail."

Addie's voice, as clear as if she were on the phone instead of her secretary or assistant.

A throat clears. *"Actually, I'd like to leave a voicemail, please."* The hypnotic voice once more.

"Mr. Black prefers a paper message."

"He prefers a paper message," the assistant says.

"Oh, for God's sake. Give me the phone." Then, louder, *"This is Addison Ames. Braden and I go way back. Connect me to his voicemail at once."*

"I'm sorry, ma'am. I can't do that."

"That's ridiculous. Give me his voicemail, or I'll have your job."

"I've been told he's in a very important meeting and can't be disturbed. He doesn't give Reception access to his voicemail. As I told the other woman, Mr. Black prefers paper messages."

Addison huffs. *"Fine. Tell him to call Addison Ames right away."*

The call goes dead.

I rise.

I just got my ass handed to me on a platter by my attorneys, and now I find out Addison Ames has abused my receptionist.

She picked the wrong day to fuck with me.

Chapter Two

I walk into the reception area of Addison's office. "Good evening." I glance toward the reception desk.

Addison's assistant, I presume—the one with the hypnotic edge to her voice—gulps, stands, walks out from behind her desk...and unceremoniously drops her purse. Its contents spill over the marble floor.

She parts her lips, and a pulse arrows straight to my groin.

She has the sexiest mouth I've ever seen—full red lips that glisten slightly, and the way they're parted... I could slide my tongue right between them.

I *want* to slide my tongue right between them.

I look down.

Front and center among the contents spilled is...a condom.

Her cheeks redden. "I'm sorry. I was just leaving for the day." She kneels and begins to gather the items.

I kneel down across from her. "Let me help."

She meets my gaze. "That's kind of you, but I've got it." She grabs the condom along with what appears to be a tube of lipstick or something and shoves them back into her purse. Then she gathers the rest and rises.

I stand as well. I'm nearly a foot taller than she is, but she's hardly small. Not a shrinking violet, this one. Her embarrassment over the condom is warranted, I suppose, but *is* she embarrassed? I'm not sure. I can't quite read her, and as a businessman, I've learned to read people pretty much on sight.

But not her. Not the woman with the luscious lips and hypnotic voice. She wears a white silk blouse, skinny jeans, and black pumps. I got a great view of her cleavage when she bent down. Very nice.

What was her name again? She said it on the message, but it escapes me at the moment.

She forces out a laugh. "That was embarrassing. Would you believe I meant to do that so you'd know I'm not hiding a knife in my purse?"

"Do you really think whether you're hiding a knife—or anything else dangerous—would be my first thought when looking at you?"

Definitely not. My first thought was those lips—those lips I'm dying to kiss.

Most likely I'm just horny. It's been a while. Too long—too long since I've participated in any kind of sexual encounter at my club or anywhere else.

For a moment, I imagine this woman—her gorgeous lips parted in that sexy way and her chestnut-brown hair unbound and falling over what I'm sure must be creamy shoulders—bound to my bed naked, her body ready for whatever I want.

And whatever she wants—or rather, what she doesn't yet *know* she wants.

"What woman doesn't want to appear a little dangerous?" she says.

I look into her warm brown eyes, which seem at odds with

her squared shoulders and crossed arms. "You don't seem dangerous so much as someone who likes to be in charge."

"Doesn't everyone?"

My lips quiver. Just a touch, but I feel it all through my body. She amuses me, but even more, she turns me on.

"I guess it depends on whether you're horizontal," I reply.

She blushes along her cheeks and neck. Damn. It's like she lit a match inside me. Still, I've embarrassed her. Should I apologize?

No way. I'm not even slightly sorry.

She draws in a deep breath and clears her throat. "What can I help you with?"

"I'm Braden Black. I'm here to see Addison."

"She's in her office. Did you have an appointment?"

"No. She's an old friend."

"Of course. I'll tell her you're here."

"No need." After what Addison pulled on my receptionist today, I'm not feeling the least bit accommodating. I cock my head toward the closed door. "She in there?"

The assistant nods. "Yeah."

I walk toward Addison's private office, discreetly adjusting my burgeoning erection.

"You can't," she says.

"Sure I can. Watch me." I approach the closed door.

Before I knock, however, the door opens.

"Skye, can you—" Addison's lips curve downward into an angry frown. "What the hell are *you* doing here?"

Addison Ames was always a spitfire, always determined to get what she wants, no matter the cost. A spoiled brat, this one. But she won't get away with treating my employees badly. I'm sure she feels I deserve her wrath, but my people decidedly do not. My past with Addie no longer angers me, but the present? She won't get away with bullying anyone around me.

"Thought I'd come over to tell you if you ever bully my receptionist again, I'll make sure every one of your followers knows the truth about you."

"Truth about *me*? Are you kidding? I'm not the one with something to hide, Braden."

"You have a lot more to hide than a hatred of coffee," I say.

"And what about you? You want your business associates to know—"

"Enough!"

My voice booms through the office as rage swirls through me like a tornado. She wants to threaten me? Bring it on. She'll go down in the dust.

Fortunately, my command seems to stop her.

I can't help looking over my shoulder at her assistant, who's stopped what she's doing as well.

Addison says simply, "Stay off my Instagram."

"I'm not sure you should be telling me what to do," I say, forcing my voice to stay calm, "but I'll play it your way for now."

"Good." Addison stomps back into her office and slams the door.

I stand still for a moment and stare at her closed door, running my fingers through my hair. Then I turn and face her assistant. Her brown eyes are the color of my favorite bourbon, Wild Turkey, and right now, they're wide with surprise.

"She hasn't changed," I say.

"You mean she's slammed a door in your face before?"

I keep myself from smiling. She's...something. Challenging, in her way. "Many people have."

She smiles, her whole face lighting up like something out of a song. "I suppose it's better than someone being nice to your face and then stabbing you in the back."

"I get my share of that, too," I say. "And I agree. It's always better to know where you stand."

I stare at her then. Really stare, taking in everything about her. Those lips, those bourbon eyes. The embarrassed blush on her cheeks and neck.

Her rack.

Yeah, the woman has an amazing rack. Even bound up in the work clothes she wears, it's impossible to miss.

She looks down for a few seconds and then looks back up and meets my gaze. "I guess you know where you stand with Addie," she says.

"Pretty much everyone does."

I allow my lips to bend ever so slightly upward. I suppress a shiver.

"I couldn't help myself," I say. "She hates coffee."

She smiles. "I know. She threw out the latte after the shoot. Perfectly good and hot. I'd have happily drunk it."

"You're a coffee drinker, then?"

She nods. "Absolutely."

"Me too." I stare at her again, unable to shift my gaze from that appealing mouth. "Care to go for a cup..."

Her eyes widen.

I glance toward her desk where her nameplate sits. I remember then, from the phone recording Cindy sent me. Skye Manning.

"...Skye?"

"It's almost six."

I don't miss a beat. "Dinner, then?"

She looks down at her wrinkled silk blouse and skinny jeans. Her gorgeous brown hair is falling out of its ponytail. Again, I imagine it unbound and free, gloriously curtained over her shoulders and back.

She eyes Addison's closed door.

"You don't need her permission," I say.

"I wasn't—"

"Sure you were. Your boss doesn't particularly like me, so you were wondering if going to dinner with me would somehow cost you your job."

She opens her mouth, but nothing comes out.

"Are you good at your job, Skye?"

Skye. I love the way her name sounds as it rolls off my tongue—like a caress.

Her cheeks redden. Again. It's off-brand for me to push a woman who's not interested, but this one *is* interested. She's just not admitting it.

More importantly, *I'm* interested. *Really* interested.

She licks her lips. "Well, I—"

"Let's attack this from a different angle. How long have you been working for Addison?"

"Almost a year."

"Then clearly you're good at your job, or she would have gotten rid of you long ago. Addison might be a pain in the ass, but she's smart. She won't let a good thing go." One corner of my mouth twitches slightly. Man, I want to smile. This woman really makes me want to smile. I've perfected my poker face over the years, to the point where I use it not only in professional situations but also personal ones.

But then I let go.

I smile.

I fucking smile like I've never smiled before.

"I'm not dressed appropriately," she says, meeting my gaze.

"I didn't say we were going to a black-tie affair."

"I don't think—"

I interrupt her. "You look fine. It's dinnertime, and I'm hungry. I don't feel like eating alone for once. Don't make more of this than it is. Your job will be safe."

She opens her mouth, and her stomach lets out a famished

growl. Adorable. Freaking adorable, this woman.

"You're obviously hungry," I say. "Let's go."

She walks toward the door of the office. "Okay. Where are we going?"

I hide my enthusiasm at her acceptance. Why do I feel like jumping for joy? Sure, I haven't had sex in a while, but I'm never this eager.

"I feel like oysters," I say.

"Sounds good," she says as I open the door for her. "Wait," she adds.

"What?"

"I don't even know you. I... I'll meet you there. What restaurant are you thinking?"

Smart of her. I like her more already. "Union Oyster House. You want me to get you a cab?"

"Sure. I guess."

"Or you can drive with me. It's not far, and I personally guarantee your safety."

She pauses a few seconds before turning to me. "As long as you personally guarantee my safety."

"Absolutely."

I lead her to a black Mercedes parked in front of the hotel. My driver emerges and opens the door. The back seat is lush with a cream-colored leather interior. I get in next to her.

"Union Oyster House, Christopher," I say to the man who's been my driver for the past several years.

"Yes, sir." Christopher closes the car door and takes his place in the driver's seat.

We don't talk at first, which is fine with me. Personally, I hate forced conversation. I got enough of that early in my career at events where I had to schmooze my way into what I wanted. I'm good at it, but like social media, I dislike it. After the day I've had, forced conversation sounds akin to torture.

And I'm never in the mood to be tortured.

So I'll wait. I'll wait for her to relax a little bit. Loosen up. I want to know this woman, and it's not because knowing her will piss off Addie. That's merely a fringe benefit. I rarely concern myself with Addison Ames—this afternoon notwithstanding—and as I regard Skye Manning, her tense countenance and her luscious lips, I don't give a rat's ass what the consequences will be.

Addie knows a lot of secrets.

But my desire—fuck, it's more than desire—for her assistant outweighs all of that.

I relax next to her. My knee touches hers, and she tenses even more. I expect her to say something, but she doesn't.

With Skye Manning, I may not always get what I expect.

And I find that realization thrilling.

The car stops, and Christopher opens the door once more. She takes his gloved hand as he helps her out of the vehicle.

"Thank you," she murmurs.

"You're welcome, ma'am."

She cringes slightly at Christopher's use of "ma'am."

I hold back a smile.

"Mr. Black," the maître d' says as we walk into the restaurant, "we're thrilled you're joining us tonight. Your usual table?"

"That'll be great. Thanks, Marco."

Marco personally leads us to my preferred table. It's near the back—a bit more isolated and a bit less noise. I sometimes do business here, so I prefer the additional privacy.

Skye sits when Marco pulls out a chair for her. "Thank you," she murmurs again.

"Sometimes I like to sit at the bar," I tell her once I sit down across from her. "Those shuckers tell the most amazing stories."

I'm not sure why I mentioned the shuckers. For some

reason, I felt like I needed her to know I don't have a habit of bringing women to my usual table.

Skye takes the menu Marco hands her and stares at it as if it's the most interesting thing she's ever seen.

I already know what I'm about to say. I've said it to many women before, but never have I meant it as much as I'm about to.

"Skye."

"Yeah?" Still staring at the menu.

I lift the menu out of her hand. "Look at me."

She meets my gaze.

"I want to take you to bed tonight."

Chapter Three

She freezes.

I stare at her, dare her to break the invisible force between our gazes. She doesn't.

And damn, it's hot.

Just when I think she may never speak again— "Excuse me?" comes out.

"I'm pretty sure I didn't stutter." I again resist the urge to smile, even though I'm sure my eyes are giving me away. "And I'm also sure there's nothing wrong with your hearing."

She clears her throat. "I'm not going to bed with you, Mr. Black."

Yeah, she is. Already I see the signals. Her gaze darts from my eyes to my mouth, and her lips part when she eyes my shoulders. She's interested.

"Call me Braden."

She squirms slightly in her seat. Her brown eyes darken slightly to an almost smolder, and I can't resist creating the image in my mind of her gaze meeting mine right as she climaxes.

It's difficult, but I resist the urge to adjust my tightening groin.

I stay in control.

Finally, she speaks. "Are you always so blunt?"

"I find it useful in negotiations to lay most of my cards on the table outright."

"I guess I didn't realize this was a negotiation."

"Everything's a negotiation, Skye."

She looks down, the first to break the laser focus between us. Nice. Her first act of submission. Where there's smoke…

"This is dinner," she says, "not a negotiation."

"That's where you're wrong. Think about it. You have a reason for everything you do. You may not think it through, but your subconscious does. For example, you have a reason for accepting my dinner invitation."

She returns her gaze to mine. "I do? Other than being hungry?"

"You didn't have to accept my invitation to sate your hunger." I lick my bottom lip, my mouth suddenly dry at the thought of her sating her hunger on *me*.

Her eyelids flutter slightly. "What other reason would I have?"

"You tell me."

"I don't know. Maybe I want to be seen with you."

"That's a crock." I hold back a scoff.

"How do you know?"

"Because you're working for Addison Ames. You work behind the scenes. You're not interested in being seen just for the sake of being seen. You're interested in furthering your career, and you're willing to put in the time."

She clears her throat. "Maybe I want to—"

"Stop this game, Skye. There's only one reason you accepted, and we both know what it is." I burn her gaze with mine. "You want to go to bed with me."

I'm not wrong. I expect resistance. Appreciate it, even. This isn't a woman who's interested in my money or my prestige. This is a woman who's willing to do what it takes to get ahead by working, not fucking. Why else would she have taken a job with Addison Ames? Scrubbing toilets would be more pleasant.

She draws in a breath. "You said you lay *most* of your cards on the table up-front. Most, not all."

She impresses me even more. Not everyone would catch that. "True. I usually keep an ace up my sleeve."

"What's that ace tonight?"

I lower my eyelids slightly, measuring my next words. "I'd be a shitty negotiator if I gave that up so early."

She draws in another deep breath. "I'm still not going to bed with you, Mr. Black."

"Braden," I say again. "And you are, Skye. You definitely—"

A server appears. "Hi, Mr. Black. I'm Cory, and I'll be taking care of you and your lady this evening. Would you like to begin with a cocktail?"

"Absolutely, Cory," I say. "Skye?"

"Vodka martini," she says. "Extra olives."

"Any particular vodka?"

"Grey Goose?"

Cory nods and then turns to me.

"Wild Turkey on the rocks." All the bartenders here know I mean one rock.

Still my favorite, even though I can afford the top-shelf brands now. I guess a guy never really leaves his roots. Coming of age in South Boston, I was lucky to be able to afford a six-pack on a Saturday night.

"Very good. Any appetizers?" Cory asks.

"Yes. A dozen of your best oysters on the half shell, please."

"Any particular ones you want to try tonight?" he asks.

"Three of the Blue Point, and you choose the rest." I nod to Skye. "Do you want anything else?"

She shakes her head. "I love raw oysters."

I smile—a big one. A woman who loves raw oysters. Not that a person who loves raw oysters is hard to come by in Boston, but I can't wait to eat oysters with Skye Manning. Already, I know it's going to drive me wild.

I say nothing. I like silence. I'm comfortable in silence. Most women—at least most women who date me—aren't. Except for Skye Manning. She doesn't try to make the dreaded forced conversation, and I appreciate her all the more.

A few silent minutes later, our drinks arrive.

I lift my glass to my lips and take a drink. The bourbon is smoky and slightly harsh, and I love it. I let it sit on my tongue for a few seconds, let it glide over every inch of my mouth before it trickles down my throat.

And I wonder how my cock will feel jammed up against the back of Skye Manning's throat.

Later, I'll find out.

"Tell me," I say after swallowing, "a little about Skye Manning. You must be something to be working for Addison."

"I have a degree in photography and media from BU. She hired me for my photography skills."

"For her influencing?"

"Yeah."

"But those are selfies."

"Actually, they're not. I take the pictures, and she positions her arm so that it looks like a selfie to the untrained eye."

Why am I not surprised? I grin. Another big one. I've got to watch myself. I never smile this much. "Sounds like classic Addie. Everything has to look perfect."

"How do you know Addison?" she asks.

Now there's a loaded question. The party line is that Addison Ames and I dated briefly when she was eighteen and I was twenty-four, and the relationship didn't end well. The party line is correct. But another several layers exist to the story—layers we don't talk about.

Not ever.

So I'm curious about what Addie may have said to Skye. She knows better than to say anything other than *we had a thing ten years ago*.

"She didn't tell you?" I ask.

"Not really. I'd love to hear it from you."

"But you witnessed the interaction between us."

"Yeah. You weren't overly friendly."

Does Skye mean the plural *you*? Or is she referring specifically to me? I don't bother to ask. I don't care, and also, Cory arrives with the oysters.

"No," I say simply.

"A dozen of tonight's best." Cory sets the tray between Skye and me on the table. "Starting here"—he points—"and going clockwise, we have the Katama Bay from the east coast of Martha's Vineyard, the Moondancers from Maine, the Molly Qs from Mashpee, and then of course the Blue Points from Long Island Sound. All nicely sweet and briny, and I agree, sir, my personal favorites are the Blue Points. Did you have any questions?"

I shake my head, take out my phone, and snap a photo of the oysters that arrived. As I was interrupted earlier, I owe my social media team a post.

Skye raises her eyebrows.

"Got to keep the followers happy," I say.

"How many followers do you have?" she asks.

"Not as many as Addison, but enough."

"I never would have thought you were the social media

type."

Boy, is she right on the nose. "I'm not, really, but people seem to want to know what I'm up to. Probably only because I'm richer than God, which still seems a little unreal to me. I'm definitely a self-made man. I wasn't born into money like Addison and her sister."

I'm not quite sure why I added the part about my being different from Addie. Though it shouldn't, what Skye thinks of me matters. I don't particularly care what people think, so this realization settles in my stomach with a weird jolt.

"Anyway, I never really got out of the habit," I say, not quite willing to tell her I only post because my team tells me to. "You on Instagram?"

"Yeah. Of course."

"What's your handle?"

Her cheeks pink up again. "@stormyskye15."

My lips twitch slightly. I can't get over how much I want to smile a lot around this woman. I'm not sure whether that's a good or bad thing yet. "Stormy? Why not sunny or blue? Or even cloudy?"

"Because I like stormy skies. They're a lot more interesting than blue or sunny skies, don't you think?"

Yes. Stormy Skye. It fits her. "I suppose I never thought about it," I reply. "What's interesting to you about them?"

"The colors. The gray that turns almost to green. The cumulonimbus clouds that stretch for miles but are fluffy on top."

"Cute," I say.

But I don't mean that cumulonimbus clouds are cute. I mean that she's cute. Her. Skye.

Damned cute.

"Why fifteen?" I ask.

"Because fourteen was taken."

Damn. So fucking cute! "I'm tagging you."

"On a photo of oysters?"

"Sure. We're sharing them, so why not?"

Nothing like oysters at my favorite place with a new friend. #oysters #dinnerout #bostonsfinest

Good thing I'm not paid to influence like Addison is. My post-writing skills suck. I tag Skye and the restaurant and then put the phone away and nod toward the oysters. "Ladies first."

She chooses one of the smaller Blue Points and squeezes a few drops of lemon juice on it. Then she scoops it expertly on the fork and into her mouth and takes a sip of her martini. Damn. I was looking forward to watching her slurp the oyster directly onto her tongue.

Fuck.

"Just lemon?" I ask.

She swallows. "Yeah. It's perfect."

"I like a little cocktail sauce."

"Amateur," she says with a slight teasing tone.

I meet her gaze as I take one of the Moondancers, dab it with cocktail sauce, and hold it an inch from my lips. "We'll see who the amateur is by the time this night is over."

Chapter Four

Before I can fully appreciate the look of surprised awe on her dropped jaw, Cory returns to take our dinner orders.

Skye quicky closes her mouth and scans the menu. "I'll have the pan-seared haddock with mashed potatoes and fresh veggies."

"Salad?" Cory asks. "Or a cup of our amazing clam chowder?"

"No thank you."

"Great. And you, Mr. Black?"

"I'll have the fried oysters with a mixed green salad." In my opinion, you can't eat too many oysters.

"Dressing choice?" Cory asks.

"A balsamic vinaigrette." I hand him my menu. "And bring us a bottle of your best white Burgundy."

"Very good." Cory nods and leaves the table.

I expertly slurp the oyster I'm still holding and let it glide down my throat. Perfectly salty and briny, with the zing of tomato and horseradish from the cocktail sauce. An explosion of flavor on my tongue, but all I can think about is what Skye tastes like between her legs.

Sweeter and tangier than any oyster, I'll bet.

Skye is eyeing me as if I'm starring in a porn flick.

Nice.

I dab my napkin to my lips. "Do you enjoy your job, Skye?"

She opens her mouth, but her phone dings. She quickly grabs it out of her purse, her eyes wide. It must be her notifications because I tagged her in the oyster post.

"Congratulations," I say. "You're famous."

She stares at her phone as it continues dinging.

"Turn off notifications," I say, "or it'll drive you bananas."

She follows my advice and then tucks the phone back in her purse. Good. She's not a social media addict. Or she's choosing to focus on our dinner over Instagram. Either way, respect.

"You going to answer my question?" I ask.

"Sure. What question?"

"Do you enjoy your job?"

"Yes and no."

"Meaning...?"

She shrugs. "I get to take pictures, which is what I love to do, but I'm not exactly photographing anything significant."

"Addie trying on scarves isn't going to make it into *National Geographic*," I say. "You're right about that."

She shrugs again. "I'm making good contacts."

"That's true. Maybe you can become the official photographer for Bean There Done That. Getting those sprinkles of nutmeg just right on cappuccinos."

No shrug this time. She goes slightly rigid. "Did you really ask me to dinner to diss my job?"

My comment was a poke at Addison, not Skye. I should apologize, but I'm not ready to be quite so accommodating. At least not yet. "That wasn't my intention. I asked you to dinner because I really want to fuck you."

Man, those words are true. Were and are and becoming even more so by the second. Already I imagine her nipples sore from my attention, her ass gloriously pink.

"How am I supposed to respond to that?" she asks, her voice shaking.

I stare at her, right into those big brown eyes. "I wouldn't be where I am today if I didn't go after what I want." The rasp in my voice surprises me. The need.

God, I want this woman in my bed. Underneath me, writhing, moaning. Tied down, blindfolded, at my mercy, as I tantalize her with my fingers, lips, and tongue.

And then I'm going to fuck her. Fuck her like she's never been fucked before.

How am I supposed to respond to that? I haven't yet answered her question.

So I do.

I raise one eyebrow. "You can tell me you'd like to fuck me, too."

She's trying not to squirm. Already I know her pussy is wet. I can tell when a woman wants me, and this woman wants me as much as I want her. It's in her eyes. It's in the tenseness of her body. It's in the way I know she's squeezing her thighs together to ease the ache in her core.

"Because you do," I say. "Don't try to deny it, Skye. I see it in your eyes." I slurp an oyster and lick a dab of cocktail sauce from the corner of my mouth.

Delicious.

But not nearly as delicious as I know Skye Manning will be.

She bites her lip. "If I were to agree to this… Where?"

"My place." Or my office. My car. Hell, a bathroom stall here at the Oyster House for all I care. I want Skye more than I've wanted any woman in recent—or distant—memory.

I find myself holding my breath, waiting on her response as if it's a lifeline.

"I don't even know you."

"Sometimes it's better that way." True words, though they taste bitter tonight. I *want* to know her. I want to know Skye.

She cocks her head slightly. Is she waiting for some kind of explanation? I won't give one. I want to fuck her, and I won't apologize for it. Sure, she doesn't know me, but she will. I have no doubt. I load cocktail sauce onto another oyster, slurp it, and again lick the dab of sauce from the corner of my mouth.

My pre-dinner drink is long gone, and so is Skye's martini. Our wine arrives, followed by our meals. She takes a bite of her haddock, chews, swallows.

I could sit here and watch her eat and not once get bored. I could tell her my life story, how my brother, Ben, and I worked for our father's small construction company in South Boston. I made some modifications to a pair of safety goggles, which turned out to be state of the art. I patented the design, and Ben and I started Black, Inc. when I was twenty-five years old. Now, at thirty-five, I'm a billionaire, and most construction workers in the world use my goggles. But I've gone far beyond goggles. My investments in real estate, luxury assets, public and private holdings, foreign currency, precious metals—you name it—have made Black, Inc. a household name.

I am the CEO, while Ben handles marketing, and our father, Bobby Black—yeah, he goes by Bobby—is chairman of the board.

Not bad for three guys who never went to college.

But Skye undoubtedly knows my story. Everyone does.

I could tell her what I want to do to her once we get back to my place. How I want to squeeze those round tits and bite her nipples. Tie her up and lick her pussy until she's raw.

Fuck her until morning.

That would scare the hell out of her, though.

So I stay quiet.

No forced conversation. I'm good with that.

"Do you have any pets?" she asks after swallowing a bite of broccoli.

"A dog."

She widens her eyes. "Oh?"

Does that surprise her? It does most, and I've never understood why. Can't Braden Black be a dog person? I love dogs.

"Yeah. A rescue pup. She's adorable."

She smiles and lifts her eyebrows. "You rescued a dog?"

"Is that so hard to believe?"

"Well…no."

Again with the surprise. Animal rescue is something I feel strongly about. I'm very generous to local shelters. I pull out my phone and hand it to her. "She's great. Part border collie and part Australian cattle dog with some other stuff thrown in. I did one of those doggie DNA kits on her."

Her eyes go wide again, this time with appreciation. She's definitely a dog person.

"She's beautiful." Skye gives my phone back.

"How about you? Any dogs?"

She shakes her head. "I love them, but my apartment complex doesn't allow them."

"Then move."

"It's not that easy when you don't have millions sitting around collecting dust like you do." She freezes, her fork halfway to her plate, and she looks away from me. "I'm sorry. That wasn't called for."

I shake my head. "No worries. I'm used to it. But, Skye, I'm not any different from the next person."

"Except that the next person can't buy whatever he

wants."

"I can't, either."

She returns her gaze to mine, her eyes almost taunting me. "Exactly what do you want that you can't buy?"

I don't even have to think about my answer. It rolls right off my tongue.

"You," I say. "In my bed."

Chapter Five

I've never paid for sex, and I never will, but from time to time, women have offered themselves to me for money. Or jewels. Or a luxury sedan. Or first-class plane tickets to Paris.

I've sent them all on their way.

Skye would never do anything so demeaning. She's too challenging. Too sure of herself. Too independent. Too focused.

She carries a condom in her purse, for God's sake. This isn't a woman who puts herself in any situation where she's not in control.

I respect her all the more for that.

I'm not interested in anything easy.

I'm interested in a challenge.

I'm interested in Skye Manning.

Very interested.

"No," she says. "I'm not for sale."

"That's why you'll come willingly." I lower my gaze to her mouth.

That gorgeous mouth, lips glistening and parted just so...

Damn. My cock is already about to explode.

I've got to have her. Tonight.

She grabs her napkin and wipes her mouth.

"Let's go," she says, and my heart pounds.

I eye her plate containing about a third of her fish and a few broccoli florets. "You didn't finish your dinner."

"I'm suddenly not hungry. You want to fuck me? Let's go fuck."

Music to my ears.

"Works for me." I motion to Cory. "We're ready for the check."

. . .

I'll give Skye credit. She doesn't gasp in awe at the sight of my downtown penthouse decorated in black and forest green. No. She's more interested in the black-and-white ball of fur biting my ankles.

"Hey, Sasha." I lean down and scratch the fur on her shoulders.

"She's beautiful." Skye kneels to scratch her behind the ears. "Hi there, Sasha. You're so pretty."

Sasha licks Skye's face for a few seconds but then grows bored and heads somewhere else in the penthouse.

Skye nods toward the black lacquer grand piano that sits in one corner. "Do you play?"

"No."

"Then why do you have a piano?"

"I hire a pianist for my parties," I say. "Guests love it. Do you play?"

She shakes her head. "We didn't have a piano. My dad plays the guitar, though."

I lead her to the piano, where a guitar also sits. "I do, too. Just dabble really. But I love playing classical guitar and then of course some folk songs. All acoustic stuff."

I hope she doesn't ask me to play something, though. In truth, I haven't touched my guitar in ages. My business occupies most of my time, a big reason why I'm not wired for any kind of long-term relationship. I have my own way of working off steam, something I hope will interest the gorgeous woman in front of me. For now, though? I'll settle for a good old-fashioned fuck.

In and out, wham, bam, and thank you, Ms. Manning. I close the distance between us and gaze down at her, zeroing in on her mouth again. I trail a finger over her upper lip and then her lower. "I've wanted to kiss those full lips since I saw you at Addie's office. You have the sexiest mouth I've ever seen."

I crush my mouth to hers.

Her lips are already parted, and I thrust my tongue between them.

She's as soft and supple as I imagined, and she tastes of crisp wine and sweet spice. I deepen the kiss, and she kisses me back as if her life depends on it.

My cock is at full attention now. Full attention—from a goddamned kiss.

A tiny groan, more a vibration than a sound, begins in my throat. Her hands drift up my arms to my neck, and she entwines her fingers in my hair. I need a haircut, but with her next move, I may never get another. She grabs my hair and pulls slightly, a gesture I feel all the way to my toes.

I growl into her mouth and roughly tug on her ponytail, my tongue still tangling with hers. We kiss and we kiss and we kiss until—

"Bedroom," I gasp, breaking the kiss. "God, I want to fuck you so bad. I need to get inside that tight little body of yours."

I need to touch her—her face, her neck, her shoulders.

Undress her, lock my gaze onto those awesome tits of hers, pinch her nipples until she squeals, slide my fingers between her legs, feel how ready she is for me.

And she's ready. Already her musk has perfumed the air in my penthouse. I inhale, close my eyes, inhale again.

Then I grab her hand and guide her down the hallway toward the closed door at the end.

My bedroom.

I touch the brushed brass doorknob, ready to turn it.

She bites her lip. "No."

Frustration wells inside me, and I narrow my eyes. "Excuse me?"

She clears her throat. "No. I can't do this. We barely know each other."

I stare at her. Force myself not to glare at her.

Why is she resisting?

She's turned on, clearly. Her heart is thumping so hard and fast that I can actually see her breasts move. Her cheeks and chest are red with blood flow, and— I inhale. Yes, no mistaking the fragrance.

Fuck. Now I want her even more. I didn't think that was possible.

But it's her choice.

I may have blue balls, but I'll never force a woman into my bed.

I'm gazing at her, into her, and though we're only inches away from each other, the distance seems like miles.

I don't want to be miles away from this woman.

I want her in my arms. In my bed. Underneath my body.

It will happen. Sometimes, patience comes in handy. I don't have a lot of it, but I've learned to fake it. The business world requires patience. Sometimes the personal world does, too. Anything worth having is worth waiting for, and Skye Manning is definitely worth having.

And worth waiting for.

I say nothing. Instead, I take her hand and lead her back to the living area. Sasha prances around us, and I lean down to give her a pat on the head.

"I'm sor—"

"Not a problem, Skye." I pull my phone out of my pocket, clear my throat, and call my driver. "Christopher? Ms. Manning needs a ride home."

Chapter Six

Cold showers suck. They don't work on aching balls, but they do make sure sleep never comes. Not a huge problem. I always have work I can get done.

I'm toweling off my hair when Christopher calls.

"She get home all right?" I say into the phone.

"Yeah."

"Tell me about her place."

"It's downtown, a decent apartment building. Walking distance or a short ride on the T to the Ames Hotel where she works."

"Did you walk her up?"

"Of course. It's late."

"Tell me."

"I didn't see much. Just made sure she got in okay. I heard the dead bolt click, and I left."

"You didn't look inside?"

"Not really. No."

Fuck. I sound like a horny schoolboy. *Did she say anything about me? Do you think she likes me?*

I stop myself before I actually ask those questions. Since when do I care if a woman likes me? I can get twenty women over here to take Skye's place in a heartbeat.

"Thanks, Christopher," I say. "Good night."

"Good night, Mr. Black."

I set my phone down on the counter and continue drying my hair. I throw the towel in the hamper and put on a pair of old jeans and a white T-shirt. I slide into my slippers, grab the phone, and leave my bedroom. Down the hallway is my home office.

Guess where I'll be spending the night?

Not a problem. I love to work. I love the ins and outs of business, finance, marketing, investing.

I see it as a game—a game I almost always win.

Funny. That's usually how I see my female conquests as well, and it's usually a game they're more than willing to play, obeying my rules. And I have some very particular rules. Very particular tastes.

But Skye Manning? I can tell she'll be a challenge.

She may not like my rules.

But she'll succumb eventually.

I'll make sure of it.

Because I can never resist a challenge.

· · ·

After spending a good portion of the night dealing with the shitstorm that resulted from yesterday's meeting with Legal, I finally fall into bed around three a.m.

But my sleep is anything but restful.

Dreams of Skye Manning plague me.

That kiss—how perfectly her lips aligned with mine, the delicious flavor of her mouth, her intoxicating scent of raspberries and roses. Red roses.

So much of her is still a mystery—the color of her nipples, the taste of her pussy, the way she'll look lying naked, her wrists bound to my headboard.

Regardless of my sleepless night, I rise at six a.m. sharp because my day is full of more meetings to deal with the fallout from the supplier who's in breach of contract. Another cold shower. They still suck, but they give me the burst of energy I need to face each day with renewed vigor. My personal physician recommends them for stress tolerance, but I learned the benefits of cold-water bathing long ago, when I was just a kid. Our water heater broke, and we couldn't afford a new one, so it was cold bathing for several months. I hated it.

But looking back, in the midst of the shitshow that was my childhood, I recall feeling better after those cold showers.

Alert.

Ready.

Alive.

From that time on, I knew if I wanted to make something of myself—and I had a burning desire to do so—cold showers would be a part of my life. They taught me willpower and courage—it takes sheer will to stay under the cold when the dreamy hot water is only a flick of the faucet away.

But as I said, despite the myth, cold showers do *nothing* for aching balls. Nothing to ease the desire for Skye Manning, either.

No matter. There's work to be done, and I have never let anything—or anyone—interfere with my goals. An hour later, I'm dressed to the nines in a navy-blue custom-tailored suit and sitting behind my desk at my offices in downtown Boston, answering emails and doling out tasks to staff members.

"Find me a new supplier," I tell them. "We'll pay whatever's necessary to get this damned contract filled with time to spare."

A chorus of *Yes, Mr. Black*s later, I'm confident the job will be done and done well. I tolerate nothing less.

And I'm right. By eleven thirty, a new supplier is located and a new contract drafted.

I allow myself a sigh of relief.

My stomach growls, and I chuckle out loud. I skipped breakfast this morning to get here and get moving on today's problem. I haven't thought about food until now.

I'm hungry.

For lunch.

And for something else.

Now that the crisis is handled, Skye Manning is back in my thoughts. It's not enough that she plagued my dreams. She's starring in my daydreams as well. And daydreams aren't something I'm used to. I focus. I get the job done. I don't waste time on daydreams.

Today, though, the daydreams are unusually persistent.

Which pisses me off.

Hell, it's time for lunch, and I've earned a break.

I know exactly where to go…and what I'll find there.

Chapter Seven

Addison's office is locked, which is odd, but no matter. I've got today's *New York Times*, and I'll wait. I lean comfortably against the wall and peruse the headlines.

And then I see her.

Skye Manning.

She walks toward me, her hair bound in a ponytail again, her clothing similar to what she wore yesterday. Skinny jeans, but this time black sandals instead of pumps, a pink button-up blouse, and a navy blazer. The blouse is like a second skin, and those tits…

Damn.

She approaches me and clears her throat.

I lower my paper, and my lips twitch slightly, seemingly on their own.

"May I help you?" she asks.

"Sure. You can open the door."

She quickly retrieves the key from her purse and unlocks the office. "Addie's not here."

"Good," I say.

She opens the door, walks in, and sets her purse on her desk. She takes out her phone quickly and checks something, her ass looking delectable in denim.

My heart is racing, but I'm determined to play it cool. Just her presence affects me in a way that's totally foreign to me. I affect her, too. I saw it in her eyes zeroing in on my lips before she scurried to her desk.

One of us must make the first move or we'll both end up wanting…and though I'd love for it to be Skye, already I know it won't be.

"Skye," I say.

She turns. "Why are you here?"

I stalk toward her. "For this."

Without so much as a thought, I grab her and kiss her. Hard. She gasps, and I thrust my tongue into her mouth, exploring at first but then taking. Another raw kiss, and she pushes her breasts into me, moves her hips.

I groan into her mouth.

And I'm lost. Lost in Skye, and all we've done so far is kiss.

My body's on fire, and I push into her, letting her feel my erect cock against her belly. I'm ready. So ready to touch every part of her, bind her and spank her, fuck her hard. Fuck her fast.

And then fuck her slowly, savoring every minute.

She grabs my head and threads her fingers through my hair, pulls me toward her, and explores me as I explore her, our tongues locked in a sword fight, our lips sliding against each other. Nothing matters. Nothing except this amazing kiss.

Until I break away.

If I don't, I won't be able to stop. And I doubt she will be, either.

I draw several ragged breaths into my chest, my heart

racing. Her lips are sexy and swollen, her chest rosy, her nipples hard and protruding against the clingy fabric of her blouse. I resist the urge to tweak one.

"Dinner tonight," I say huskily. "I'll pick you up here at seven. And this time, Skye, you're coming to my bed. Get used to the idea. It's going to happen."

I turn and walk out the door.

. . .

Sitting next to me in the back seat of my car, Skye clears her throat. "Where are we eating tonight?"

"My place."

"Oh? You cook?"

"I have a personal chef. She's taking care of everything."

Skye nods.

Marilyn's been with me a few years now, and she knows my tastes. Her skills as a chef are top-notch, and I pay her more than she'd earn in a five-star restaurant. The hours are better, too. She's adept at all cuisines, but Italian is her specialty.

A robust Italian dinner will set the perfect mood for what I have planned for tonight.

Odd, how I want this woman—Skye—so badly. Is it the thrill of the chase because she turned me down last night?

No.

It doesn't happen often, but I've been turned down before. I simply move on.

So what is it about her?

She's an enigma to me. A woman who's focused and values control, yet something about her screams submissive to me. My instincts about submission haven't been wrong yet, so I trust them.

Beyond instinct, though, I know little about Ms. Manning

and how she'll react to my particular tastes in the bedroom.

I know only that I must have her.

We arrive and take the elevator to my place. Sasha greets us at the door.

"Hey, sweet girl," I say, petting her. "Annika will take you out, okay?"

"Is Annika the chef?" Skye asks.

"No. She's my housekeeper. She's probably upstairs." I quickly send a text.

Within a few minutes, Annika, gray-haired and spry, whisks into the room, leashes Sasha, and walks her out, never saying a word. I prefer my staff to be the silent type. We get along well that way. Christopher's the most talkative of the bunch, and he's hardly a conversational wizard.

A sweet yet pungent fragrance punctuates the air—tomato and basil from the Italian meal Marilyn prepared. I inhale the scent again, my mouth already watering. I specifically requested that she not cook lasagna. It's too filling for what I have planned for later this evening. Penne arrabiata, full of spicy heat, and veal Marsala, less spicy and more filling but not so much to make a person uncomfortable after the meal.

Skye stands, fidgeting with her hands and looking delectable.

"Make yourself comfortable," I say.

Her lips quiver just a touch, and she continues fiddling with her fingers.

She's nervous, of course. But I don't want her to be nervous. Perhaps a drink will help.

"Wine?" I ask. "Or something stronger?"

"Wine is good."

"Red?"

"Sure."

"How about a Chianti Classico? It'll go well with dinner." I pull a bottle from my ornate wrought-iron rack.

She nods and removes her blazer. "What's for dinner?"

"Penne arrabiata and veal Marsala. You like Italian?" I open the bottle, pour two glasses, and hand one to Skye.

She takes a sip. "Yes. Love it."

"Good."

She smiles hesitantly, and I get the feeling she's trying to draw one out of me.

As much as I want to smile in Skye's presence, some inner instinct tells me not to give in.

So I keep my lips together.

"Marilyn set out some antipasti for us. Follow me."

I lead her to the kitchen. She widens her eyes at the marble and hardwood as I show her to the island surrounded by barstools. The antipasti—olives, melon, salami, prosciutto, and small blocks of white cheese—rests on a silver platter. A cruet of extra-virgin olive oil and another plate holding short wooden skewers sit adjacent.

"Please." I wave my hand over the platter. "After you."

"No, go ahead," she says. "I'd like to enjoy the wine for a few minutes."

"Of course." I take a skewer, load it up with the antipasti, and then drizzle olive oil over it. I hold a napkin to catch the drips and pull the green olive off with my teeth.

And I imagine those teeth around her nipple.

My groin tightens further. The peppery and slightly bitter flavor of the olive oil always tantalizes my tongue. Why is Italian food so sexy? All I want to do at this moment is tear all her clothes off and drizzle olive oil over her naked body, lick it off in its peppery glory.

Damn.

She stands frozen, watching me intently, not making any move toward the food.

"Please," I say again after swallowing.

She nods, grabs a skewer, and pushes a piece of cheese

onto it. Then an olive, a piece of folded prosciutto, and cantaloupe. She moves it toward her mouth.

"You forgot the best part, Skye."

She lifts her brows.

"The olive oil." Even I notice the rasp in my voice. Olive oil. Dripping over Skye. Glistening. Our bodies sliding together like—

"I'm watching my fat intake," she says.

I eye her body. No problem with fat intake. None at all.

"It's only a bit. Here." I take the skewer from her and drizzle the light-green liquid onto the food. "Try it."

She pulls the chunk of cantaloupe off with her teeth.

I inhale sharply.

Fuck, she's sexy. That mouth. Those lips. That perfect way she parts them.

She pulls the next piece, the prosciutto, off her skewer.

I inhale again. "Your mouth. Watching you eat is better than porn."

She widens her eyes and meets my gaze.

Her brown eyes are shining.

She's turning me on...and she knows it.

Which turns me on even more.

My flesh is hot, so hot. Damn. We're only on antipasti, and I'm ready to fuck her senseless.

She sets the skewer down on a napkin, takes another sip of wine, and winces slightly.

"You don't like the wine?" I ask.

"No, it's fine."

"You made a face."

She widens her eyes, which have darkened to a milk chocolate. Fuck.

"I did? I didn't mean to."

"You winced a little."

"Did I?"

"Yeah, what were you thinking?"

She hesitates for a few seconds. Then, "Just thinking I'd rather be drinking Wild Turkey."

I can't help myself. I laugh. I really, really laugh, and damn, it feels good, and I can't remember why I was holding back earlier. Wild Turkey? She's a fan of my favorite bourbon? Perfect. Just perfect.

"Why didn't you ask for it, then?"

"I don't know. You offered wine."

"Ask for what you want here, Skye. Trust me, I plan on asking for what *I* want and then taking it."

I pick up her wineglass and leave the kitchen. At my bar, I pour a lowball glass of the distinctive amber liquid and then walk back to Skye.

"I'm a Wild Turkey fan myself," I say.

"I know. You ordered it last night."

"But you didn't. Why?"

"I like a vodka martini with oysters."

"Good call, but this goes with everything." I hand her the glass. "I added one ice cube. Hope you like it that way."

"Yeah, I do. I think watering it down just a touch brings out the flavor."

"A Wild Turkey connoisseur, huh?"

"I'm from Kansas, so—"

Her admission surprises me more than a little. I'd pegged her for an East Coaster like myself. "You're not from here?"

She takes a sip of bourbon and smiles. "You didn't notice my lack of accent?"

"Yeah, but I just figured you were from somewhere else on the East Coast. Not the Midwest."

"Why?"

I could go into a long tirade about how she screams East Coast to me. How she's fast-paced and focused, how she's working toward a career in photography by taking a position where her photos will get noticed, how she dresses in body-hugging yet classy clothes. Of course, I'm generalizing, but most people I know from the Midwest or West Coast move slower. I simply shrug. "You look like a city girl."

"Kansas has cities."

"True, but not like the East Coast."

"Also true," she says. "I come from a farm, anyway."

"A farm?" I lift my eyebrows. She astonishes me once more. "A real, honest-to-goodness farm?"

"Uh…yeah. Does that surprise you?"

"A little. Do you milk cows and everything?"

She rolls her eyes. "I didn't grow up on a dairy farm, Braden. I grew up on a corn farm. You know, knee-high by the Fourth of July?"

"That's interesting." Not the corn so much as the fact that Skye Manning is so *not* a farm girl in my eyes. She's the antithesis of a farm girl.

"Why did you leave?"

She lets out a short laugh. "Because I've taken about all the photos of corn I want to take in my career."

I resist the urge to join in her laughter. "Right, photography. Makes sense." I gaze at her, my eyes never leaving hers, as I take the last sip of my wine. "Ready for dinner?"

"Sure, let's eat." She takes another small sip of the bourbon, sets the glass down, and licks her lips.

God.

That mouth.

My cock is straining against my pants. I'm done waiting. So done.

I meet her gaze and burn her with my own. Her eyes are wide with an answering need, her lips parted and glistening.

I stalk toward her, my chest already rumbling with a groan.

"Fuck dinner."

Chapter Eight

I grab her hand and lead her to my bedroom.

I gaze at her for a moment as we stand in front of the closed door. The door to the room where I'll finally fuck Skye Manning. Maybe get her out of my system.

But I know already it will take way more than one fuck to get this woman out of my system. The thought both frightens and exhilarates me.

Her ponytail has come slightly loose, her cheeks are pink, her nipples hard. A lovely picture, but again, my gaze is drawn to her mouth.

That fucking amazing mouth.

I pull her toward my body and push my erection into her belly. "Feel that?" I whisper, tugging on her earlobe—God, her flesh is like silk beneath my tongue—with my teeth. "Feel what you do to me. You won't leave me wanting tonight, Skye. I'm going to fuck you."

I let her go and open the door to my bedroom.

She walks forward, her demeanor almost trance-like.

Not the first time a woman has reacted with awe at seeing

my bedroom. It is truly spectacular, decorated in mahogany with navy-blue and ivory accents. All my furniture is custom designed and my bedding made of the finest silk imported from India. But the pièce de résistance is the window—which is actually a whole wall that overlooks the Boston Harbor.

Skye walks toward it, still moving as if an unseen force is manipulating her.

Little does she know that unseen force will soon be me.

I stand next to her, looking out over the yachts in the marina.

"One-way glass," I say. "We can see out, but no one can see in."

"Is one of those yours?" she asks.

"The *Galatea*, yeah. Ben's got her out tonight."

"Ben your brother?"

"Only Ben I know. He's more into the boat thing than I am."

"How can you *not* be into the boat thing? They're so beautiful." She sighs softly.

"They're a damned lot of work." True words, but I want to take Skye out on the *Galatea*. Just the way her eyes are shining makes me want to buy her a fucking armada.

"But don't you—"

I tug on her ponytail, resisting the urge to give it a harder yank to bring her to her knees. "Do you really want to talk about boats right now?"

She turns and assesses the decor with wide eyes. She seems to zero in on my headboard—or rather, the notches and blunt metal objects placed just so. The design is my own, and each piece serves a vital purpose.

One I hope to share with her.

She turns and regards my highboy dresser and chest and then the mahogany wardrobe next to my walk-in closet. I keep secrets in that wardrobe—secrets I'm definitely going to share with Skye.

She turns toward the opposite wall where two wingback chairs in navy with gold flecks sit. Then she returns her gaze to the bed.

"This is amazing," she says.

Oh, she has *no* idea. I'll introduce her to all the pleasures of pain and submission. And if she takes to my lessons well...

New York.

Black Rose Underground.

But that's way in the future.

Damn. The future. I don't think of women in terms of the future, so why the hell am I considering any of this?

For now, I'm going to fuck her into tomorrow.

"It's a nice place to come home to at night," I finally reply.

"I'll say. If this were mine, I'm not sure I'd ever get out of bed."

I resist the urge to groan as I remove my suit jacket. "I like the sound of that."

I stand in my white shirt, tie still knotted but loosened, pants, and glossy black leather oxfords. I don't plan on undressing anytime soon, even though my cock has other plans and really wants to be free.

"Take off your clothes," I say, "slowly."

Will she obey?

I swallow as I wait to find out.

Then she begins to unbutton her blouse.

I warm all over, and I'm abruptly aware of the thumping of my heart.

One button. Two buttons. Three—

Was slowly my idea? Big mistake.

I yank the shirttail out from her jeans and finish the job by ripping the two halves apart. Buttons fly, one pinging the wardrobe door but most of them falling quietly onto the plush ivory carpeting.

"Couldn't wait," I say huskily.

Her nipples press against the lace of her bra.

Nice. She likes it when I take charge. When I get rough.

I flick one nipple over the fabric. Time to see more of her gorgeous flesh. "Take it off," I growl. "I want to see those tits."

Again, she obeys. Damn. She fucking obeys.

This is going to work between us. Sweet Skye Manning, who's focused and prepared and always in charge, is going to submit to me.

Fuck.

She unclasps her bra slowly, eases her arms out, and lets it fall to the floor at her feet. Her ample breasts fall gently against her chest.

They're even more beautiful than I imagined. A C cup, I'm guessing, and perfectly round and taut, her nipples pinkish-brown buds against larger-than-average areolas.

I lower my eyelids and groan. My tie isn't binding, but it's too much now. I need freedom from any restriction around my neck, freedom to enjoy the rest of Skye's striptease. I remove the tie and toss it on the floor. Then I unbutton the first two buttons of my crisp white shirt. Yes, freedom. I inhale deeply, resolving to soothe my pounding heart.

I'm in deep with this one. Too fucking deep. I know this already, but I have no intention of stopping. My cock aches, and I desperately need release.

But first, those tits. Are they as soft as they appear? As lovely to the touch as they are to my eyes?

I reach toward her, and she shivers as I cup her breasts.

Damn. Twice as good to the touch. They're perfectly round in my palms, soft as satin.

"Beautiful," I murmur and thumb both her nipples.

She sighs softly.

"Do you like your nipples sucked? Or pinched?"

"All of the above," she says.

"Oh, baby. We're going to get along just fine." I twist her nipples just hard enough to make her groan. "You like that?"

She closes her eyes. "Mm-hmm."

"Say yes, Skye. Always say yes. I need to hear the word."

"Yes. I like that, Braden."

My cock jerks at the caress of my name on her lips—those gorgeous lips and that hypnotic voice. I want to hear it again and again, like a soft symphony playing in the background of my mind.

"Your voice is sexy. I love the way you say my name. Say it again."

"Braden."

"Again."

"Braden."

I close my eyes and imagine what's to come. Then I open them and meet her gaze.

"Now, tell me what we're going to do here tonight."

"You're going to fuck me, Braden."

"Yes, I'm going to fuck you."

She's standing in front of me, her sandals and jeans still on, her breasts exposed, her nipples hard and ready.

"You say you like your nipples pinched."

"Yes," she says on a soft sigh.

"What else do you like?"

"Whatever you want to do to me."

The words seem to fall off her tongue with no thought or effort.

Just as I hoped.

"Take off the rest of your clothes, Skye."

"Are you going to take yours off?"

"Does it matter?"

She opens her mouth to respond, but I stop her with a gesture.

"Undress."

She swallows, kicks off her sandals, and then unsnaps and unzips her jeans. She slowly lowers them over her hips and peels them off her legs until she's standing only in her panties.

Her body is long and lean, her tummy a delicious curve. I resist the urge to gawk at her like an adolescent, but man, she makes me feel like I'm untried.

It's uncomfortable.

And extremely erotic.

"Keep going," I say.

She wiggles out of the panties and kicks them a few feet away, next to my tie. Her mound is stubbled with a few days' growth of dark hair, and her pink pussy peeks out at the apex of the triangle. I lick my lips in anticipation.

"Very nice." I inhale, breathing in her musky scent. The sweetest perfume. "I can smell you. You're ripe. Wet. Aren't you?"

She bites her lower lip. "Mm-hmm."

"What did I tell you?" I say sternly. "About using the word?"

"Yes. Yes, I'm wet."

"Who are you wet for, Skye?"

She clears her throat. "For you. I'm wet for you, Braden."

I grab her then and crush our mouths together. Her tongue wanders out to meet mine in another raw kiss. I slide my lips against hers as I plunder her mouth.

I trail one hand over her shoulder to her chest, cupping a breast and pinching a nipple. She inhales sharply, breaking our kiss just slightly. Then I travel downward with my hand, over her belly, and touch her clit gently.

"Oh!"

I swirl the tip of my finger over her clit again, and then I tweak it. Hard. She groans, and I move lower to slide my fingers through her folds.

Slick, wet, and silky. God, paradise.

I can't fucking wait.

This time, I break the kiss. "So wet," I growl in her ear. "I'm going to drive my cock into you, Skye. I'm going to drive so far into you that you'll be sore tomorrow. Every time you move, you'll think of me inside you, taking you, fucking you. You'll know I was here."

Chapter Nine

I slide a finger deeper into her heat.

She inhales sharply.

Heaven. Pure heaven. She's going to be perfect around my cock. "God, you're so tight. I can't wait to fuck you."

For the moment, though, my finger is at home like it's never been before. I slide it in farther, probing the anterior of her wall, searching for her G-spot. It's different in every woman, and when she sighs softly, I know I've found it. I massage it lightly. Just a touch. No need to send her over the edge yet. Despite my aching dick, I've learned not to rush these things. A ripe woman, like a fine wine, is best savored.

I continue to finger fuck her, adding another while working her clit with my thumb. Her legs wobble, but I steady her, keeping her in the perfect position for the things I'm doing to her.

"Feel good, baby?"

"God, yes," she sighs. "So good."

I nip her earlobe with my teeth. "By the end of this night," I whisper, "I promise this will be the least of what you remember."

Words I take to heart.

Already, she's so responsive to every touch, every feather of my fingers inside her. I'm so fucking hard, but first…

I push her down on the bed, move to spread her legs, kneel down, and close my eyes.

"I need to taste you."

I slide my tongue over her clit, finally sampling her juices that have consumed me since I first inhaled after our kiss at the door. That intoxicating mixture of tangy and sweet, with an extra zest that is Skye's alone—like a hard peach cider. So delicious.

I lap at her, licking the wetness from her inner thighs and then shoving my tongue into her heat.

"God, you taste good," I say against her thigh.

She raises her head and looks at me between her legs. "Are you ever going to undress?"

"In time," I say. "But if you ask again, I won't."

No time like the present to let her know who's in charge here.

I am.

No one else.

And a quick, hard fuck will prove it better than any words can. I'll savor her later.

With a brisk move, I flip her over so she's lying facedown, her legs hanging off the bed. I pin her in position. "Don't you dare move."

I fumble with my belt, my zipper. Then I remember… A condom. A fucking condom. God, how I wish I could experience her unsheathed, cock to pussy with no barrier.

I grab the foil packet out of my pocket, rip it open, push my pants and boxer briefs over my hips to mid-thigh, and sheath myself as quickly as I can.

She looks over her shoulder—

I push her back down harshly. "I said don't fucking move!" Then I groan as I position myself and plunge deep into her. "Fuck, yeah."

Fuck. Yeah. Nothing poetic about those words, but they say what my whole body feels. She's tight and snug, warm and perfect against me, and for a moment, I wish I didn't need the rubber. That's how perfect she feels, how much I want her, and I know it would be ten times better with no barrier between us.

But I know better. I'm always careful. For now, though, I lean down, trapping her under me to give her a slight taste of the control I expect in the bedroom. "Don't move, Skye. I'll stop if you do. Do you understand?"

"Yes," she whimpers.

I suck her earlobe between my teeth. "You're so damned tight. Fuck, you feel good."

I rise slightly, still inside her, and plant my hands on her shoulders—not hard enough to hurt but hard enough that she can't move. She's trapped, at my mercy.

Exactly as I want her.

Completely under my spell.

I pull back and thrust into her again, relishing how well she grips me. How her body encases mine. I close my eyes then and surrender to the feelings in my body. Sparks ignite between us—sparks that are new to me. Slightly disconcerting, even, but that thought is fleeting. I open my eyes, fully expecting to see a visible current between us.

I plunge in and out of her, slowly at first and then increasing my speed. My shirt brushes her lower back as I push back inside her, her walls gripping me and turning me inside out.

She grasps the comforter in her fists, still immobile, as I fuck her and fuck her and fuck her. She tightens around me, and I know she's getting close to orgasm. The thought enthralls me.

I want this to last… To last…

But already my balls have tightened, and my time's up.

"I'm going to come." I thrust and thrust and thrust, each time her pussy grasping me more tightly, more perfectly. "Come with me, baby. Come with me."

My words are a command—one I know already she'll obey.

"Oh my God!" she cries.

And that's all it takes for me. I burst, shoving into her so hard as my seed shoots from my balls through my cock and outward. Every cell in my body seems to pound in time with my heartbeat. Skye pulses in time with me, each stroke, as I finish inside her.

Chapter Ten

Skye's eyes are heavy-lidded, dreamily satisfied yet with a touch of surprise. Shock, even. Yes, she just climaxed, but I know that look. I've seen it before.

This was her first orgasm. Ever.

I resist the urge to smile smugly. This isn't the first time I've granted a woman her first orgasm. Will it be the last?

The fact that I'm even thinking that question disturbs me more than a little.

I'm not done, not by a long shot. After disposing of the condom, I undress. Quickly. Really quickly. So quickly I actually surprise myself.

Skye gasps.

She stares into my eyes and then drops her gaze to my semi-erect cock sans condom.

"Move to the head of the bed," I say. "Lie on your back and grab two of the rungs of the headboard."

She widens her eyes and continues staring at me. Will she obey?

"Now, Skye." My voice is firm.

She hastily scoots backward as I demand, rests her head on one of the pillows, and grabs the headboard.

"I'm not going to bind you," I say.

I almost never bind a woman the first time, unless she asks for it. I want to ease Skye into my world slowly. I don't want to scare her. I want to entice her.

Will she let her guard down? Will she relinquish her control to me?

As if she's testing me, she lets go of the headboard and meets my gaze, hers on fire.

Yes, I expected this. Someone as focused and driven as Skye will resist. I won't punish her for defying me.

Not yet.

"Grab the rungs," I say calmly but darkly.

"No, I won't. You can't tie me up."

"I think I just said I wasn't going to."

"I—"

"Grab the rungs, Skye. Now."

She grabs the rungs.

Nice. I didn't have to prod her. She obeyed my last command instantly. I warm inside. This will work. I'm determined.

"Good," I say and scoot on the bed so I'm straddling her, my cock dangling at her mouth. "Get me hard again. Use that sexy mouth of yours."

She parts her lips—God, she's fucking hot—and slowly trails her tongue over the bottom one. I push my cock between her lips slowly, letting her go at her own pace. When I hit the back of her throat, I'm only a little over halfway in. She lets go of one rung—

"Don't let go!" I say through clenched teeth.

She quickly re-grabs the rung.

Nicely done, Skye. Mental binding is the ultimate test of submission. After tonight, I'll know if she fits in my world.

Full introduction takes time, and with Skye Manning, I'm suddenly willing to invest all kinds of time.

I want her that badly.

I still move in and out of her mouth slowly. My erection has returned in full force. I could stay in her mouth forever—that's how good it feels. That's how much I love watching my cock slide between those sexy lips, feeling the soft pressure, the warm wetness. A good blow job will suck the life force out of a man, bring him to his knees. It's a fucking art. Skye may not be the most experienced, but my God, she makes up for it in enthusiasm.

She worships my cock with her mouth.

And it's driving me wild.

So wild that I must stop, or I'll shoot down her throat.

And that's not my plan. Not yet.

First a little worship of my own.

I remove my cock from her mouth and ease down her body. "Your tits are perfect," I say, and then I suck one between my lips while lightly pinching the other.

Goose bumps erupt on her flesh.

I suck, nibble, bite.

Her beautiful tits are swollen, pink, nipples hard and taut—their texture like silk over a rigid pencil eraser. Each nibble inches its way straight to my dick. She's so responsive, writhing and grinding under me. This woman loves to have her tits sucked, pinched, bitten.

I can't wait to get nipple clamps on her.

The muscles in her arms go rigid. She wants to let go of the headboard. She's dying to let go. But she won't. Already I know she won't.

Skye Manning is a perfectionist. Her control will be her undoing, because her control requires perfection. I told her not to let go, so she won't. To do so would be to fail. Skye won't fail. I don't know how I know this about her so soon, but I do. It's written in every soft groan she makes, every tightening of her hands on the rungs.

And I find that beautiful.

"You're beautiful," I say after releasing her nipple. I move down her body, raining soft kisses on her belly and then her vulva. "I want to eat you again, but damn, I need to get inside that hot pussy. Fuck." I move from the bed and return with a condom.

"Let me do that," she says.

Her offer is tempting, but perfectionist or not, she still has much to learn about being in my bed.

I meet her gaze, my teeth clenched. "Don't you fucking move."

"Braden, I want to—"

"I said don't move!"

She inhales sharply and looks up.

"I'm going to fuck you again, Skye, and this time, I'm going deep."

God, so deep.

I put the condom on and maneuver her legs over my shoulders, opening her.

Then I thrust in.

She bites her lip as I tunnel all the way into her body. So tight and so welcoming. I wonder if I'll ever get enough of her suction around me.

"That's good," I grit out. "Sweet pussy. Sweet Skye."

Her shoulders are creamy, her lips glistening. I long to lower my head, kiss her mouth, her cheeks, her neck.

But that would require me to shift angles, and I don't want to lose the depth I'm getting. God, she feels good around me. So fucking good.

Though I can tell she wants to, she doesn't let go of the rungs.

She watches me, gazes into my eyes, and her pussy

responds. Already I feel her walls clenching, her climax imminent.

"God, Braden!"

She grasps the rungs with white knuckles as I pound into her, grazing her clit, my balls slapping against her ass.

She moans.

She screams.

"That's it, baby. Come. Come all over me. Come for me. Only me."

I fuck her harder and harder.

She pulses around me, and a tingling intensity builds in my balls. I'm ready again.

"Fuck. Skye. Yes!" I roar as I thrust deeply and come, our climaxes in perfect tandem.

My God.

I'm in deep. Again, both frightening and exhilarating.

She meets my gaze.

I roll off her onto my back, one arm across my eyes.

Pure euphoria consumes me, and I lie immobile for several moments, trying to quiet the thoughts that jumble inside my mind. This first time was too good. Too damned good. Already I know I need more of her. The problem is— will I ever get enough?

Finally, I move off the bed, stand, and throw the condom in the trash. Then I bend down, pick up my pants, and take my phone out of my pocket to text Christopher.

Skye needs to leave. Now. I have a big day of meetings tomorrow. Important meetings. If she stays, I won't get any sleep. I may not get any sleep anyway.

"Going to Instagram this, too?"

I regard her. Her eyes twinkle. She thinks she's being funny. She has no idea I'm texting my driver to get her out of here. I don't want to do it. I want her to stay. I want to spend the entire night fucking her into next week.

But I can't. Already I know it's too dangerous.

Still I say nothing as I finish my text. Then, "I just called Christopher. He'll drive you home."

She lets go of the headboard.

Without waiting for my permission.

Chapter Eleven

Christopher is on call at all times, and he's paid very well to be. Still, when he needs time off, I give it to him. Tonight isn't one of those times, and he texts me back quickly that he's on his way.

I leave my clothes strewn where they are and stride slowly—a forced slowly—to my walk-in closet. I grab my black velour robe and wrap it around my body, knotting the belt.

I have to leave the bedroom. If I stay here, I'll fuck her again. I'll do things she's not ready for, and that would be a mistake. A big mistake. She may even let me do those things, but then she'll have regrets. I don't want that to happen.

What's truly frightening, though, is that I have the desire—fuck, it's almost an urge—to lie with her. To wrap my arms around her and spend the night with her, here in my bed. That the urge is nearly as strong as my urge to fuck isn't lost on me.

Which is why she's leaving as soon as Christopher gets here.

And why I'm leaving the bedroom.

I clear my throat and hold up my phone. "I have an important message I need to respond to right away. Get dressed, and Christopher will meet you in the front room."

I try not to look at the regret in her warm eyes as I walk out of the bedroom, closing the door behind me.

I try not to think about how she must be feeling. Probably a mixture of confusion and abandonment along with awe that she experienced an orgasm for the first time tonight. She's no doubt thinking that whatever this is between us is over. That I'm done.

That's okay. She can think that for now.

But she's wrong.

This is far from over.

And I *will* make this up to her.

. . .

Sleep eludes me again for most of the night, and my cold shower this morning is like icicles piercing my flesh. Still, I'm up by six a.m. Only 1,440 minutes in each day, and I've learned never to waste one.

After dressing and grabbing a quick cup of coffee and the breakfast sandwich Marilyn prepared for me, I head to the office, where a new set of emergencies greets me. After I gather the resources to put out the necessary fires, it's nearly lunchtime—my usual time to hit the gym and then grab a healthy meal.

Not today, though. Today I have lunch with my brother and father at the Oyster House. It's a monthly date that I never break. I definitely won't break it today, as I'm famished. Sure, I ate a small breakfast sandwich this morning, but I went without dinner last night because I couldn't wait to get Skye in bed.

Ben peeks into my office. "You ready?"

I nod and gulp down the last sip of lukewarm coffee in my mug. "Yeah. Where's Dad?"

"He's ditching us today. Wants to take the new legal intern out to lunch for some kind of orientation."

I wrinkle my forehead. "We have a new legal intern?"

"Apparently. Kathy something."

Interesting. I don't recall an intern at the meeting where Legal handed me my ass on a silver platter. Whatever. My legal team is the best, so if they need an intern, I'm good with it.

I rise. "Let's go. I'm starved."

· · ·

My brother is younger than I am, much more talkative and charismatic, and a bit of a loose cannon. Still, he's smart as a whip and works nearly as hard as I do. His contribution to the company is unequaled, and I depend on him as my right-hand man. He may not have invented the product that put us on the map, but his skills at promotion and marketing led to our success just as much.

"The good Misters Black." The maître d' smiles. "Your regular table?"

"Is there any room at the bar today?" I ask.

"For you two? Of course."

Union Oyster House is the oldest restaurant in Boston and even claims to be the oldest restaurant in continuous service in the United States. Daniel Webster and JFK were big fans. The place epitomizes the American dream, and I love everything about it—especially the oyster bar. Nothing like watching a fresh oyster get shucked, dabbing it with cocktail sauce, and sliding it onto your tongue. One time, right after Ben and I started Black, Inc., one of our favorite shuckers, Mickey, invited us behind the bar and taught us how to shuck. It's a lot harder than they make it look. Mickey retired a few years ago, and today, as I take my place at the bar, I don't recognize any of the shuckers.

The din of conversation is white noise around us. This isn't the best place to conduct business—it's too noisy—but that's not what these monthly lunches are for. They're for family, to remember what's important. I often need that reminder as I get so engrossed in my work, I neglect my brother and father.

Ben and I have a good relationship. Brother squabbles sometimes, sure, but we're pretty close. My father and I? That's another story. Sober for over two decades, Robert Black is smart but trying in some ways. Due to things I don't allow myself to think about, he and I have a love-hate relationship. But he's my father, so I let him into my business, and he does an excellent job with the board of directors, of which he's chairman. He's a natural leader in many ways—he owned a small construction company before Black, Inc. made it big—and I learned much of what I know about running a business from him.

In truth, I'm glad he bailed today. This way, I can talk to my brother about the woman he's currently dating. Not my business, of course, but Ben seems to attract gold diggers. Not that I don't. I'm just good at ferreting them out before things go too far.

Of course, I never let things go too far anyway.

I open my mouth to start the uncomfortable conversation when—

"I hear you're seeing Addison Ames's assistant."

I keep my mouth from dropping open. Barely.

Addison Ames isn't someone I speak of. Ever. Just responding to her Instagram post the other day went way over the line as far as I'm concerned, but I couldn't help myself. Her hypocrisy gets to me sometimes.

"Where'd you hear that?"

"Her sister."

"And you were talking to Apple Ames…why, exactly?"

"We hang out every once in a while."

I pick my jaw up from the bar again. "You what?"

"There's a little history there."

"Yeah, but you know damned well—"

"Easy, Bray. Jeez. We get together. We shoot the breeze about nothing in particular."

"And…?"

"Yeah. We fuck. What's wrong with that?"

"I thought you were seeing that other woman. Morgan something or other."

Ben takes a sip of his water. "That? That's over."

This isn't entirely bad news. At least now I don't have to have the Come to Jesus talk with my brother about gold-digging women. Morgan What's Her Name had "get a prenup" written on her forehead.

That's where the "not bad news" part of this ends, though. Ben got together with Apple Ames, Addie's twin sister. Yeah, they had a thing once. But Ben and I had an agreement. At least I thought we did.

"The Ames sisters are off-limits," I say. "Or did you forget about that when you got a chance to get laid?"

"Apple is as casual as they come," he says. "She doesn't want anything from me, and I don't want anything from her. Other than the occasional fuck. She's a tigress in the sack, so…"

"If it's a fuck you want, you don't have to get it from Apple Ames."

"Apple's not Addie," Ben says. "She's the anti-Addie and then some."

"Still, with our history…"

"Bray, honest. She's not her sister. She can't even stand Addie. Which is why she was only too eager to tell me how pissed off Addie is that you're dating her assistant."

"*Not* dating. And how does she even know?"

"Hell if I know."

A plate of freshly shucked oysters appears in front of me. I inhale their tangy brininess. Not that I give a shit anyway. I'll see whomever I please. I've never cared what Addison Ames thinks of any decision I make. I rarely give her a thought, except when one of her posts comes up in my feed. Ordinarily, I scroll on by.

Why did that one coffee post irk me so much?

I have no clue, but I'm glad it did. It led me to Skye Manning.

"Apple says Addie's seeing red about it. I swear to God, more than ten years and the woman's still hung up on you."

"She's not," I say.

"I know that's what you want to think, but why else would she care about you dating her assistant? What's her name, anyway?"

"Skye." My lips curve upward slightly just saying her name. Damn.

I pick up an oyster, dab a bit of the red sauce on it, and slide it into my mouth. For a split second, I'm lost in the spicy tang.

Then I swallow.

"It's none of Addie's business who I date. And I'm not *dating* Skye."

"Oh?"

"I don't date, Ben."

"Semantics," he says. "Is she a candidate for the club?"

"You know I don't have an interest in anyone who's not." I pick up another oyster. Dab of sauce. Slurp.

Ben slides a few oysters into his mouth and then picks up his buzzing phone. "Sorry, I need to get this." He rises and walks away from the bar.

I take the opportunity to check my own phone. If he can interrupt a family lunch with a call, so can I.

Instead of checking calls, though, my fingers seem to tap on their own and pull up Instagram. My post from this very restaurant is still front and center—the oysters Skye and I shared.

I miss her. I actually fucking miss her.

Damn.

I tap on her tag to see her profile.

Except it's set to private. Smart woman. Within another second, I've asked to follow her—the first such request I've ever made.

I put my phone away and slurp another oyster.

Chapter Twelve

Later that afternoon, I pick up my phone to see if Skye accepted my request.

Another post from Addison Ames appears—in this one she's wearing a horrendous grape-colored lip shade—complete with obsequious comments.

Absolutely in love with @susannecosmetics new Burgundy Orchid lip plumper! Grab yours before they sell out! #sponsored #bigkisses #kissme #lipgloss #lips #kiss

So luscious! Ordering mine now, @realaddisonames. Gorgeous!

What a great color on you!

Their lip plumper is the best. Love this new shade!

I have no problem letting this one go by. It's classic Influencer Addie, like always.

I check my notifications, and—yes!—@stormyskye15 accepted my request.

I scroll through her posts. Some yoga poses, some cute sayings, some selfies with a gorgeous dark-haired woman who she refers to as her bestie. But in the midst of the everyday

Instagram photos are some that are truly art.

Skye has talent.

A close-up of an eastern bluebird, the yellow of its chest as vivid as sunshine and its blue back the color of the Pacific Ocean off Kauai. How did she capture the hues so brilliantly, when the bird could have flown away in an instant?

Another photo is an old man—face wrinkled, a Red Sox cap on his head—riding through the cobbled streets of the Freedom Trail on a retro blue Schwinn bicycle. He's clearly in motion, but Skye somehow captured him in perfect focus, his gaze intent on the road in front of him.

My favorite are her two most recent photos. They're raw in their simplicity. A black fire hydrant with a red top—which looks like a hat to me—sits on a busy Boston street as a shadow plays over it. The first photo is taken from above, and the shadow juts straight out, perpendicular to the hydrant. The second photo is from a different angle, and the shadow looms in the back, as if it's a phantom coming from behind. I'm mesmerized.

My God…

Her photos are pure brilliance.

I want to help her with her career. Get her work in galleries, magazines. I have connections. I can make this happen for her.

Except she has to ask.

And if I know Skye Manning, she'll never ask.

Which makes me want to help her all the more.

For now, though, I have my own work to do.

Ben and I are on a plane in the morning to New York for meetings, and I wonder whether I should pay a visit to my club.

It's been a long time, and I miss it, but…

I want to go with Skye.

And I'm not sure I'll enjoy it without her.

What the hell is happening to me?

• • •

Black Rose Underground.

My leather club on the bottom floor of my Manhattan residence tower. After a shower to get the grime of travel to New York cleaned from my body, I dress in simple black pants, a black button-down, black casual shoes. I pull the key card out of my wallet and take my private elevator down. I have my own entrance to the club. One of the perks of owning it.

My tastes are varied, and none of the clubs in Manhattan quite suited me, so I built my own.

Confidentiality is a must, and members leave their inhibitions at the door.

Claude Bonneville sits at his desk, burly and threatening. No one gets into Black Rose without Claude's okay.

"Hey, Mr. Black," he says. "Long time no see."

"Been busy. How are things going here, Claude?"

"No issues. Everyone's cool. A couple new membership applications for you to approve. They're in your inbox."

I nod. "Thanks. I'll take a look." I don't check my Black Rose email except when I'm here. I have a private server in the back that I can't even access from anywhere else. What happens at Black Rose truly stays at Black Rose.

I walk through the main room, its bloodred carpeting speckled with members. Some are dressed casually, as I am. Others are dressed in club gear—leather, chains, corsets. Some are naked.

Anything goes at Black Rose Underground—well, anything pertaining to wardrobe. I don't allow edge play here, for which I have my reasons.

I walk to the bar, where a topless woman gives me a

dazzling smile. "What'll it be, Mr. Black?"

I don't know her name. I don't allow myself to get close to anyone who works at the club, other than Claude and Rick and Steve, my managers. "Wild Turkey, one ice cube."

"You got it."

A minute later, my drink appears. I bring it to my lips and let its aroma waft around me before I take a sip and let it float on my tongue. When I swallow, it burns. That's what I like about Turkey. It's a good slow burn. The other billionaires can have their top-shelf brandies. Give me good old Turkey any day of the week.

Rick Myers, the manager on duty tonight, approaches me and sits next to me at the bar. "Braden, haven't seen you in a while. Anything you need tonight?"

"A scene, Rick."

"Did you bring someone?"

I shake my head, picturing Skye in my mind. "Not this time. Anyone available?"

"Aretha's here."

Aretha Doyle, a New York model, was my arm candy for a year until we parted ways a few months ago. We never dated. I don't date. She's gorgeous and intelligent and very nice, but there wasn't really any connection beyond that. Still, she was always up for a scene.

"Is she?" I take another sip.

"You want me to set it up?"

I down the rest of the bourbon in one swallow. "Sure. Bring her to my suite." I set the glass down, rise, and walk through the door leading to various exhibition rooms. My private suite is at the end of the hallway. I slide the key card through the door and enter.

And I wait.

Fifteen minutes later, a knock on the door.

I unlock the dead bolt. Aretha Doyle stands before me

clad in nothing but a thong and platform heels that make her eye to eye with me. Her dark hair falls over her broad shoulders, and her tits stick out like cereal bowls. They're not fake, just small and perky—fashion-model tits.

Nothing like Skye's.

But I'm not here to think about Skye. My earlier thought that I may not enjoy Black Rose without her spooked me more than a little. I'm here to immerse myself in a scene with a willing participant.

Aretha is willing.

I take her hand. "Come in."

"I'm surprised you wanted to see me, Braden."

"Why?"

"Well…you said we were over in no uncertain terms."

She's right. I did say that. She was getting too close to me, and I knew if we continued, she'd end up getting hurt. I don't like hurting women. Not emotionally. Physically? That's a different story, as long as the hurt ultimately leads to pleasure for both of us.

"That doesn't mean we can't enjoy each other's company now and again. You're still a member of this club."

She nods. "What do you want tonight?"

Skye.

The word emerges in my mind seemingly by itself.

I want Skye.

Yes, I want a scene, but I want Skye more.

Damn.

I lead Aretha to the leather table. "Lie down."

She complies, like a good submissive. I bind her arms above her head but leave her ankles free. I walk to the wall, choose a riding crop, and return to Aretha splayed out on my table, beautiful and ready and willing.

I bring the crop down hard on her tits.

Chapter Thirteen

I'm back in Boston Friday morning, still unsated.

One lash to Aretha's tits, and I knew I couldn't continue with the scene. I wasn't hard. I wasn't excited. I apologized and sent her away. As much as I craved a scene with a willing partner, I craved something else more.

Skye Manning.

And with Skye Manning, I have to go slowly.

No scenes at the club, at least not yet.

My workdays are always jam-packed, but by mid-afternoon, I can't wait any longer. I have to see Skye.

Even if it means running into Addison Ames.

I text Christopher, and a half hour later, I arrive at the Ames Hotel. I walk through the marble lobby past the elevators to the offices on the first floor. The door to Addie's office is open. I stand in the doorway.

Skye covers her computer monitor and steps out from behind her desk. "I'm free as a bird!" she says, smiling.

"Good to know," I say.

She jerks her gaze upward, her eyes wide. "How did you

get in here?"

"Same way I get anywhere. I walked through the door."

"Sorry. Addie's already gone for the day."

Damned good news, as far as I'm concerned. "Why would you think I came to see Addie? You witnessed our last encounter."

She opens her mouth, but nothing emerges. She shuts it quickly.

"I came to see *you*, Skye."

She crosses her arms. "You could have called."

"Why? And miss that look of adorable perplexity on your pretty face? Besides, you never gave me your cell phone number."

"You know where I work."

"Maybe I didn't want to put you in the awkward position of taking a phone call at work."

"So you showed *up* at my work instead?"

"I figured it's nearly quitting time."

"What if Addie had been here?"

"Then Addie would have been here."

"But you... She..."

I take a step toward her. "Do you really think I give a damn if Addison Ames crosses my path? She doesn't scare me, Skye. In fact, she's probably first on the list of everything that *doesn't* scare me."

God, that's the harsh truth. Addie would like to think she scares me, but she doesn't.

"Oh?" Skye says. "What *does* scare you, Braden?"

I regard her, my body already tensing, aching, wanting. I meet her brown-eyed gaze and pierce her with my own, trying to singe her with my eyes.

One word.

One word will answer her question, and it's the unadulterated truth.

"Nothing."

She gapes at me, her lips parted in that enticing way. I want more than anything to touch her. Cup her soft cheek. Rub my thumb over her full lower lip. Pull the band out of her hair and let the waves fall over her shoulders.

Then take her back to my place and fuck the daylights out of her.

"Why are you here to see me, then? Can I help you with something?" Her voice is so soft, it's almost a whisper.

I close the distance between us. "You can come back to my bed."

She moves away, stumbling slightly. I steady her with my hand, her skin warm. Tingles flash through me when I touch her. Goddamned tingles. What am I? Fourteen?

She eases away from me until the backs of her thighs hit the desk.

"You going to answer me?"

"With all due respect, you didn't exactly ask a question," she says.

"True. *You* did. You asked if you could help me with anything, and I answered. Still, I think my response is worthy of a reply."

She inhales deeply, and for a moment, I wonder if she's going to speak to me at all.

Finally, "You're not even offering me dinner this time?"

I resist a smile, remembering the cold penne and veal I found in the kitchen the morning after our encounter. Marilyn had to throw it away.

"We didn't exactly get to dinner the last time."

Her cheeks are adorably crimson as she clears her throat. "A girl still has to eat."

"Then dinner it is. What's your pleasure?"

She stares at me. Again I wonder if she's actually going to speak. Then she does.

"You told me I was something your money couldn't buy, but now you think dinner will buy me?"

Oh, fuck. Enough of this game playing, dancing around each other. I grab both her shoulders. I gaze into her eyes. "I haven't been able to stop thinking about you, Skye. I want you in my bed. What's it going to take?"

She shudders, rubs her hands on her upper arms. "I—I can't be bought."

"I'm not trying to buy you. I *am* trying to bed you."

"You just want sex, then? Not a date?"

A date? I don't date. But to have Skye, I'm willing to go an extra mile. I give a half-hearted shrug. "We can go out on dates if you want. If that's what it takes for you to feel comfortable coming back to my bed. But it will be simply dating. I can't give you any more than that."

"Why not?" she asks boldly.

"Because I can't."

She narrows her eyes. "Nice try. But I'm looking for a reason, Braden. I'm twenty-four years old. I'm young, and maybe a purely sexual relationship would be fun. A day will come, though, when it won't be enough for me."

"If that day isn't here yet, why not come back to my bed?"

"I have my reasons."

"Care to enlighten me?"

She wets her lips. "I'm not interested in being your fuck buddy."

I'm not looking for a fuck buddy, but I don't say this. She's not yet ready to hear what I'm actually looking for. Slowly. I must go slowly or this will blow up in my face before I can get her where I want her.

"What will it take to get you back into my bed, then? I told you we could date."

"Tell me why it can't lead anywhere."

I shrug once more. "I can't give you a reason."

"You mean you won't."

Smart girl. "Stickler for semantics, are you?"

She nods.

"Then you're correct. I won't."

She's still standing against her desk, and the tops of her breasts—visible in the low-cut, clingy shirt she's wearing—are rosy. I imagine how soft and warm they'll be against my fingers, my lips.

She's holding back quivers, forcing her body not to respond to mine.

She knows how to stay in control. Damn, she's good.

But I'm better.

"I… I'll…think about it," she finally says.

Think about it? It's her right, of course, so I'll make damned sure she has something to think about. Something long and hard that can give her another one of those orgasms she's only begun to experience.

I crush her to my body, my erection apparent. I press it into her belly. "This isn't a game, Skye."

"I never said it was."

"There's nothing to think about."

"There's a *lot* to think about. I'm not someone's toy, Braden. I have some self-respect, you know."

"Of course you do. Do you honestly think I'd want to bed a woman who has no self-respect?"

She steadies herself. "Honestly, I don't know what to think."

"Think about this." I cup both her cheeks and smash my lips to hers.

She opens, letting her tongue wander out to meet mine.

The intensity of the kiss surprises me.

I feel like I'm drugged, aware of nothing else but Skye's lips on mine, her tongue tangling, teasing mine. Her kisses are addictive, and I want more of them. More of everything Skye Manning.

Her body splayed out and bound, her skin red from a riding crop, her nipples sore from a clamp. Better yet—sore from my lips and teeth.

I want her any way and every way.

But first I have to get her back to my bed.

She deepens the kiss, groaning into my mouth, pushing her breasts into my chest. Her nipples are hard. She rises on her toes and rubs against my bulge. Yes, yes. I feel her begin to surrender, begin to need this as much as I do.

There's only one thing for me to do.

I pull away, breaking the kiss with a loud *smack*.

She falls back against the desk, gripping the edge.

"I want you," I say. "You do something to me, something I don't quite understand but want to." I grip her with my gaze. "Don't think too long."

Then I walk out the door.

Chapter Fourteen

I toy with the idea of going back to New York, to the club, but I ultimately end up at the gym working out for three hours. When my body finally reaches its limit, I head home and sit in my Jacuzzi listening to jazz.

When I've effectively turned into a prune, I get out of the tub, towel off, and head to the kitchen. It's after ten p.m., and Marilyn's off duty. She left me dinner in the refrigerator—coq au vin with French bread—but I'm in the mood for something else.

Something…spicy.

I order some Thai from a place that has all-night delivery, alert the night staff that it's coming, and head into my office to check on a few emails. I have business all over the globe, so emails come in at all hours.

I expect mail from China, India, Australia.

I don't expect anything from Addison Ames. She emails me a couple of times a year, reminding me how much I owe her. It's all a crock. I read and delete. Really, I should just delete.

But curiosity is my downfall, and I open it. Weird. It's blank, just her signature block. She must have accidentally hit Send before she wrote anything. Just as well.

Delete.

Easy enough.

I still do business with Addie's father. The Ames Hotel is the best in Boston, so why wouldn't I?

I've worked hard, and I deserve the best.

I deserve Skye.

Skye isn't the most beautiful woman I've ever met, and she's far from the most worldly. She's a Kansas farm girl.

A Kansas farm girl who I can't get out of my mind.

Skye *is* beautiful, though, in a refreshing way that most of the women I go out with aren't. I seem to attract women who like to apply makeup with a putty knife and waltz around in Dolce & Gabbana.

I bet Skye doesn't own any Dolce & Gabbana. I bet she shops at Target.

Honestly, I'm not a fan of Dolce & Gabbana, though I do love a nice Armani suit. For the most part, though, I'm still a boy from South Boston at heart. Hell, we couldn't afford Target. We shopped at the Salvation Army thrift store and sometimes even had to get free food from the local food bank.

Skye grew up on a corn farm, so she most likely never had to take charity.

In her way, she's more worldly than I am. She's a college graduate. I'm not. Lack of higher education hasn't held me back at all, though.

You had some help, you know.

I ignore the devil on my shoulder. It's gotten easier over the years.

What is Skye doing right now? I could call her, but I still don't have her number. Easy enough to get, but I doubt any of my team would be excited to hear from me at eleven on a

Friday night.

Damn! She pisses me off. I shouldn't be wanting to call her. I want her almost too much, and it's disorienting. It's throwing me off my game, and I can't be off my game.

Ever.

. . .

I rise early Saturday morning and take Sasha on a long walk, and we end at a dog park where I let her off her leash and she runs around and plays with the other dogs. I find a bench, sit, and—of course—check my phone. As usual, some business requires my attention. Time to go.

I whistle. "Come on, Sasha!"

She looks up, her cute puppy eyes pleading, and then she continues her play.

Nice try.

I walk over and leash her. "Sorry, girl. Time to go."

She reluctantly comes along.

Back home, I hand my pup over to Annika's capable hands and head into the office. The real office. Yeah, I'm wearing jeans and a Grateful Dead T-shirt, but it's Saturday. I really want to call Claire and ask her to come in and lend a hand, but I resist the urge. My staff works hard during the week, and most of them covet their weekends.

I don't blame them.

Years ago, when I did construction for a living, working for my father's small company, I was one of those people who coveted time off. We didn't get much. We worked six days a week most weeks, for up to fifteen-hours stretches sometimes.

I learned hard work from my father. Once he got sober and got his act together…

Well, it wasn't just the sobriety that forced him to get his act together.

And I really don't want to think about any of that shit right now.

So I dive in and tackle what I do best.

Work.

• • •

Two prospectuses and four phone calls later, I rise and stretch. The sun has gone down, and dusk shades the view from my office window. What the hell time is it, anyway? I've had my phone on speaker this whole time, and I haven't bothered to check the hour.

Eight thirty? Not surprising. I lose track of time a lot. Ben says I'm a workaholic, though he works nearly as much as I do. He's not here now, though. He's probably out with a woman.

Smart man.

I could find a woman easily. I'm horny as hell, so I give it a minute of thought.

Then I dismiss it.

Because I only want one woman.

I pick up my phone to check Skye's Instagram. What's she doing right now? Most likely she's home or possibly out with friends. Perhaps the good-looking bestie who makes appearances in her posts.

Before I even click on her profile, though, a photo appears on my feed.

It's Skye and her bestie.

Hanging out at the MADD Gala with the bestie! @ tessalolita #madd #gala #bestiesforever

Skye looks gorgeous. She's fucking glowing. And those tits. They're nearly spilling out of the clingy little black dress she's wearing. Her hair is down, tumbling in soft waves over her shoulders, and her eyes are bright, long-lashed, and sparkling. And those lips… Painted with a red tint and parted…

I adjust my groin.

Skye is out on the town. Not only out but at the MADD Gala—an event I was asked to sponsor but turned down.

Fuck it all. I could be there right now. With Skye and her little black dress and her glistening red lips.

I could be there.

And I'm not.

But I can fix that.

Chapter Fifteen

"Mr. Black!" Lila Marquez, a prominent member of the Junior League of Boston and head of this event, rushes toward me as soon as I ease into her peripheral view outside the ballroom. "You came!"

"Good evening, Lila. You're looking lovely as always."

Lila smiles, a blush gracing her cheeks, and her eyelids flutter slightly.

"I'd like a ticket, please."

"Mr. Black—"

"Braden, please."

She blushes again. "Braden… Dinner's over. We have dancing and the auction results, of course, but I'm afraid there aren't any tables."

"I don't need a place at a table. Just a ticket to enter the event."

"But you won't—"

"Not a problem, I assure you. I only want to enter the event. There's a…person inside I'd like to confer with."

"Of course! You don't need a reason. Go ahead in, Mr.—

Braden."

"I'm happy to pay for a ticket."

"I wouldn't dream of it."

"Then you'll find a generous donation in your inbox Monday morning. Thank you, Lila." I whisk past her and enter the ballroom, scanning the dimly lit space for Skye.

A band is playing swing music, and quite a few couples are dancing. I recognize Skye's bestie, @tessalolita. She's wearing a red dress and dancing with Garrett Ramirez, a local architect whose firm, Reardon Brothers, put in a bid on my new building.

They won't be getting it. I don't like how that particular firm does business.

Skye. Where is Skye?

When I don't locate her right away, I follow Bestie with my gaze as she and Garrett leave the dance floor. Bestie makes a beeline to—

Skye.

She sits at a table by herself. Bestie wipes her brow as she sits down next to Skye.

They chat, but of course I have no idea what they're saying, as they're across the room. Skye picks up a nearly full drink and downs it. Just like that.

Then my hackles rise.

Garrett Ramirez and another young architect, Peter Reardon, son of the boss, Beau Reardon, approach Skye's table. The four of them head to the dance floor while I curl my hands into fists.

I could go cut in. Drag her away. Force her back into my bed. She may not even resist.

Instead, I watch from afar as she moves in that dress that hugs her body the way I want to be hugging it. Her smile seems pasted on, but still she dances, and she's damned good on her feet, too. Who knew Skye Manning could swing?

Then again, why would I know? I just met the woman.

Four numbers.

Four fucking numbers I wait through—tempted to chew off my own arm to get out of this trap—before Skye finally leaves the dance floor.

Peter Reardon follows her, and they head to the bar.

I'm right behind them, staying just far enough away that they won't notice me unless someone pounces on me to kiss my ass, which happens a lot at these kinds of events. Someone's always trying to get a hand in my pocket. I'm generous by nature, but tonight, I hope like hell no one notices me.

I'm behind them now, and I can hear their conversation. The bartender hands Peter a Guinness and what appears to be a Wild Turkey for Skye.

"What's your name?" Skye asks her companion.

"What?" Peter yells.

For God's sake, asshole, I can hear her. But my senses are on high alert. I could hear Skye whisper at this point.

"What's your name?" she asks again.

"Peter. You?"

"Skye."

"Nice to meet you." He hands her the bourbon.

Skye takes a sip. "What do you do, Peter?"

"What?"

For crying out loud.

"I'm an architect. I work for my father, also an architect. You?"

"I work for Addison Ames."

"The heiress?"

"Yeah. I'm her personal assistant, but I'm really a photographer at heart. That's what I want to do full-time eventually."

"What?"

"I said I'm her personal assistant. But I want to eventually make a living as a photographer."

"Cool," Peter says.

Cool? My God, she's way too good for the likes of this asshole.

Skye takes another sip. "You want to dance again?"

I take a step closer.

"Sure." He grabs her hand.

I'm ready to intervene when he speaks again.

"I'm sweating. You want to get some fresh air first?"

Oh, hell no. I see where this is going. I close the gap in two giant steps.

"No," I say firmly. "She does *not.*"

Chapter Sixteen

"What are you doing here?" Skye demands.

I can't help an assessing gaze. That dress is even more amazing up close. It was made to form fit her body. A fine silver chain sparkles around her throat.

I imagine, for a moment, that she's wearing my collar. That she's mine—body, heart, and soul—for safekeeping, always and forever.

I drop my gaze down her bare legs to her strappy silver sandals, her pretty toenails painted bright red.

Fuck it all.

I raise my head and meet her glaring eyes. She asked me a question. *What are you doing here?*

"Keeping you from getting yourself into trouble," I say without apology.

Peter goes rigid next to her. "Nice meeting you, Skye," he says, turning.

"Wait! Aren't we going to dance?"

"Another time." He disappears onto the dance floor.

Good. Let him go. She's way too good for him. I've heard

rumors about Reardon Brothers. Rumors I'm definitely going to look into now.

"Come with me." I pull her out of the ballroom, through the hallway, to the hotel lobby, her heels clacking on the marble floor as she runs to keep up.

"What are you doing?"

"Keeping you from sneaking into someone else's bed."

"Seriously?" she huffs.

"You've been drinking."

"You don't know anything about me. I'm not drunk. I never get drunk. And I can sleep with whomever I want. How did you find me anyway?"

I pull my phone out of my pocket. "Instagram."

"I'm going back in," she says, hands on her hips.

"Not without me."

"Do you even have a ticket to this event?"

"Do you think I need a ticket?"

She shakes her head. "Fine, come along, then. I can't leave Tessa in there alone."

Tessa? Ah, the bestie. @tessalolita

"Tessa's a big girl. She can take care of herself."

"Interesting take. Tessa's my age, Braden, and you obviously don't think *I* can take care of myself."

"Not true. I didn't show up because you can't take care of yourself. I showed up to keep you out of someone else's bed."

She shakes her head. "You're unbelievable. What makes you think I'd end up in someone's bed?"

"Look at you. You're beautiful with a killer body. Damn, that dress…"

She taps her foot and scoffs. "Please…"

"Do you really not see yourself the way I see you?" I cup her cheek. "Your hair is the color of roasted chestnuts, your eyes the warmest brown I've ever seen. Your skin is like the richest cream, and God, Skye, your mouth…" I inhale, willing my cock to behave itself. "Your lips are pink and plump and heart-shaped, and fuck, I can't leave them alone. I've never seen a mouth like yours. The way your lips are always slightly parted drives me wild."

For a moment she seems to soften. But only for a moment.

"You're acting like I was in there gyrating for ten-dollar bills in my panties. It's a hotel charity event for MADD, Braden, not a strip club."

"That dress—"

"Isn't even mine. It's my friend's."

"It can't look anywhere near as good on her as it does on you." My voice cracks a little. Damn it.

She swallows. "I need to go back in."

"Why? Dancing? You want to go dancing? *I'll* take you dancing. Be sure to wear that amazing dress."

"I told you, it's not—"

"Your dress," I finish for her. "It should be. It was made for you."

As if in response to my voice, her nipples tighten and protrude out against the black fabric. In response, something of mine protrudes as well.

"What are you doing here anyway?" I ask.

"Addie gave me the tickets."

"Of course," I say. "Addie. I should have seen her fingerprints all over this."

"So what? I got the tickets, and I wanted to go out with my friend."

"Like I said, I'll take you dancing."

"I don't want to go dancing," she says.

"What do you want, then?"

Please say you want to go back to my place. Please.

"I want to go back inside. My friend will be worried."

"If I take you back inside, the men will be all over you."

"Braden, one guy was paying attention to me. *One.* And

you scared him off."

"He's not good enough for you." She doesn't even know the half of it.

"You don't even know him."

She's wrong there. "Neither do you."

"Of course I do. He's an architect."

"You're wrong, Skye. I *do* know him. That's Peter Reardon, and his father is Beau Reardon of Reardon Brothers Architecture. His friend is Garrett Ramirez, also an architect with the company. Beau is trying to get the contract on my new building."

She wrenches her arm out of my grasp. "What are you saying? That the two of them are paying attention to us because of *you*?"

"I'm not saying that at all."

"Sounds like it from where I'm standing."

"Not at all. They didn't know you were with me before— but now they do. They're playboys. I guarantee you they both have two things on their minds tonight. That contract—which probably means a huge bonus from Daddy—and getting laid. I'll let you guess which one is foremost in their minds on a Saturday night."

"Interesting. What do you have on *your* mind tonight, Braden?"

I can't help a slight smile. "Not a contract."

Damn, no lie there. All I can think about is getting Skye back in bed. Yeah, I'm acting like a territorial ass, when I know damned well she's not mine. Not yet, anyway.

I should apologize. I even open my mouth to do so, but before I can—

"I'm going back in," she says.

"Fine. I'm going with you."

"Suit yourself."

I follow her back to the ballroom. She struts in and heads

for a table.

The gorgeous brunette in the red dress runs toward her, nearly knocking over a server and her tray full of drinks. "Skye, are you all right? Peter said—" Her eyes morph to circles when she sees me behind Skye. "It *is* you."

She clears her throat. "I'm fine."

Bestie regains her composure and lifts her lips in a dazzling smile. "Aren't you going to introduce me?"

I hold out my hand. "Braden Black."

"Braden, this is Tessa Logan, my best friend."

"It's an honor, Mr. Black." Tessa flutters her ridiculously long eyelashes as she shakes my hand. She's a flirt. I'm used to it. She *is* a bombshell, but not what I'm after at the moment.

"Call me Braden. Any friend of Skye's." I turn to her. "Drink?"

"I've had enough, thanks."

"You?" I nod to Tessa.

"I'd love another banana daiquiri," she says coyly.

"Done. I'll be back." I head to the bar.

"Two Wild Turkeys, one ice cube, and a banana daiquiri," I say to the young woman tending bar.

She drops her jaw. "You're Braden Black."

"Guilty."

"Wow. Sure. Give me just a minute." She fumbles with the stainless steel shaker for the daiquiri.

Lila Marquez pushes her way toward me. "Braden!" she gasps out. "A table opened up for you."

"Lila, I don't need—"

"Oh, I insist. It's right up front."

"A table right up front opened up?"

"Yes. Isn't that lucky?"

Lucky, indeed. More likely one of the bigger donors just went home. It's nearing eleven.

"I'll be with you in a minute, Lila," I say. "Just getting

drinks."

"I've put your name on the table," she says. "You can't miss it. Enjoy the rest of the evening!"

"I will. Thank you."

The bartender finishes the drinks, and I pick them up and push through the crowd, not spilling a damned drop, thank you very much, as I reach Skye's table.

"One banana daiquiri." I hand the canary-yellow drink to Tessa.

"Thanks so much." A grin splits her face.

"I took the liberty of getting you Wild Turkey in case you changed your mind." I hand Skye a glass.

"I didn't."

"Great. Then two for me. Follow me. I've got a much better table."

"I'm sure being Braden Black has its perks," she says dryly, a lock of hair falling over her forehead and into her eyes.

I lower my head and softly blow her hair out of the way. "Being *with* Braden Black also has its perks."

Chapter Seventeen

Tessa takes a long sip of her banana daiquiri and then heads back to the dance floor.

Nice. Now I can talk to Skye alone. I take a drink and then slide my tongue across my bottom lip. The bourbon warms my mouth and throat.

"Did you notice how Peter Reardon made a quick getaway when I showed up?"

Skye grits her jaw. "Yeah. I'd have to be blind to have missed it."

"You said I thought he was hanging around you because of me," I say, "but that's not what I thought, and that's not why."

"Oh?"

"He was pursuing you because you're sexy as hell, Skye."

She gulps, pink spreading again to her lovely cheeks.

"He made a quick getaway because when he saw me stake my claim—"

She crosses her legs slowly. "Excuse me? Stake your claim?"

"You think that was a bad choice of words?"

"I do. I'm not something you can plant your flag on. I'm a person, Braden."

"A very intriguing person," I say. "At any rate, when he saw that I was interested—are those words better?"

She nods.

"He put the contract ahead of bedding you. Which is fine by me."

"I see," she says, clearly trying hard to sound nonchalant but failing.

"Sure you don't want a drink?" I nod to the second Wild Turkey sitting in front of her.

Tessa returns to the table and sits down, her brow line sporting a fine sheen. "This band is fantastic, but I need a break. Care to accompany me to the little girls' room, Skye?"

"Yeah. Sure." She stands and grabs a silver clutch. "Excuse me for a minute," Skye says to me.

"I'll be here." I hold back a smile.

Several guests clamor up to me as Tessa and Skye turn to leave the ballroom. Everyone wants to shake my hand, which is the usual way of things at these events.

I exchange greetings with the mayor, the district attorney, several MADD board members, and a few people schmoozing to get my business. Then Peter Reardon appears.

"Mr. Black," he says.

"Hello, Peter."

"I just want to… I mean…"

For God's sake, spit it out, man.

"I'm sorry," he finally blurts out.

"For what?"

"For dancing with Skye. I didn't know that you and she were…you know."

"I'm afraid I don't know."

"She's obviously your…" He drops his gaze to the floor.

"I'm just sorry." He rushes off.

I actually feel for the guy. His father wants that contract, and he thinks he just blew it. Little does he know I've already decided to go with another firm.

I rise to head to the auction table. A tall blonde has other plans for me, though.

"Mr. Black"—she holds out her hand—"Laurie Simms from Carter and Amos. I'd love a minute to speak with you about your legal needs."

I shake her hand. She has a firm grip, which I like, but I'm going to have to let her down nonetheless.

She takes a seat at the table. I guess the auction items can wait. I'm not a rude person, so I sit down next to her.

"We represent several big businesses here in Boston," Laurie says. "Our corporate law department is top-notch."

"I've heard great things about your firm, Ms. Simms—"

"Laurie, please."

"All right. Laurie, I've heard great things about your firm"—not a lie—"but Black, Inc. handles most corporate matters in-house, and for those issues we need extra help with, we have a retainer with Johnson, Mahoney and Crabtree."

She nods. "I can't say I'm not disappointed, but Johnson, Mahoney and Crabtree is an excellent firm."

"But not as good as yours?" I prompt. I'm interested to see how diplomatic she'll be.

"I like to think we're the best corporate firm in Boston," she says shamelessly. "All our partners and a majority of our associates were written up in *Legal All Stars* this year, myself included."

"You're a partner, I take it?"

"I'm on track for next year. I won't lie to you, Mr. Black. If I could snag Black, Inc. as a client, it'd be a huge feather in my cap."

"Call me Braden," I say. "I admire your boldness."

She laughs. "You mean my audacity?"

"Laurie, audacity is often required to get ahead in any area. I'm pretty audacious myself when it comes to business." And other things, but that's none of her concern.

"I had to try. Are you enjoying the gala?"

"I am," I say. "I may make a few bids."

"One of our senior partners, Jack Carter, is on the MADD board, but he had a family emergency earlier."

"Is everything all right?"

"Yes. One of his kids was in a car accident, but she's just scraped up a little."

"Good to know."

"That's why I'm here. I've been his associate for the past five years, and he asked me to come in his place."

"Lucky you."

She smiles. "I enjoy dressing up and getting wined and dined. After working seventy hours a week, it's a nice break."

Laurie Simms is quite beautiful. Tall, with honey-blond hair in a loose knot, blue eyes, and fair skin. Another time and place, I'd probably consider seeing her outside of business.

But I only have eyes for Skye Manning tonight.

"Did you bring anyone to the gala?" she asks.

I clear my throat. Not technically, but, "Yes, she's in the ladies' room. Skye Manning."

Laurie cocks her head. "That name sounds vaguely familiar to me."

"She works for Addison Ames."

"Right!" Recognition dawns on Laurie's pretty face. "Her assistant. I remember now. Addie and I have lunch from time to time."

"Oh?" Clearly Addison never mentioned her past with me to Laurie. Good thing.

"Yeah. I interned with Brock Ames when I was in law school. I worked in the legal department for the hotel chain."

"How did you end up with Carter and Amos?"

"Actually, I—"

I stop listening.

Skye and Tessa have reentered the ballroom and are only a few feet away from the table.

And Skye's jaw is dropped open.

Chapter Eighteen

Tessa drops her purse on the table and heads to the dance floor while Skye brings her jaw back in place, returns to the table, and smiles. It's a fake smile, though. She's jealous. Jealous that I'm sitting with another woman.

Nice. I don't mind a little jealousy. Not at all.

I stand. "Skye, meet Laurie Simms."

Skye holds out her hand and glues on the smile once more. "Skye Manning."

Laurie takes Skye's hand and gives it a strong shake. "Braden was just telling me about you. You work for Addison Ames?"

"I do."

"She's a doll," Laurie says.

I resist an eye roll. "Doll" is not a word I'd use to describe Addison Ames.

"Please have a seat," Laurie continues.

Except Laurie is sitting in the seat Skye vacated only minutes ago. I hold out the chair on my other side, and she sits. The extra bourbon I brought for her is within reach. She grabs it.

"Addie and I go way back," Laurie says. "I used to work for her father."

"Oh?" Skye says. "What do you do?"

"I'm an attorney." She slides a card toward Skye.

Nicely done. Skye probably has no need for a corporate attorney, but Laurie's thinking bigger. She's getting her name out everywhere she can. I admire that.

"I interned with Brock Ames when I was in law school," Laurie continues. "He got me set up with my current firm."

"So how do you two know each other?" Skye asks sweetly.

"We don't, actually," I say.

"Oh?"

"Shameless self-promotion." Laurie smiles. "Of course I recognized Braden and had to come introduce myself."

"As I said, Ms. Simms, I'm happy with my current representation."

She stands. "Can't blame a girl for trying. Nice to meet you, Skye."

"You too." She smiles back. This time it seems more genuine.

Skye has a beautiful smile. Her whole face lights up, and her lips... I resist the urge to cup her cheek right here in the middle of the MADD Gala.

"Thanks," I say.

"For what?"

"For getting back here. Seemed like you were gone forever. When I'm alone, people pounce. Laurie is the umpteenth person who came up to me while you were gone."

"Were the others beautiful females as well?"

I smile. "Does it matter?"

She looks at her drink. "I suppose not."

"One was Peter Reardon. Apparently he was waiting outside the ballroom, and when he saw you and Tessa leave, he came back in and sought me out. He apologized for dancing with you."

"Oh, for God's sake. That's ridiculous. He had a perfect right to dance with me. I enjoyed his company."

"I'm sure he enjoyed yours as well. He just didn't know you were with me."

"I *wasn't* with you."

"You are now, and I aim to keep it that way."

She squirms in her chair. I can't tell if she's angry or turned on by my comment. Most likely both, which is exactly what I was hoping for.

"Have you thought any more about coming back to my bed?" I ask.

"I don't want to talk about that here," she says.

"Why?"

"Why? Because we're nearly screaming at each other to be heard above the band."

She's exaggerating a bit, but I'll indulge her. "Let's go out to the lobby, then."

"I can't. I have to watch Tessa's bag."

"Tessa's bag will be fine. If it's not, I'll replace everything in it." I rise. "Come on."

"She'd never forgive—"

"For God's sake." I reach for her hand and tug her behind me.

We walk along the outer edge of the ballroom to the entrance and then through the hallway into the lobby.

"Why did you come here, Braden?"

"I already told you. To keep you from getting into someone else's bed."

She tilts her chin upward. "Why is that any of your concern?"

"Because I want you in *my* bed, Skye. Haven't I made that clear? And I'm not very good at sharing."

"What about what *I* want? Has that occurred to you?"

"You seemed to have a good time in bed with me." I'm tempted to mention her first orgasm, but I keep that to myself.

She doesn't reply.

"You're not denying it," I prod.

"No, I'm not. The actual act itself was...acceptable."

I let out a boisterous laugh. Acceptable? Given her responses and reactions, I'd wager it was way more than simply acceptable. I've got to hand it to Skye, though. I've never met a woman yet who can hurl it back at me as well as she can. I never realized I'd find that trait so attractive.

I finally curb my laughter. "Acceptable? You're something else, Skye."

She crosses her arms. "Making fun of me again?"

"No, I'm not, actually. You are a challenge, Skye Manning, and I never back down from a challenge."

Never have I meant words as much as I mean the ones that just left my mouth. I will have Skye Manning. She *will* submit to me.

It's just a matter of when.

"The act itself was acceptable," I continue. "Are you saying something else about our time together *wasn't* acceptable?"

"Yes, that's exactly what I'm saying."

I smile. "Don't leave me in suspense."

She clears her throat. "Fine. I didn't like how it ended."

"I seem to recall it ended with both of us climaxing. What was wrong with that?"

"That's part of the act. The act was acceptable, as I've told you. I'm talking about *after* the act."

Interesting. I didn't behave any differently than I ever do when I'm done with sex. I said goodbye and I contacted Christopher to take the woman home.

"I believe you left," I say.

"That's not how I'd phrase it. You didn't say a word to me other than to tell me Christopher would take me home. You left me alone to get dressed—"

"Did you want help dressing?"

She uncrosses her arms and extends her fingers. "Would you let me finish? God." She pulls her hair off her neck.

Her neck is fabulous—long and creamy and ready for my kisses. "Fine. Go ahead."

"You kicked me out, Braden. It was…"

"It was what?"

"Humiliating, all right? It was fucking humiliating. I felt…disposable."

Humiliating? I treat women well. I always have. I leave them satisfied. Every fucking time. Besides, I will never be held responsible for someone else's feelings. I stopped that long ago.

"I don't regulate how you feel, Skye. *You* do."

She shakes her head and glares at me. Damn, she's beautiful when she's angry. All hot and bothered and ready for a good fuck.

But I glare right back at her. No way will I take the blame for how *she's* feeling. "I don't consider you disposable, so why do *you*?"

She curls her hands into fists. "I *don't* consider myself disposable, which is why, Braden, if you want me in your bed so badly, you can't treat me as if I am. You can't just kick me out when you're done."

"We were *both* done."

"Maybe *you* were," she says. "Personally, I had several more orgasms left in me."

Really? I resist the urge to chuckle. Does she truly think I'm that ignorant? That I can't tell when a woman experiences something she's never experienced before? She's young. So young. Eleven years my junior. I need to remember that. She's not nearly as experienced as I am, and she probably thinks I don't have a clue that she never climaxed before me.

I run a hand through my hair. "I don't normally let anyone spend the night at my place."

True. I don't. It's nothing personal. I'm just not wired for a long-term relationship, and the sooner a woman understands that, the better. Allowing a woman to stay the night—to sleep in my bed—sends the wrong signals. It's not that I don't want a woman to spend the night. I believe I'd enjoy it—holding her, waking up next to her, fucking her in the morning. Of course I'd enjoy it. But so would she, and she'd continue to want more that I can't give her.

"Then don't," Skye says, her brown eyes glowing. "I won't go back to bed with you if you're going to make me leave afterward. Simple as that."

Fighting words. True fighting words. And if any other woman stood before me and said them, I'd nod, tell her goodbye, and walk away.

But I can't walk away from Skye. My feet feel like they're mired in cement, and the rest of my body seems caught in a force field.

This woman—this young and focused and, in some ways, immature woman—holds me in some kind of a thrall, which should bother me a lot more than it does.

I don't beg women to go to bed with me. Ever.

But Skye somehow planted a feeling inside me, and it's growing.

I want her back in my bed.

I will do whatever is necessary to get her back there.

I sigh, rubbing my forehead. "Fine. If that's what it takes to get you back in my bed, you can stay until morning. Does that suffice?"

She shrugs. "I don't have to stay. I just would like the option."

I cock my head, resisting a smile. I understand this woman better than she realizes.

It's control she wants.

She won't get that with me, but for the moment, I'm willing to give her the *illusion* of control.

"I'm beginning to see what you really want," I say. "It's not so much that you want to stay. It's that you want to be the one to decide, isn't it?"

She stays silent for a few minutes as people bustle around us in the lobby. The MADD Gala must be breaking up.

Finally, when the chaos in the lobby settles a bit, "I can't go back to your bed, Braden."

I sear her with my gaze. "You *can*."

"No, I can't. It just doesn't feel…"

I move into her space, feeling the heat that surrounds both of us. "You want to say it doesn't feel *right*, Skye. But you're not that good an actress. It's a lie, and you know it."

I close what little distance remains between us, bend down, breathe onto her ear.

"Come home with me," I whisper, "and you can leave whenever you want."

Chapter Nineteen

She goes limp in my arms for a timeless moment.

And I know I have her.

I pull back slightly.

"I…have to tell Tessa," she says.

I take her hand and lead her back to the ballroom. Tessa is sitting at our table when we get there. Her purse is still there, too, and she doesn't seem the least bit annoyed at Skye for abandoning it.

"What have you two been up to?" she asks.

"We just—" Skye begins.

"We're leaving," I say. "Can I give you a lift home?"

"I think I'll stay, actually. Garrett and I are hitting it off. Peter's a mess, though."

"What's wrong?" Skye asks.

"He's terrified of *you*," Tessa says to me, smiling. "Though you don't seem all that scary to me."

She's flirting, and Skye doesn't like it. I can tell by the way she goes slightly rigid.

I like that Skye doesn't like it. I like it a lot.

As for Peter, good. I want him scared of me. I don't want him near Skye. I don't particularly want Garrett near Tessa, either, but that's not my business.

"He just wants a contract with my company," I say, "and he thinks I won't give it to him because he was dancing with Skye."

"Oh. Is that true?"

"No. I'm not giving it to him anyway. The decision has already been made."

"Does he know?" Tessa asks.

"He will." I turn to Skye. "Ready?"

"Yeah, sure. See you, Tess."

"I'll call you tomorrow," Tessa says.

Within a few minutes, we're sitting in the back of my car again with Christopher at the wheel. I inhale and get a whiff of everything Skye. Her raspberry-scented hair, her soft floral cologne, a hint of bourbon, and…her sweet musk.

Skye leans into me and yawns.

"Tired?" I ask.

"No, I'm okay."

"Good. You need to be awake for what I have in mind tonight."

She quivers. Just a touch, but I can't help but notice. I'm always tuned in to my women, but with Skye? I'm on a whole different level. I feel everything with her.

And I'm disturbed at how much I like it, how much I'm beginning to crave it.

Christopher stops the car in front of my building, and we stay quiet as we walk through the lobby toward my private elevator.

We stay quiet as I slide my card.

We stay quiet as we step into the elevator and it zips up to my penthouse.

We stay quiet, and with every passing microsecond, my

need for Skye grows *ad infinitum*.

The elevator halts, and the doors slide open, revealing my foyer and living area.

We're hardly through the door when—

"Fuck," I growl and pin her against the wall beside the entryway, the door still hanging open. "I've wanted to kiss you all night. That sexy mouth of yours...and this dress. I ought to rip it off you so no other man can see you in it."

She trembles. "It's Tessa's."

"Don't care. I'll buy her a new one."

"But I like—"

"Still don't care." I crush my mouth to hers, grab one of the straps of her dress, and pull sharply as I thrust my tongue between her lips.

The low screech of the ripping fabric turns me on almost as much as this kiss. It means the dress's days are numbered. Soon I'll have a naked Skye in my arms...

She melts into the kiss as I deepen it.

This is a kiss of determination—a kiss of my will over hers—and I groan when I feel her surrender. Surrender to my lips, teeth, and tongue as our mouths slide together. Her heart beats rapidly, so strong that I feel it as we're mashed together, her body still pinned against the wall.

Th-thump. Th-thump. Th-thump.

Her heart's cadence matches my own.

I'm rough and merciless as I devour her. I rip the other strap of her dress and push it over her shoulder and then downward, until it's banded around her waist. I slide my hands up her sides and cup her breasts, and then I pull back, our mouths parting with a *pop*.

God, a black strapless bra that barely contains her ample tits. Her cheeks and chin pink from the roughness of my stubble against her soft skin. And her lips...

I gaze at her, focusing on those full lips. "I wish you could see your mouth right now, Skye. Your lipstick is smeared, and your lips are swollen and glistening and parted in that slight way that's all you." I drop my gaze. "And these tits. Spectacular."

"Bra," she says, panting.

"Yeah, fucking sexy. Made for your tits." In my head are images of the many ways I can relieve her of it, none of them ending with the garment intact.

"Bra," she says again. "Don't rip it."

I ignore her command and rip the black lace off her, freeing her breasts. "I'll buy you a hundred bras, Skye. A new one for every time I fuck you, just so I can rip it off."

Her nipples are tight and hard, so ready for my touch. But I don't touch them. I'm still cupping the rosy flesh of her breasts, still gazing at them.

"Please," she says.

"Please what?"

"My nipples. Touch them."

I can't help a surly smile. "You want me to touch your nipples, Skye?"

"Yes, God. Please."

I brush my lips against the top of her throat. "How do you want me to touch them, baby?"

"I don't care. Just touch them. Please."

"What if I don't?" I tease. "What will you do?"

She meets my gaze. "I... I'll leave."

Interesting choice, and one I'm not expecting.

I don't like games as a rule, and Skye is definitely playing one. I want to get in her pants more than I want my next breath, but I *will* remain in charge here. Even if it means blue balls tonight.

I move backward, releasing her breasts. "Go ahead. You're not obligated to stay here."

Already I know she'll renege. She clearly wants me as

much as I want her. Her breasts are swollen and her nipples erect. A sheen of perspiration shines on her flesh, and her fragrance. Damn. She's wet and hot and ready.

No, she doesn't want to leave. But she'll claim to, because she doesn't want to give me the upper hand.

Fuck. Skye Manning. A challenge.

And I love a challenge.

She clears her throat. "Fine. But I'll need a…shirt or something."

I glare at her. How far is she willing to take this? Because I *will* win this battle.

She opens her mouth, but I push her back against the wall, my hands gripping her shoulders. I move toward her slowly until our lips are only millimeters apart. God, I want to close the minute gap and kiss her, slide my tongue between those luscious lips and head into the bedroom. And I know she wants the same.

But I didn't get where I am today by giving in, and I won't give in now.

She will.

And she does.

She closes the distance and presses her lips to mine.

I pull back, still gripping her shoulders. "I thought you wanted to leave."

"I thought you *wanted* me to leave."

"When did I say that?" I ask. "You're the one who brought it up. What kind of a game do you think I'm playing, Skye?"

"I…don't know."

"That's because I'm not playing a game. You may think this is a cat-and-mouse thing, but it's not. I enjoy making you want me."

"Braden, you know I want you, but if you ever tell me to leave again, this whole thing is over."

"Is it?"

She gulps. How far will she truly go? Will she leave just to remain in control?

"I'm afraid so," she finally says.

I'm hard as a rock. I could so easily whip out my cock, push her against the wall, and shove into her from behind. She'd let me, and God, I want her so badly.

But I release her, walk through the entryway to a closet, and open it. I pull a blue cardigan out, walk back, and hand it to her. "Go ahead, Skye. Leave."

Chapter Twenty

I don't want her to leave.

She doesn't want to leave.

Her eyes tell the tale—their bourbon-hued depth defies her and shows the truth. She glances downward and then toward the blue sweater I hold.

She doesn't move, even when I take a step toward her.

I don't ask her to leave again. I simply stand three feet away from her, the sweater dangling from my hand.

Stalemate.

She has two choices. She can take the sweater and leave, or she can stay, effectively giving up control over this situation. Already I know which side will win, and I know what it will cost her.

She opens her mouth, and I finally close the distance between us, dropping the sweater and again gripping her shoulders.

"No more games, Skye," I whisper darkly. "Give in to me tonight, and I promise you more pleasure than you've ever known."

"No more games," she whispers.

I kiss her. Hard.

Harder and deeper than ever. Her own ache and hunger pour into me through the kiss. I feel every bit of it, and it mirrors my own. I break the kiss and then scrape my teeth over her jawline and down her bare shoulder. Her nipples are still hard and wanting, and this time I take one between my lips and gently kiss it.

I strengthen my hold on her, remaining gentle with the nipple, even though I want to bite down. Hard.

My cock pulses in time with my heart, and I have to force myself to go slowly. I tease her other nipple with my fingers while I continue to suck at the first, gradually increasing the pull. She gasps and threads her fingers through my hair as I bob against her breast. I finally release the first nipple, glide my lips over to the second, and clamp my mouth around it. No teasing this time. I full-on suck it. Hard. A low moan emerges in her throat, and she pulls at my hair.

I groan without meaning to.

"Is your pussy wet for me?" I say against her flesh.

"God, yes."

"I can smell how much you want me."

The fragrant aroma wafts around us, has my cock straining. I'm like a horny kid with her. I release the nipple. Inhale. Exhale. Regain control over my body.

Then I slide my hands down her abdomen, pushing the dress off her to the floor. She stands only in her black panties. I lower my head and inhale. Deeply.

She has the scent of a goddess. But she's not a goddess. She's Eve. She's Delilah. She's a temptress like no other woman I've known. She has no idea how much inner strength I required to hand her that sweater, to tell her to leave.

Because my God, I want her. I want to do everything to her.

I inhale again and then slide her panties over her hips.

They land within the circle of the dress.

She's naked.

Naked and wet and completely at my mercy.

Perfect.

I trail my tongue over the top of her vulva, which is freshly shaven and smooth this time. I spread her thighs and flick my tongue over her clit, savoring the brief taste of her. She inhales sharply and I tilt my head, meeting her gaze.

"Bedroom," I rasp. Then I stand and pull her—naked while I'm still fully clothed in my tux—to the bedroom.

I leave her standing by the bed and walk to my highboy. I open a drawer and pull out a black silk blindfold.

Tonight it begins.

The education of Skye Manning.

The submission of Skye Manning.

I return to the bed, place the cool silk over her eyes, and tie it around her head, taking care not to tug on her beautiful hair.

She opens her mouth, and I wait. I wait for her to tell me to stop. I will always stop if she wants me to, but she doesn't want me to. Already I feel this.

She closes her mouth, and I smile, knowing she can't see my expression.

"Don't speak," I say. "Just enjoy."

"Enjoy what?"

I hold back the urge to give her a light smack to the breast for her disobedience. "I told you not to speak."

She presses her lips together.

"Because I've taken your sight," I say, "your other senses will be enhanced. You won't see what I do to you, but you'll smell it, taste it, hear it."

"What if—"

"Skye," I say, forcing my voice to sound gentler than I

actually feel, "if you speak again, I'll punish you."

She rips the blindfold off her eyes. "I didn't sign up to be beaten."

I expect resistance. Actually want it. Skye's strength and take-charge attitude are part of what attract me to her, and it will make the end that much sweeter. For both of us.

"Who said anything about being beaten? What kind of man do you think I am?"

"You said you'd punish me. What other kind of punishment is there?"

I meet her gaze. "You're about to find out."

Chapter Twenty-One

She shudders, and her nipples and areolas tighten further.

I suck in a breath.

Watching her reaction to my words, my actions, thrills and sends sparks skittering over my flesh.

Her mind is working. I can almost see the cogs turning in her brain. She's thinking about punishment, and she's not sure if she'll like it or hate it.

She's wrong on both counts.

She's going to love it.

"Are… Are you going to hurt me?" she asks.

"Only if you want me to." I slip the blindfold onto her eyes once more. "Keep it on this time."

"But are you—"

"Punishment doesn't have to hurt, Skye. At least not physically."

"So you're still going to…?"

"Punish you? Oh yes."

Shivers rack her body. "How—"

"No more talking," I command. "You're used to being

in control, Skye, so I'm trying to be lenient. But I have my limits."

She opens her mouth—

"Do you want to be gagged?"

She shakes her head vehemently.

I lower my head and nip at her soft earlobe. "The first thing I noticed about you was your sexy mouth. The second thing was your amazing rack. But the third thing, Skye, was what truly drew me to you. Do you know what it is?"

She shakes her head.

"When you dropped your purse, you wouldn't accept my help. You had to maintain a semblance of control in the situation. Then there was the condom."

She bites her lip. And damn, I want to bite it for her. Hard. Leave my mark on that sexy mouth.

"Yes, I saw it," I continue. "Another way you keep your life in control."

"Because I don't want to get pregnant?"

I resist the urge to berate her for speaking again. "It's more than that, and you know it. If a situation arises where you want to have sex, you're ready. You don't have to rush to the pharmacy for protection."

"A lot of women carry condoms around."

"Less than you might think. Some depend on other methods, or they run to the pharmacy as needed. Some are concerned only about pregnancy and not diseases."

"And you know this because…"

"I've been with a lot of women."

Well, she asked. I've always been amazed how many women expect the man to provide protection. It's never a problem, as I'm always fully stocked with condoms, but so many women think only about unplanned pregnancies and not diseases, which can be far worse.

"I had a feeling about you." I resist the urge to caress her soft cheek, trail a finger over her gorgeous neck. "About your need for control. Then, after our first dinner and my attempt to seduce you, I knew for sure."

Her mouth twitches, but she doesn't respond.

"I recognized it in you. I recognize it in people because it's part of who I am as well."

She nods.

"I wouldn't be where I am today," I whisper darkly, nipping her earlobe once more, "without knowing how to exercise control in every situation."

She nods again and attempts to suppress a quiver unsuccessfully.

"That includes controlling *you*, Skye. Right now, I control your pleasure. I have leverage over you. Do you understand?"

She doesn't respond.

"I asked if you understand."

This time, she nods once more.

I gently push her onto the bed. "Lie down."

She obeys.

I kneel, spread her legs, and draw in a breath, relishing the whiff of her sweet sent. She jars slightly. Already I see her sense of hearing is heightened. She's aware of my intake of breath.

"Your scent intoxicates me, Skye," I whisper. "I can sit here between your legs forever and never get tired of it." I inhale again, this time holding my breath longer until I exhale.

A soft sigh emerges from her throat. She goes rigid.

"Relax, baby. No need to tighten up right now." I inhale once more. "As much as I adore your smell, you taste even better."

I begin at her perineum and slide my tongue upward until I get to her clit. She gasps sharply. I glide over her clit, swirling around, and then I close my lips around it and suck ever so slightly.

She sighs, and a moan follows. I give as much pleasure as I take, all while staying in control in the bedroom. Eating Skye's pussy is as pleasing to me as it is to her. She's that delicious, that responsive.

I don't berate her for releasing the sounds. I commanded only that she not speak. Her sexy gasps spur me on, and I increase the speed of my tongue. She grips the comforter in both her hands and arches her back, undulating her hips. I'm deliberately ignoring her clit now. I've lit the fuse. Now it's time for the long tease. I shove my tongue into her pussy and then lick and pull on her labia.

Her moans fuel my desire, and I move up and flick my tongue over her clit. Once. Just once.

She writhes beneath me. I know what she wants, but she's going to have to wait.

I go back to eating her pussy. "You're so wet," I say against her flesh. "God, you drive me wild, Skye. You're so responsive to everything I do."

Yes. Yes, I am. Please. Please. Please let me come.

I hear the words in my mind. In her voice.

She's done well, but I'm not ready to reward her yet. No. I'm ready to keep her on the edge.

I slide my tongue up her pussy and grab hold of her clit once more, this time nipping harder. Once. Twice. Then three times.

I thrust two fingers into her heat, and— I release her clit.

Is it an asshole move? Not really. The penetration from my fingers inside her along with clitoral stimulation would equal instant orgasm.

But it's the climb that's the real pleasure. I want to drive her just as wild as she drives me.

I push her thighs forward and lower my tongue, sliding it over her asshole. She tenses.

"Oh!"

Not surprising. Ms. Manning has never had a rim job. I'll remedy that with pleasure.

I jab my tongue into her ass gently. Then I bring my palm down on the cheek of her ass with a loud—

Smack!

She jerks against the slap as her ass turns a lovely shade of pink.

"That's for talking." Then I slide my tongue back over her asshole and up her pussy again.

Her hand wanders to her vulva. She's so ripe. I know what she's feeling. If she can just touch herself, just once, she'll shatter.

Not on my watch. Time for another lesson in who's in control in this bedroom.

I grab her wrist. "No, you don't. That clit is mine tonight. No one touches it but me."

"But I have to come."

I move forward and slide the blindfold off her eyes, chuckling. I can't help it. I know what's coming, and so does she. "I told you I'd punish you for talking."

"The smack?" she says.

"No, that was for pleasure."

She liked the smack. I could tell from her reaction. She doesn't deny it.

I suck on her clit once more while ramming my fingers in and out of her pussy. She shudders on the bed, her hips moving frantically against my lips and tongue.

She tastes so sweet, and she grinds against my face, rubbing her juices into my skin. Fuck. My cock is on fire, so ready to slide right into her, but I know control better than anyone, and I can wait.

And so will she. I pull away from her clit and remove my fingers from her pussy.

I move forward, letting the fabric of my shirt slide over

her nipples.

I press my lips to one nipple and then the other before I kiss her lips chastely, letting her taste her own sweetness.

"Do you understand now, Skye?"

"Understand what?"

"That punishment doesn't have to physically hurt."

Chapter Twenty-Two

Skye is slick with perspiration, her body pink and taut, so ready.

"I was right," she says. "You knew what you were doing the whole time."

Smart woman. "Of course I did."

"You freak."

"What's freakish about denying you a climax?"

"Most men love it when their partner comes," she says.

"I've never in my life been 'most men.' That's not to say I don't enjoy it when you come. I do, actually. I enjoy it a lot."

"Then why—"

"You *know* why."

She wants to deny my words, play innocent. She even opens her mouth to say something but then closes it. Tension is still coiled inside her—tension I will relieve.

But not yet.

"You're still resisting, Skye," I say. "If you weren't so determined to be in control, you could have come three times by now."

"Why?" she asks.

"I've already answered that. You know why."

She shakes her head. "No. I mean, why do you need me to give *you* control?"

"I don't need it."

Her eyes widen. "You *don't*?"

"That's what you asked. You asked why I need it, and the truth is, I don't."

She shakes her head. "I don't understand."

"I don't need it. I *want* it."

"Why, then? Why do you want it?"

Why? I've never thought about why. It's what I like in the bedroom. It's what I've always liked in the bedroom, and I see no reason not to have what I want, as long as my partner is willing.

"Does there have to be a reason?" I finally say.

"Yeah, there does," she says. "How am I supposed to understand if there isn't a reason?"

"Still trying to stay in control, aren't you?"

She sits up. "Just because I want answers—"

"Means you're not giving up control."

"You said if I gave up control, you'd show me pleasure like I've never known. Then you deny me a climax. That's not showing me pleasure, Braden."

"True, but there's still an element missing to that agreement."

"What's that?"

I trail a finger over her cheek, a gesture so pure that it's almost loving. I find it freeing. And disorienting. "You *haven't* given up control."

"But you want me in your bed, Braden. You've said that from the beginning."

"I don't deny it."

"Why not take me as I am?"

"Because you and I will both like it better my way."

"What makes you so certain?" she asks.

I slide my finger over her lower lip, my cock about ready to burst. "I see it in your eyes. You're a beautiful woman, Skye, but you're the most beautiful when you let go and surrender to your body."

My own words ignite the embers burning deep within me. She zeroes in on my still-clothed crotch. My erection is more than apparent.

"You want me," she says.

"Of course I do. I'm not made of clay. I'm a man, baby, and any man who lays eyes on you wants you."

I burn her with my gaze. She's so young—and so innocent in so many ways—but damn, I've never wanted a woman more than I want Skye.

She clears her throat. "Is my punishment over?"

"That's up to you."

"Meaning…?"

"Meaning…are you ready to give up control?" I gesture for her not to respond yet. "Before you answer, know this. I want to fuck you. I want you more than I've wanted anyone in a long time. I think I've made that abundantly clear."

She nods.

"I *will* fuck you tonight," I say. "The only question is whether you get a climax."

"But if you fuck me—"

I quiet her with a touch of my fingers to her lips. "Trust me. I can still fuck you and keep you from coming."

I'm a master at bringing a woman to the edge and then denying her an orgasm. It's a punishment much more effective than any flogging or binding. I love when a woman comes for me, but I will withhold it to exert my power.

And Skye is determined to resist my power.

"Do you want to come tonight, baby?"

She nods.

"Tell me. Tell me you want to come."

"I want to come tonight, Braden."

I narrow my eyes but only slightly. "Then don't disobey me again."

She's assessing me, trying to figure me out. She won't. I haven't even figured myself out. In the end, though, she won't resist. She'll come to my bed, and she'll give me what I desire.

Her control.

She clears her throat. "Tell me what you want, Braden."

"I want to fuck you into next week."

She curves those delectable lips into a teasing smile. "You're in luck. I've got all next week open."

Chapter Twenty-Three

I grab the silk blindfold and tie it over her eyes again. "No talking, Skye. Understand?"

"I have a question first."

My God, she'll be the death of me. "For God's sake. What kind of question could you possibly have? No talking means no talking."

She lets out an exasperated sigh. "It's a valid one, Braden. Can I sigh and moan? Groan?"

"Sexual sounds are permissible."

"Okay. But you got me last time for saying 'oh.' Isn't that a sexual sound?"

"No. 'Oh' is a word. 'Oh God' are words. 'Yes, Braden, yes' are words."

"But those words are indicating that I'm enjoying myself."

"So what?"

"So...don't you want to know I'm enjoying myself?"

"I know you're enjoying yourself by how your body responds to me. The words are superfluous."

She scoffs. "Seriously?"

I can't help a chuckle. I love her words, but what I love even more are her nonverbal responses. How her body reacts, how her flesh becomes flushed, how her pussy gets swollen and wet. And what she doesn't yet understand is that, without words, all response comes from her body. It reacts more, feels more. Wants and desires more.

In turn, I want and desire more.

It's a win-win concept.

"You become more of a challenge every second, Skye Manning. You're my Everest, and I'm determined to conquer you. Now, be quiet."

She presses her lips together and makes a locking motion with her hand. She's something all right. The sarcasm ripples off her.

That's fine. She'll understand. Eventually.

I gently push her until the backs of her legs hit the bed. "Lie down."

She obeys.

I head to my antique mahogany wardrobe and open the door. Before me—on shelves, in drawers, and hanging—are my various playthings. Tools I use to give pleasure. I zero in on a stainless steel anal plug.

How I'd love to lube it up and begin training on Skye's ass. Just the thought has my cock growing even harder, if that's possible. Licking her ass tonight intoxicated me.

But that has to wait. She's barely ready for an introduction, so I must go slowly. If I try too much, she'll bail. She can't bail. I want her too much. She has it in her psyche to submit. I just need to draw it out slowly.

I pick up the stainless steel plug anyway. It's cool to the touch, and I have a use for it—one Skye and I will both love.

I return to the bed, where she lies supine before me, naked, blindfolded, and exquisitely appetizing. I suck in a breath and adjust my groin.

She squirms when I come near her. Though I'm being quiet, she hears me with her heightened senses. Sensory deprivation can be very erotic. I'll introduce her to it further another time. For now?

I trail the end of the anal plug around one of her hard nipples.

She gasps and arches her back. I trace the swell of her breast and move to the other nipple.

I enjoy using toys on women. They offer different sensory excitement to a partner, and consequently, they elicit different sensory responses. I love watching how their bodies react.

But with Skye...

The anal plug traces her rosy breast, and somehow I feel her soft flesh beneath my fingers as if I'm actually touching her, as if the plug has become an extension of my arm, of my body.

Prickles erupt on her creamy flesh, and in tandem with her, I'm tingling as well. I continue, going from nipple to nipple and then trailing down her abdomen, feeling her warm skin beneath the anal plug as if we're meeting flesh to flesh.

I close my eyes a moment, savoring this new sensation I've uncovered.

I want Skye's submission. I yearn for it. I crave it. So much that I don't have to actually touch her to feel her.

Unreal.

I stop at her belly button. It's a sexy indentation, and I imagine a platinum and diamond barbell laced through it. I circle the toy around the little notch. She arches again, and her clit is visible and swollen, protruding slightly from her gorgeous pink folds. I want so much to drag the stainless steel downward, circle her clit. But I linger at her navel.

"So beautiful, Skye. You should have this pierced."

She opens her mouth but then closes it. Was she going to say something?

I'm glad she decided not to. I really don't want to have to

withhold her orgasm. I get just as much pleasure as she does from her climax.

When I finally trail downward to her vulva, she lets out an excited moan. Still I tease, though, gliding over her pubic bone and down the sides of her opening. I nick her soft labia, suck in a breath as it glistens with her wetness.

As much as I don't want to leave that paradise between her legs, I trail the anal plug down over her inner thighs to her knees.

Then I begin the trip back up. The ultimate tease for both of us.

I trail the steel back over her slit. "Mmm. Nice and wet. How much do you want me, Skye?"

She opens her mouth and then slams it shut.

"Good girl." I don't need her words. The slickness of her pussy is more than enough answer. I slide the plug over her.

She moans and circles her hips. Arches her back and undulates...

But I move the object back up her vulva to her breasts and then to her lips. I poke it into her mouth. "Taste yourself. See how delicious you are."

She swirls her tongue over it—that sexy, silky tongue— and I imagine the pointed end of the anal plug is the head of my cock. Fuck. I swear I feel it, as if she's licking me, caressing that most sensitive part of me with that warm tongue.

Damn.

I take the anal plug away from her lips and set it on the night table.

Enough is enough.

I remove my clothes as quickly as I ever have, leaving them in piles on the carpet, and quickly put on a condom.

Skye squirms on the bed, twisting the covers with her hands.

"Don't move your hands, Skye," I say.

She releases her fists.

"Bend your legs so your feet are flat on the bed."

Again, she obeys.

I stare for a moment at the sheer beauty before me. Her pussy, engorged and juicy, just waiting for me to plunder it. I crawl forward and nudge her slit with my cock.

She reaches—

"I said don't move your hands!"

She quickly jerks her hand back.

I understand. She wants to touch me. Normally I don't need a woman's touch, but with Skye...

Damn. I want it.

But not. I gave her a command, and she will obey.

I tease her pussy again with my cock, sliding it back and forth from her clit nearly to her ass. It's a tickle that has my balls on fire already. I want to thrust into her. No more waiting.

But I wait.

She says nothing. She keeps her hands flat.

And still I wait.

One minute ticks by. Another. My cock is so sensitive I may explode...but still I wait.

Until—

One powerful thrust, and I'm inside her. A vibrant groan squeezes out of me. Skye cries out, not in words but in pure emotion.

Yes, this is what I'm after. Words are fickle. They lie. When I take away her speech, I get honesty. Pure, raw honesty. It's a powerful aphrodisiac.

I pull out, and she whimpers.

I tease again, letting just the head of my cock breach her pussy. Tiny shallow thrusts, just enough to make her want me more.

And God, it makes me want her more, too.

My determination is waning.

I have to have her.

Now.

"Fuck it." I thrust into her, tunneling through her with my cock, burning through her flesh and taking what I need.

She groans. Her nipples are tight and hard, and though I ache to lean down, touch my chest to hers, I don't. That would give her friction against her clit, and she'd come. I'm not ready to let her come yet, so I concentrate on my cock in her pussy. I simply fuck her. I fuck her hard.

Again and again, I invade her pussy with my harsh thrusts.

Each time, she gloves me more completely, swallows my cock more generously.

Until I can't wait any longer.

I lean down, cover her body with mine, and kiss those beautiful lips, still thrusting, thrusting, thrusting, and giving her the jolt against her clit that she needs.

And that's all it takes.

Her pussy contracts, pulsating against my plunging cock. Moans emerge from her throat.

"That's it, baby," I say. "Give it to me. Give it all to me. It's mine."

Thrust, thrust, thrust—

"God, yes! So tight, baby. So good."

All mine. That orgasm is all mine.

My cock is so deep inside her, and still she quivers around me. I give one last strong thrust and release into her hot pussy.

I pulse, pulse, pulse, as she continues to come, milking every last ounce of semen from my dick.

Fuck.

Even *I* can't believe how good it is.

When my cock finally calms down, I pull out, roll off her, and remove the blindfold.

"You can speak now and move your hands."

But she has no words.

Chapter Twenty-Four

I can't help a glint in my eye. "Have I truly rendered you speechless? Seems unbelievable." I'm on my side, my head propped on my hand. I stare down at Skye.

She reaches forward and pushes a stray hair over my forehead. "What do you want me to say?"

"You can start with, 'Wow, Braden. You rocked my world.'"

I laugh. "Isn't that pretty obvious?"

"See what happens when you give in to me?"

She smiles but says nothing.

Already, I know why. She thinks she's still in control, and in a way, she's right.

Submissives don't realize how much control they truly wield.

She did what she had to do to make sure she climaxed. I can't blame her for that. I wanted that climax from her as much as she did, but I was willing to put it off if she disobeyed me.

She wasn't.

I know your secret, Skye Manning.

But for now, I'll keep that knowledge to myself.

Finally, she speaks. "It was amazing."

I kiss her lips softly. "Go to sleep."

Something jars me then, as I dispose of the condom quickly and lie down beside her.

I'm feeling…content. Content to be sleeping next to Skye in my bed.

I lie back and close my eyes, and I wonder…

Why do I like this feeling so much?

• • •

I'm up at dawn the next morning, and still strangely content to see a sleeping Skye, naked and gorgeous, next to me. I kiss her chastely on the forehead and rise, take a shower as quietly as I can, dress in jeans and a T-shirt, and pad barefoot to the kitchen.

Marilyn isn't up yet, so I start the coffee and fire up my iPad to check the morning news and then my email.

A half hour later, Marilyn appears, her hair—which I can't decide if it's blond or brown, depending on the day—knotted on her head. She's the only one on my personal staff to commute. The others have private bedrooms on the third floor of my penthouse.

"Good morning," she says cheerfully. "Was I supposed to be in earlier this morning?"

"No, you're right on time."

"Oh, good. What can I make for your breakfast this morning, Mr. B?"

"Bacon and eggs, I think. And toast. Lots of toast." After last night, I need to do some carb loading.

"You got it." She opens the refrigerator and grabs eggs and bacon.

While Marilyn lays strips of bacon in her large cast-iron skillet, I peruse my email. Mostly good news, though I'm going to have to travel to New York again this week. Normally I don't mind travel, but Skye…

I wipe the thought from my mind. Skye is not an issue. Work goes on as scheduled. I've never changed my plans for a woman, and I'm not about to start now.

I'm knee-deep in the middle of looking over a résumé for a new marketing manager when a soft "ahem" drifts to my ears.

I look up.

And suppress the urge to gasp as my cock reacts to the sight of Skye—wearing one of my white button-down shirts. It hangs on her, leaving her entire body to the imagination.

It's the sexiest thing I've ever seen.

I hold back a groan as I turn toward her. "Good morning."

"Good morning," she replies.

"Coffee?"

"Absolutely. Thank you." She walks in and takes a seat next to me.

Marilyn turns away from the stove and eyes her. "Good morning. I'm Marilyn."

"Hi," Skye squeaks out.

"How do you take your coffee?" Marilyn asks.

"Black."

A moment later, she slides a cup of steaming black coffee in front of Skye.

I turn to her. "Hungry?"

"No. I'm good."

"Are you sure? Marilyn always makes enough to feed a small army."

"That's because you have the appetite of a small army." Marilyn smiles and sets a full plate of bacon, eggs, and toast in front of me. "Sure I can't get you anything?"

"No." Skye takes a sip of coffee and then sets the cup down quickly, spilling a few drops on the marble counter. "Sorry," she mumbles.

"Not a problem." Marilyn wipes up the mess with a flourish.

Skye burned her tongue on the hot coffee, but I won't embarrass her by mentioning it. This goes beyond a burned tongue, though. Something is bothering her. I place my iPad on the counter. "Could you excuse us for a few minutes, Marilyn?"

"Sure, Mr. Black. Just buzz if you need me." She exits the kitchen.

I turn to Skye. "What's going on?"

"Nothing."

"You're acting strange. Are you uncomfortable here?"

"No. Not exactly."

"You're the one who wanted to stay," I remind her. "To leave on your own terms."

She nods. "Yes."

"Okay. Just so we're both on the same page—you're welcome to stay as long as you like. I have a few hours of work to do."

"Oh. Okay. I should check in with work, too." She takes another sip of coffee. "Braden?"

"Yeah."

Her cheeks are that delectable shade of pink again. "I'm going to need something to wear home."

I resist a smile, though the memory of shredding Skye's little black dress is worth a face-splitting grin. "Of course. Find out where Tessa got the black dress, and I'll have it replaced. You can wear the cardigan I gave you last night."

"Okay... What about pants?"

I nearly smile again. "I guess I didn't leave your dress in working condition as a skirt."

"No, you didn't."

I stand. "I'll find you something. Next time, bring a change of clothes."

She widens her eyes slightly. Is she surprised? I'm nowhere near done with Skye Manning.

"In fact," I continue, "bring over several things. Or if you want to leave me your sizes, I'll have some stuff delivered."

"That's okay. I have plenty. I can bring some over."

"Good," I say, my voice going darker, "because I plan to destroy a lot of them."

Chapter Twenty-Five

Work and a ten-mile run fill the remainder of my Sunday—
except for the call I make to my tailor after Christopher leaves
to take Skye home. Rather than wait to find out where Tessa
bought the dress—since I may or may not be able to find the
same one, especially if it's not from the current season, which
I'm betting it isn't—I take the matter into my own hands.

"Miguel, it's Braden Black."

"Good morning, Mr. Black. What can I do for you?"

"I've got a project for you, if you're free today."

"I'm always free for you."

"Great."

Miguel Moore and I have an arrangement. I pay him ten
times what he gets from anyone else, and in return, he drops
everything and sews his ass off for me with a twenty-four
hour or less turnaround. It started back when I'd made my
first hundred million, and Sasha, who was just a pup at the
time, chewed up my tuxedo. I had an event the next day, and
a rental wasn't going to cut it. I put out a plea on social media
and Miguel answered. His work is top-notch, and over the

years, we've kept up the arrangement.

I plan to take advantage of it today.

"I need a dress."

Miguel laughs. "I'm guessing your usual measurements? Or is it for a young lady?"

I chuckle lightly. "For a young lady, thanks. I need you to work your magic. I have the tag from the back of the dress and some photos of a woman wearing it at a gala last night. Other than that, it's in tatters."

"Must have been a fun night."

Right. And none of his business. I clear my throat. "I'll have what's left of the dress couriered to you right away. I'll need two exact replicas of the dress created. Just a minute, and I'll text you the photos."

A moment later, Miguel says, "Got them. It looks like a basic mini sheath with spaghetti straps. I can replicate it no problem."

"Excellent. Send one dress to Ms. Tessa Logan. I'll find her work address and text it to you. I'll pick up the other. Then bill me, of course."

"You got it, Mr. Black," Miguel says. "I won't let you down."

"I know you won't. Sorry to make you work on a Sunday, Miguel. Thanks."

After ending the call, I take a quick side trip to the MADD website. Front and center is a photo of Skye and me dressed to the nines. The caption reads, "Braden Black and friend."

I roll my eyes. The usual. Most women would find that caption humiliating. I hope Skye isn't one of them. She's much more down-to-earth than the women who usually inhabit my orbit.

Except it's not Skye's reaction that concerns me.

It's my own.

It's the realization that I don't want to just be Skye's "friend."

I want more.

. . .

The next morning, because of an early meeting with a potential investor, I don't get into my office until ten thirty.

"Good morning, Claire," I say absently as I head straight through the door. "Any messages?"

Claire rises and enters my office to lay down a handful of message slips. "Mostly mundane stuff," she says, "except for these three." She shoves them toward me.

I read the name.

Kay Brown.

"You've got to be kidding."

"Three calls before ten," Claire says. "I'm expecting the fourth any minute now."

"What does she want?"

"What do you think? She wants the scoop on the MADD Gala."

"She doesn't need to get that from me."

Claire smiles. "You're going to make me spell it out for you, huh? Apparently you had a new woman on your arm. I've been hearing gossip all morning."

"My personal life isn't any of Kay Brown's business. Or this office's."

"I didn't say *I've* been spreading gossip, Mr. B. I've been hearing gossip."

"From whom?"

"I'm not a snitch. But you can count on me not to spread any."

I nod. Claire's not a gossip. If she were, she'd be long gone by now. With a staff the size of mine, there's bound to be some talk, though. I know this, and I usually let it lie.

Today, for some reason, it rubs me the wrong way.

I've been on the receiving end of libelous gossip stories in all the rags. I ignore it. Always. But I don't want Skye subjected to it.

"Call Kay and tell her I'm not interested in talking," I tell Claire.

"I will. Just so you're aware, though, Kay knows the name of your date last night. She mentioned Skye Manning."

I lift my eyebrows, though I don't know why I'm surprised. Boston's resident bloodhound can easily sniff out that kind of information.

"Very well. Make the call anyway."

"Will do. I don't expect that to stop her, though."

I sigh. "Neither do I. Thanks, Claire."

Kay Brown is relentless. She's a hired gun for the *Boston Babbler*, our local gossip rag where all the stories use an "unnamed source." I swear to God, they just make most of the shit up. I normally let it roll off my back. All the stories are forgotten as soon as the next issue rolls out.

But again, I don't want Skye involved.

Why am I feeling so protective of her? She's a grown woman, for God's sake.

The emotion bubbling inside me is becoming more than disorienting.

It's agitating.

And I don't like feeling agitated.

My mind is racing. This day is no different from any given day in my world. I have no fewer than twenty projects in the works, no fewer than fifteen calls to return.

Definitely a lot to do.

Instead, I rise.

I know Kay Brown. She'll be dogging Skye in no time, so I should warn her. That's all it is. The fact that I'm itching to see Skye doesn't enter my mind.

But I've never been a good liar, especially to myself.

I want to see Skye. She has to eat. I'll take her to lunch.

"I'll be out until two or three," I tell Claire. "I'm heading to the food bank after lunch."

She nods. "Got it. I put in the call to Kay, but she's not answering her cell."

I roll my eyes. "Don't worry. She'll call back."

Twenty minutes later, I'm walking into the Ames Hotel, my shoes clacking across the marble lobby, past the elevators, to the offices.

The door to Addison's office is open, and as I get closer—

Skye's voice. "Yeah, I eat early. Since Addie's not in, I need to close up the office. Please excuse me."

I walk through the door.

Chapter Twenty-Six

Skye, purse in hand, is standing in front of her desk.

Five feet away from her is none other than Kay Brown. Christ.

"Kay," I say. "I can't say I'm surprised to see you here, since you've already called my office three times today."

"Mr. Black." She holds out her hand. "A pleasure as always."

I take her hand and shake it firmly. "If you'll excuse us, I need to talk to Skye."

"Of course. How long have you two been dating?"

To Kay Brown, "of course" apparently means "not until I ask you myriad questions." I'll throw her a bone.

"We only met about a week ago," I say.

"And your date at the gala?"

"We didn't arrive together. Ms. Manning and I saw each other at the gala and talked a bit."

Skye's audible gulp doesn't escape my notice. Is she upset at my response?

Kay turns to Skye. "Your lunch date, Ms. Manning, is

with Mr. Black?"

"No, it's—"

"Yes, it is," I say, taking advantage of the situation to get Skye out of there. "Are you ready, Skye?"

She clears her throat. "Yeah, I'm ready. I need to lock up."

"Of course." Kay walks out the door and then turns and looks over her shoulder. "I'll be in touch. With both of you." And then she's gone.

"Thanks for the save," Skye says. "I thought she was here to see Addie."

"I figured she'd bother you this morning after she called my office and mentioned you by name."

"You came here to warn me?"

"In part."

"In part?"

"Yeah. I thought you might be up for an early lunch."

"Sorry. I'm meeting Tessa in an hour."

I narrow my eyes and burn her with my gaze. "Cancel." The word comes out on a low growl.

She grasps the edge of the desk. "I can't. Tess and I always have lunch on Mondays."

Her phone buzzes. "Excuse me for a minute," she says to me. "Hey, Tess."

Pause.

"Oh?" Skye's eyes widen.

Pause.

She clears her throat. "He said he'd replace it."

Pause.

"Hold on a minute." She mutes the phone and turns to me. "She got the dress."

"Good."

"She says it's perfect. Did you get it repaired?"

"It was beyond repair, as you know."

"Then how did you...?"

"I gave the remains to my personal tailor yesterday, along with your Instagram photo. He was able to replicate it."

Her jaw drops. "In a day?"

"I'm a very good customer." I smirk.

She unmutes the phone. "His tailor replicated it yesterday," she tells Tessa.

Pause.

"You can tell him yourself." She hands the phone to me.

"Ms. Logan," I say.

"Mr. Black...I mean...Braden. Hi. I'm not sure what to say. This could totally be the same dress. Thank you so much."

"You're very welcome. Anytime."

"You didn't have to," Tessa says. "What's a dress between best friends? I wish there was some way I could repay you."

"Actually, there *is* something you can do for me."

"Of course. Anything."

"Let me take Skye to lunch today. You can have lunch with her tomorrow."

"Are you kidding?" She laughs. "Of course! And thank you again."

"I appreciate that. And you don't have to keep thanking me. Have a good day." I hand the phone back to her.

"Tess?" she says. Then she wrinkles her brow.

Tessa must have hung up.

I stare at her. "Seems you're free for lunch after all, Skye."

Chapter Twenty-Seven

"Tessa said you sent the dress to her office," Skye says to me after we order our meal at a little French bistro. "How did you know where she works?"

"That kind of information isn't hard to find," I reply.

"Not when you can pay for it," she says. "Just out of curiosity, how much did that dress cost you on such short notice?"

I try to stop my lips from twitching into a smile. "I never discuss personal purchases."

"Oh?"

"No. It's no one's business how much I pay for anything."

She drops her gaze. "Well, it was nice of you. Very nice."

"I said I'd replace it."

"I know, but I didn't expect you to actually replicate it. Why would you do that?"

I take a sip of water. "Because I can."

She doesn't reply right away. An adorable look of confusion spreads over her face instead. Why does it surprise her that I don't discuss purchases? I have the resources to replicate a dress in twenty-four hours, so I use them. I got to tear the dress off Skye, and Tessa gets a brand-new one. A great deal, as far as I'm concerned.

"Skye," I say.

"Yeah?"

"It might interest you to know that I had my tailor make *two* dresses."

She swallows the sip of water she just took. "Oh?"

"I did. You'll be wearing that dress again, but the next time you'll be on *my* arm, and there won't be any question as to who you're with."

"Will you destroy it again?" Her lips quiver slightly.

I stare at her. "Yes. Definitely."

Her cheeks go red, and her brown eyes darken slightly. "When exactly will I be on your arm?"

"You decide."

She lets out a short laugh. "It's a cocktail dress, Braden. It might surprise you to know that I don't frequent a lot of formal affairs."

"You will now. I'm invited to a lot of them, and since you insist on dating, you'll be accompanying me."

"If *I* insist?"

Oh, she drives me to drink. Those eyes. Those lips. Those needling words that tumble out of her mouth.

"I want you in my bed, Skye. If taking you out sometimes is the way to make that happen, I'll do it."

"What if I want more than that?"

"What more is there?"

"A…relationship."

I tap my fingers on the table. "I've told you I can't be in a relationship with you."

"Yeah, but you haven't told me why."

I wrinkle my forehead. She's not the first woman to ask why I won't begin a relationship. But she *is* the first woman I want to actually answer.

Except my only answer is that I know I'm not wired for long-term. I've never met a woman who challenges me enough to make me want to commit.

I don't let my mind get to the inevitable suggestion it wants to make.

Instead, I say, "The only reason I can give you is that I don't want a relationship."

"Why?"

I rub my temple. "You're persistent. I'll give you that. But there is no answer."

"You mean there's no answer that will satisfy me."

"Semantics, as you like to say."

"I like you, Braden."

I want to smile at her words. But I hold back. "I like you, too. I don't sleep with people I don't like."

"You didn't let me finish. I like you, but why me? You can have any woman out there. You must know that."

"I've told you."

"Yeah. You like my lips and my breasts. So do plenty of other men, and sexy lips and big tits aren't that hard to find."

"I won't deny that those are fine features of yours, but I also told you the thing I like most about you. Your need for control."

She takes a sip of water and sets her glass down harshly. "So I'm a game. If I give you control, you win. Is that it?"

How wrong she is. I don't play games. I've made that clear to her. But this isn't a conversation to have in a restaurant. I can see how she might perceive some of what's between us as a game. Soon, though, she'll see it's something much more exciting than any game.

"If you give me control," I say, "we both win."

"And how long do you expect this arrangement to last?" she asks. "Until you get tired of me?"

This time, I can't hold back my chuckle. "As long as you want it to."

"I find that hard to believe."

"Why is that?"

She huffs softly. "Because you can have anyone. You'll get tired of me long before I get tired of you."

"Don't be so sure of that."

"Why do you say that?"

"You'll see."

The waiter brings our meals, and she stares at the coq au vin on her plate.

A minute passes. Then another.

I take a bite of my sole and swallow. "Nothing to say? That's not like you." I know how to break the ice. I rise and lay my napkin across the back of my chair. I remove my phone from my pocket, crouch down next to her, and snap a selfie of us. "What the hell? Let's get them talking."

"You're Instagramming?"

"Kay will have the whole city talking about us within a day anyway, so why not? You're not embarrassed to be seen with me, are you?"

"Of course not."

"Then there's no problem that I can see." I edit the photo slightly to adjust the lighting and then post it.

Her phone dings in her purse.

"Tagged you," I say.

She pulls out her phone.

"You should make your profile public," I say.

"Why?"

"Because my followers will want to know you."

"I'm a private person, Braden."

"Not anymore."

I hope she understands the truth of those words. If she wants to "date" me, she's going to be in the public eye. Kay

Brown accosting her at her workplace is clear evidence of the situation.

She lifts her eyebrows. "I didn't sign up for this."

I laugh. I really, *really* laugh. The things she says… "You did, though. You wanted to date, Skye. This is what dating *me* is like." I thrust my phone back in my pocket. "In fact, I'm on my way to do some charity work. Why don't you join me?"

"You do charity work?"

"Does that surprise you?"

"No."

Right. Her eyebrows nearly shooting off her forehead gives her away. But why would this surprise her?

"I give a lot of money to charity," I say, "but there's no substitute for diving in and getting your hands dirty."

She looks down at her work clothes. "I'm not really dressed to get my hands dirty."

"Just an expression, Skye. Though I do help with a community garden in my old neighborhood, that's not what I'm doing today."

"Yeah? What are you doing today?"

"You mean 'what are *we* doing today?'"

She smiles. "Okay, what are *we* doing today?"

"Wait and see."

Chapter Twenty-Eight

I remain mum about the plans while we finish our lunch. Once we leave the restaurant, Christopher picks us up and drives us to a food pantry in South Boston.

I know the place well.

My mother brought Ben and me to this place when I was a little boy, but I don't advertise that fact.

"I come here once a week for an hour and hand out food," I tell Skye. "Let's go."

We exit the car and walk past the line of people waiting and into the building.

Several people rush to greet me.

"Nice to see you, Mr. Black," Denny, a young man who volunteers often, says.

I wave and give him a pat on the back.

"Braden!" Cheryl, who runs the place, grabs my hand. "I see you've brought a friend."

"Cheryl, this is Skye."

Cheryl holds out her hand. "Nice to meet you, Skye."

"Cheryl's an old friend," I say. "We used to be neighbors."

"When he was just a little guy," Cheryl says. "We're all so proud of his success."

Skye's good. She hides her shock well from Cheryl, but I can still see it. I'm connected to this woman in a way that's new to me, hypersensitive to her every reaction.

This time, it's not as frightening as it was when I first made the realization. It's more enlightening. Makes my chest tighten.

"You all had a hand in it," I say to Cheryl.

"He's an amazing person," she says to Skye. "Never forgets his roots. His donations keep us in business. We're able to help more people than ever these days."

Skye smiles.

She's happy about this side of me, and that makes me happy. I've never brought a woman to the food pantry. Never had the desire to.

I grab a shopping cart. "This place means a lot to me. Come on, Skye. I'll show you the ropes." I take the cart to the person at the head of the line. "I'm Braden." I hold out my hand.

A young woman carrying a toddler places the child in the buggy seat and then shakes my hand. "Elise."

"How many people in your household, Elise?" I ask.

"Just Benji and me."

Benji.

The name shifts me back in time. Benji. My mother called my brother Benji. Brady and Benji.

Each of us took one of her hands when we came here to get free food from the volunteers.

"It's Brady and Benji!" someone always said, handing us each a Dum Dum sucker.

We lived for those sweets each week.

I have happy memories of this place. It wasn't until I was older that I realized we came here because Mom and Dad couldn't afford to feed us.

This Benji has light-brown hair and blue eyes. "And how are you today, Benji?" I hold out my hand to him.

He looks away.

"I'm sorry," his mother says. "He's shy."

"Not a problem. I was a shy kid myself. This is Skye."

"Hi." She holds out her hand to Elise. "Nice to meet you."

Elise shakes her hand weakly. She's a pretty young woman wearing jeans and a sweatshirt. Benji's hair is combed and his face is clean. Elise takes pride in her little family, like my mother always did.

"You'll need some powdered milk for Benji," I say. "We'll have fresh milk soon, once the new refrigeration unit is installed. I'm so sorry for the inconvenience. Refrigeration is down during installation."

"Benji doesn't like milk," Elise says. "I wish he'd drink it."

"Not a problem. We can give you some sugar-free chocolate flavoring to put in the milk. Guaranteed to please." I should know. I hated milk, too, as a kid. Strawberry Quik was its own food group as far as I was concerned.

I lead the way down the first aisle. Skye follows, walking next to Elise.

I don't wonder about Elise and Benji's story. I already know. Life is tough sometimes. I don't ask questions because people don't want to talk about these circumstances. Benji's father may be in the picture or he may not be. It's not our business at the shelter to ask. We simply supply food and let our patrons keep their dignity. That second part means more than most people know.

Skye smiles at Benji, and he smiles back. He's an adorable kid.

"What do you like to do, Benji?" Skye asks.

He looks away then.

"He's not talking much yet," Elise says. "Benji, you should speak to the nice lady."

"Oh, no. That's okay. He's a beautiful child."

"Thank you." Elise smiles.

I pull items off the pantry shelves and put them in the cart. Powdered milk, canned fruits and vegetables, sliced bread, peanut butter and jelly. Pasta and sauce, boxed macaroni and cheese, and some apple juice. Down another aisle I find cereal, oatmeal, and instant coffee.

"Is Benji potty-trained?" I ask Elise.

"Yes and no. He still wears a diaper at night."

I turn down a new aisle and pull a pack of toddler-size diapers off the shelf. "Anything else you need from this aisle?"

Elise shakes her head.

"Is there anything special that you'd like today?"

"No, I don't need anything," Elise says. "Just the food is fine."

I'd be very happy to write Elise a big fat check, but I don't push. Pride and dignity are important to her, as they are to most. I help her bag her groceries, and then Skye and I pack them in the little red wagon she left outside the pantry.

"Do you live near here?" Skye asks.

"About twenty blocks away," she says. "It's a nice walk."

"There's a bus stop right there." Skye nods. "Let me give you—"

"No, thank you," Elise says. "Benji and I enjoy the walk. Thank you very much for the food."

"You're very welcome," I say. "You come back anytime."

Elise smiles and nods and then places Benji in the wagon among the bags of food and begins the walk home. Skye watches them for a moment. Benji pulls a loaf of bread out of the bag and squeezes it. I shift back in time once more, remembering my own Benji squeezing the day-old loaves we got at the food pantry. Mom admonished him every time. He promised never to do it again. Until the next time we got a loaf of bread. My little brother couldn't resist.

Skye smiles. "Thank you for bringing me here."

"No need to thank me."

She looks over my shoulder. Cheryl is leading another woman with a small girl hanging on her hand into the panty. Another volunteer takes a young man from the line.

"Why this place, Braden? You could volunteer anywhere."

"Because," I say, "my mother used to bring Ben and me here when we were little to get food."

Skye's mouth drops open.

"Apparently I'm full of surprises today," I say.

She doesn't know the truth of those words. She's the first person I've said them to in a long time. But I've opened something up inside me, and now I want something in return.

Skye touches my arm lightly. "I think it's wonderful that you volunteer here and also support the pantry financially."

"It's the least I can do. Never forget where you came from, Skye. It's a part of you. Always."

We head to the Mercedes where Christopher waits. I open the door for her.

I slide in next to Skye in the back seat. "I showed you a part of my past today. Now I'd like to know something about you."

Chapter Twenty-Nine

"What do you want to know?" she asks.

"Something that had an impact on you. Helped define who you are."

"Okay. But I want to say something first." She drops her gaze a moment.

"Go ahead."

She doesn't look at me. "I didn't know you ever went hungry."

"Did you give it a second thought?" The words come out in monotone. I'm not trying to make her feel bad. I just know most people never give food a second thought because they've always had it.

"No, I didn't," she says, finally bringing her head up to meet my gaze. "I've never gone hungry, and I never realized how lucky I am. I'm going to try not to take things like that for granted anymore."

I trail a finger over her cheek. "Good. You should never take anything for granted. It can all be gone in a minute."

I'm happy Skye has never known hunger. I don't wish for

her to know anything that feels so hopeless. Hunger did do something very profound for me, though. It gave me drive. It gave me passion. It taught me to never turn my back on any opportunity, no matter how small.

And it taught me to never give up. To never lose the drive to be better. Because…it can all be gone in a minute.

I know.

"I'm sorry," she says. "The thought of you going to bed hungry makes me so sad."

"Don't be sorry, and please don't be sad. Everything in my past has contributed to what I've become. Just as it has for you. Maybe you don't have one thing you can pinpoint. But tell me something about your past. Something that helped shape who you are today."

"Do I really have to go into this?" She bites on her lower lip.

I'm so close to letting her off the hook, but I lob a softball at her. One I'm pretty sure she won't resist. "No. I'll never force you to tell me anything."

"Thanks."

Silence for a few minutes. Then she speaks.

"When I was seven, I was playing by myself in our cornfields."

She closes her eyes for a moment, while I imagine a carefree little girl, long hair flying, amusing herself among the tall stalks.

"By yourself?" I ask.

"Yeah. I'm an only child, and none of my friends lived close by. I saw them only at school until I got older. Anyway, I got lost."

"In the cornfield?" I raise my eyebrows.

"Don't look so surprised. Our cornfields are huge. We have more than two hundred acres. I was only allowed to play at the very edge of the field where someone could keep an eye on me. Anyway, I got caught up chasing a praying mantis."

"Somehow, I never took you for an entomophile."

"I was seven, Braden, with the attention span of a praying mantis myself. They're green, as you know, and it was a challenge to see it as it hopped from one stalk to another. I followed it with my camera I'd gotten for my birthday. I wanted to take its picture."

I smile. "You were having fun."

"I was. There wasn't much else to do."

"Except outrun tornadoes."

She gives me a good-natured smack on my upper arm. "I won't deny taking shelter from a few in my day, but you can't outrun a tornado. You shouldn't try."

"Dorothy did."

"You watch too much TV."

"I don't watch *any* TV." Did she notice I have only one television in my entire penthouse? Probably not, since she hasn't seen my entire penthouse.

"That was a clear *Wizard of Oz* reference."

"I read books, Skye." Actually my mother read *The Wonderful Wizard of Oz* to Ben and me at bedtime. The word "wonderful" was dropped for the movie.

"Anyway," she continues, "it hopped away from me again and again, and it was great fun to follow it, until I realized I had no idea where I was. I was shorter than the corn, and all around me was more corn. I freaked out. I can still feel my little heart pounding against my chest. It was like my whole body became my heartbeat. I started running in no particular direction and kept tripping over roots and stalks."

She's clearly agitated just telling the story. Part of me wants to stop her. Her discomfort makes me feel uncomfortable myself. She stops talking for a moment, inhales slowly. Exhales. Then—

"I started screaming bloody murder, and eventually I ran

into a scarecrow and knocked myself out. The next thing I remember is waking up in my bed with my mother next to me holding a clammy washcloth on my forehead."

"So they found you."

"They did. I wasn't very far from the yard. It just seemed far to a frightened little girl."

I understand better than she realizes, and I'm moved— moved that she shared something that obviously still frightens her to this day. She went out of her comfort zone to tell me this story, and she'll be rewarded. I think about telling her how much her little story means to me. I think about grabbing her and kissing her senseless. I think about the feelings flowing through me, how they're new and vibrant and all linked to her. I think about all of this, and then I say, simply, "Thank you for sharing that with me."

• • •

I'm back in the office by three thirty, and I have a rare couple of hours without meetings. I tell Claire that I don't want to be disturbed, and I close the door and sit behind my desk.

After returning a couple of phone calls that can't wait, I sit back and put my feet up on my desk. I rarely relax in the office, but Skye's story of the cornfield haunts me.

It haunts me as much as my own childhood, which I don't let myself think about often. Ben tries to talk to me about it once in a while, but I always tell him to shut up.

He does.

The older-brother card still works when it comes to discussing the past.

Seeing my brother and father every day has become as natural to me as air. I'd take a bullet for my brother. As for Dad? He wasn't a perfect father. Far from it. But I've moved past his shortcomings as a parent and husband. He's an asset to the company. He's more than proven his worth.

Still...

Skye's story...

And little Benji at the food bank.

Though I finance the place and volunteer, I rarely let myself think about those days when Ben and I would walk in there with our mother, each of us holding one of her hands, part of her lovely face always hidden by a scarf. Most of the time the volunteers were kind.

Except for once.

• • •

"Come on, Brady," Momma said, urging me along.

I'd stopped to watch a teenage girl with a new puppy. The puppy was wriggling out of her arms and wagging its tail. It had brown fur and striking blue eyes. I couldn't stop looking at it.

"The puppy, Momma," I said.

"You know we can't have a puppy. Now, come on."

Momma always said we couldn't afford a dog, but dogs were free. You could go to the pound and get one. I didn't understand.

Frowning, I left the puppy with its new owner, wishing I could feel the love of a puppy's kisses on my face. Wishing I could throw a ball and have it bring it back to me and then wag its little tail.

We walked into the shelter. The line was short today. That was a good thing. Until—

"Hurry up, lady!" a gray-haired woman said to Momma. "We ain't got all day here."

"Yes, ma'am," Momma said. "Come on, Brady, Benji."

Benji and I were used to the nice ladies at the food bank who gave us Dum Dums. Where were they today?

The mean lady with stringy gray hair yanked a shopping cart and moved toward the first aisle. Momma followed, dragging us along to keep up with Meanie, as I had named the gray-haired lady.

"I suppose you'll need diapers?" Meanie said, shaking her head.

"No. My boys are toilet-trained."

I'd been using the potty for years, and Benji hardly ever had an accident anymore. We were big boys. Why did Meanie think we needed diapers?

"Milk, I suppose, for the kids."

"Yes, please, and some Strawberry Quik."

Meanie scoffed. "You'll get milk. Strawberry Quik is a luxury."

"But we've gotten it here the last several times," Momma says, still using her polite voice.

I wanted her to yell at Meanie. Meanie deserved to be yelled at. Momma should give her a time-out.

"We don't have any. This is a food pantry, not a convenience store."

Momma said nothing, just followed Meanie to the next aisle to get a couple of loaves of bread. "Peanut butter or jelly?" Meanie asked.

"Both, please."

"You get one or the other. Like I said—"

"Yes, this isn't a convenience store," Momma finished for her. "I get it. We'll take the peanut butter, please."

"I want jelly!" Benji cried out.

"Peanut butter is more nutritious, Benji," Momma said. "We'll get jelly next time."

We walked through aisle after aisle, Meanie snarling at Momma as she filled up the grocery cart with cereal, spaghetti noodles, cans of food, tissues, toilet paper, and finally, a package of raw hamburger. That meant beef stew. Yum.

"You're done," Meanie said. "Get on out of here. We got more people to deal with."

Momma smiled at Meanie. "Thank you very much. We appreciate your hospitality."

"Where's my Dum Dum?" Benji said sadly, his eyes wide.

"What's he talking about?" Meanie demanded.

"The volunteers always give the boys a sucker," Momma said. "Don't be rude, Benji."

"Candy?" Meanie said. "To rot their teeth so you'll have to take them to a dentist you can't afford? I don't think so. Go on, now."

Momma held her head high. "Come along, boys."

We took the cart outside, and Momma loaded up our old car. She called it a station wagon. But she didn't get in the driver's seat. Instead, she grabbed our hands once again, and we walked back to the door of the food pantry.

"Brady, hold Benji's hand," she said to me. "You can see me through the glass. Stay here, and I'll be right back, okay?"

As long as I could see Momma, it would be okay. She walked back into the food pantry and talked to a different volunteer. I held tight to Benji and waited. Soon a man walked up to Momma. They talked for a few minutes, but of course I couldn't hear what they were saying. The man left for a minute, and then he came back and handed something to Momma. They shook hands.

Momma returned to us. "Were you good, boys?" she asked.

"Yes, Momma," we both said.

"Good." She held up a whole bag of Dum Dums! "You can each have one every night after supper until they run out."

I went home happy that night. I might not have a dog, but I had a smiling momma and a Dum Dum every night.

And we never saw Meanie at the food pantry again.

Chapter Thirty

I leave for the day at six p.m., earlier than normal, but I want to see Skye. I've been thinking about her and the cornfield and the food pantry the better part of the afternoon. Plus, I want to fuck her. I really want to fuck her.

As Christopher drives me to her place, I absently pull up Instagram.

Skye has apparently taken my advice and turned her profile to public.

And it's taken off.

She responded to a comment asking about her lip color on the post I'd tagged her in at the gala.

@krissmith4009: @stormyskye15 your lip color is gorgeous!

@krissmith4009 Glad you like it. It's Susanne lip stain in Cherry Russet.

The selfie of Skye and Tessa has also exploded.

You look gorgeous! Beautiful ladies.

Wowza!

Who's your friend? You're both hot as hell.

And then—

You're so lucky to be Braden Black's girlfriend! #envious

I go rigid.

Apparently, Instagram thinks that Skye Manning is my girlfriend.

Oddly, I don't hate the idea.

Christopher pulls in front of Skye's building, and I call her.

"Hi, Tess," she says into the phone.

"It's not Tess."

"Hi," she says, her voice a bit breathless.

"I see you're gaining quite a following," I say.

"Yeah. It's pretty weird."

"Get used to it."

"I'll try. I can always put my account back to private."

"You can," I say, "but you won't."

"Why wouldn't I?"

I could go into detail, but that's for another time. "Just trust me. Do you want to get dinner?"

"I'm heating up leftovers."

"Enough for two?"

"Well, yeah, but—"

"Great. I'll be there in three minutes."

"In three minutes? What—"

"I'm right outside your building."

"How did you— Never mind. Christopher knows where I live."

"He does, but I didn't need him to find you. See you in a few."

I exit the sedan and head up to Skye's apartment. A minute later, I'm knocking on her door.

She opens it, looks me over, and sucks in a breath.

I try not to show how pleased I am at her reaction, but I fear she sees right through me. If I can tell what she's feeling, can she tell what I'm feeling? I'm not sure I want to know the answer to that question.

I love that my appearance pleases her. I removed my tie in the car on the way here, and I unbuttoned the first few buttons of my white shirt. I'm still wearing my black suit jacket.

I stride in, making the room my own. I learned early on in business that you have to own every room you enter. People take you seriously when you make it clear you belong, even if you don't feel as confident as you act. Confidence is an illusion—one I've perfected. My mother told me once that I had confidence and a knack for leadership. Apparently she was right.

Skye's modest studio is a large closet compared to my place. Her queen bed is made, and a love seat sits adjacent to it. A small two-person table is arranged between the bed and the kitchenette.

The place suits Skye. Simple with a touch of elegance, as she sees herself. Except that Skye is anything but simple.

"Smells good," I say.

"Beef stew. One of my specialties. My mom's recipe, a staple from my childhood."

My lips quirk. Funny. I've been thinking about my childhood all afternoon. And now…beef stew.

"I love beef stew."

"Good. Though I'm sure Marilyn could prepare you a gourmet version that totally puts mine to shame."

"Marilyn has never made beef stew."

Because I've never asked her for it. Beef stew was a staple during my childhood, too—but only when we could get beef, and it was usually ground. Still, my mother could make a delicious meal out of a package of hamburger.

Skye meets my gaze, her lips parted in that sexy way. "So much for small talk. Why are you here, Braden?"

"To join you for dinner."

"We just saw each other at lunch."

I raise an eyebrow. "I'll go if you'd rather I not be here."

"That's not what I meant."

I say nothing. I'll go if she asks me to, but I'm betting she won't. I'm hoping she won't.

"Stay," she says.

"All right."

"I just meant...you said you didn't want a relationship, but here you are."

"And...?"

"And...we've seen a lot of each other in a short time. Doesn't that make us...*something*?"

I rub my jawline. "It makes you my girlfriend, Skye. Isn't that what you wanted?"

"Girlfriend?" Then she shakes her head. "You saw the comment on my Instagram post."

"I did. I'll ask again. Isn't that what you wanted?"

"I don't know what I want, honestly. I only know I want more than a purely sexual arrangement."

"Which is why I've agreed to date you."

"Then let's date."

"Isn't that what we're doing right now?"

She looks down at her feet. "No. I don't normally date in bare feet and sweats. Why are you really here, Braden? Because I'm absolutely sure it's not to eat my leftover beef stew."

"Do you even have to ask?"

She gulps. "Yeah. I have to ask."

"I'm here to fuck you, Skye."

Her knees wobble. Only slightly, but I notice.

"Then I definitely need to eat."

I smile. Almost. "So do I."

She motions to the small table. "Have a seat. Dinner will

be ready in a minute. Can I get you a drink?"

I remove my suit coat, hang it on the back of a chair, and sit. "Wild Turkey."

She smiles. "I always have that." She pulls the bottle out of a top cupboard, grabs a lowball glass, and pours me a double. Then she adds one ice cube and hands me the glass.

I take a sip. "Going to join me?"

"Not tonight, no." She dishes up the stew, slices a baguette, and sets it on a plate. She pours two glasses of water and brings everything to the table.

"Dig in," she says.

I nod, spoon up some stew, blow on it, and taste it.

She watches me intently, clearly waiting for my approval. It's fragrant and meaty with a spike of thyme. The meat isn't ground beef, though. It's round steak or chuck, cut into chunks. They're braised to perfection and melt in my mouth.

Funny. This is a hundred times better than my mother's stew, yet I find myself missing hers. At the same time, I'm delighted that Skye is a good cook.

"Delicious," I say.

She lets out a breath, nods, and takes a bite herself. "Bread?"

"Yeah. Thanks." I take a hunk. "Do you have any butter?"

"Oh, yeah." She rises and finds a stick in the fridge, unwraps it, and places it on the butter dish. "Here you go."

"Thanks."

A few minutes pass. Then—

"You're a good cook, Skye."

"Thanks."

"This is the best stew I've had in a long time." No lie there.

"I'm glad you like it. I wasn't sure you were a stew kind of guy."

"Are you kidding? My mother made stew all the time while I was growing up."

"Right. It's easy to forget sometimes."

"What do you mean?"

"Well… You grew up like I did. You didn't always have billions."

"You're saying stew is a poor man's meal?" It was the way my mother prepared it. It was also a delicious treat.

"I don't know what I'm saying. Forget I said anything."

"I still enjoy the simple things," I say. "A walk in the rain, watching the sun rise, a warm bowl of stew, and a slice of crusty bread. Money doesn't change who a person is."

"I didn't mean that it did."

"Okay. No big deal."

"If you like stew so much, Braden, why don't you have Marilyn cook it for you?"

I don't hesitate. "It wouldn't be the same."

"As your mother's?"

I nod.

My mother passed away before I made my billions. It's common knowledge, so Skye no doubt knows. I don't talk about her, though. Just eating this stew brings back a lot of memories that are better left buried.

"Tell me about your mother," Skye says.

I swallow a bite of stew and dart my gaze to the side. Nope. Not going there. "I don't talk about her."

"Why?"

I meet her gaze this time. "It's too hard."

She doesn't press, thank God. "What about your dad? Can you tell me about him?"

"You can google him and find out everything."

"I don't want to read it in some rag, Braden. I want *you* to tell me."

"I don't talk about my family."

In fact, all this talk has got me needing to relieve some stress, and I know exactly how to do that.

I wipe my mouth with a napkin and stand. "Your stew is delicious, Skye, but I've had enough talking for one night."

Chapter Thirty-One

I yank her out of her chair, pull her against me, and smash my mouth to hers. I invade her with my tongue.

She tastes of beef stew and sweet spice.

She tastes of Skye.

And she melts into the kiss as I explore every inch of her mouth.

I pull her closer, grinding my thick cock into her. In truth, I've been semi-hard since I read the comment about her being my girlfriend.

It felt odd.

It felt dangerous.

It felt…right.

But I'm not here to be her boyfriend. I'm here to fuck her. To give us both what we need.

I kiss her with passion and lust. It's a kiss of possession, of power, and she's beginning her surrender.

If only I could surrender to the power she has over me. I've never wanted that kind of a relationship. Hell, I've never wanted a relationship at all.

But I've always known a true submissive wields great power—and I fear Skye may possess enough power to bring me to my knees.

Not tonight, though.

Not ever. I won't let it get that far.

Tonight is for fucking.

Her nipples are hard, and I want to touch them, tweak them, suck them hard between my lips.

She threads her fingers through my hair as our kiss deepens, and it's like our mouths are fused together.

I don't want to break the kiss, but I need to breathe.

I pull away. "Bed."

I drag her to the alcove where it sits and shove her down. She bounces lightly on the mattress as I strip off my shirt. Her eyes are wide as she gapes at me, her gaze sliding from my chest to my abs and then to the bulge in my pants. Good. *Look all you want, baby, because tonight it's going between those sex-on-a-stick lips of yours.*

I've thought of sliding my dick into her mouth since I first laid eyes on her in Addison's office. I got a tiny taste of it the first time we were together, but tonight I'm going all in.

I'm going to fuck her mouth.

I kick off my shiny leather shoes and unbuckle my belt. In a flash, I push my pants and boxer briefs over my hips and step out of them.

I'm naked, my big cock as erect as it's ever been.

Skye is still fully clothed. Usually it's the other way around. I love having a naked woman laid out for my pleasure while I still wear clothes. It's a power thing. A control thing. And it's hot as hell.

But damn, being naked for Skye, watching the pleasure she gets from gazing at every part of me…

That's another kind of power, and I'm loving it.

Besides, I'm about to pull the ultimate power play.

I meet her gaze. "Get on your knees, Skye."

"Braden, I—"

"On your knees!"

She sits on the bed, immobile.

I lower my voice. "Don't make me say it again."

She drops to her knees.

Nice. She's so beautiful on her knees, her hair falling out of her ponytail, her lips parted just so.

My dick bobs in front of her, and she reaches toward me—

"No," I say. "Stay still. Don't touch me."

She widens her eyes.

"I'm going to fuck your mouth like I fuck your pussy. You stay still."

"But it's better for you if I can use my hands."

"Maybe I'll let you do it your way sometime. Tonight, we do it mine. No hands. And no more talking." Not that she'll be able to get any words out with her mouth full of my hard cock.

I nudge it over her lips. "God, your mouth is so sexy. Open for me."

She drops her lips into an O, and I slide my cock between them. Fuck! Fucking paradise. Her mouth is soft and warm, and she glides her tongue along the bottom of my shaft. Then she grabs onto the backs of my thighs.

I don't stop her, even though I didn't give her permission to touch me.

It feels too fucking good.

I pull out and then shove myself back into her mouth, going as far as I can until I hit the back of her throat. Nice. She doesn't gag. I won't have to ease her in.

I pull out and then slide into her again. I hold it before pulling out, resisting the urge to thrust.

I'm all about control.

It's the wait. The thrill of the chase. The intensity of knowing what's coming.

My release will be that much better.

Besides, I won't be coming in Skye's mouth. Not tonight. I came over here to fuck her, and I *will* fuck her.

I slide inside her mouth once more, and this time she sucks me slightly harder. I'll give her the lead she seems to want because I'm horny and it feels so fucking good. I go faster. Faster. And she sucks me harder. Harder.

I'm doing what I told her. I'm fucking her mouth. And damn, she's hot as hell.

Saliva drips from her lips, creating a slick lubricant.

"Yeah, that's it, baby. Your sexy lips feel so good around me. Perfect. Just perfect. Fuck!" I withdraw quickly before I explode down her throat.

She gasps in a breath.

"I need to come, but I want to come inside you." I grip her shoulders and bring her to her feet, turn her around, and slide her sweats and panties over her hips before nudging her onto the bed. Her sweats are around her knees, so she can't spread her legs. Exactly as I want her. She'll be nice and tight.

I thrust into her.

"Damn, you feel perfect," I groan. "So good."

She gasps as I thrust once, twice, three times—

"Fuck!" I propel into her, plunging in as far as I can. I slap one cheek of her ass as I release.

Into Skye I pour every frustration of this day.

Kay Brown and the *Babbler*.

Gone.

Elise and Benji and how I wish I could do more for everyone in their position.

Gone.

The horrific volunteer who my mother got fired.

Gone.

And Skye. Little Skye, lost in the cornfield, helpless as she ran into a scarecrow.

Not gone, but at least I can deal with it as I leave the stress of this day behind me.

As I bury it all inside the warmth of this woman.

I stay locked inside her for a few moments, breathing heavily, my eyes squeezed shut as the waves of euphoria crash over me and nudge all the unpleasantness away.

Skye doesn't move or speak.

Finally I pull out.

Then—

"Shit. Shit, shit, shit."

I look down at my naked cock and gasp, my heart racing. What have I done? How could I be so irresponsible?

She looks over her shoulder. "What? What is it?"

"I forgot the damned condom."

Chapter Thirty-Two

Skye swallows audibly, and then she flattens her full lips.

Yeah, she's freaked out, too.

She turns over, pulls her sweats and panties back up, and sits on the bed. "Do I have reason to worry?"

"Not from me. I get tested every three months." Physician's orders. I'm always careful—present situation excluded—but my doctor knows that I engage in scenes at a private club, and she insists on the testing. I can't fault her logic. She's the expert.

Do I think Skye has herpes or HIV? Of course not. But she's a woman of child-bearing age who carries a condom in her purse, which could mean…

"Every three months? Whatever for?" Then she clamps her hand over her mouth.

"Because it's good policy, Skye, that's why. What about you?"

"I'm good. Clean."

"That's not what I'm concerned about."

"What's the problem, then?"

"Pregnancy. I don't want a kid. You carry a rubber around in your purse. Does that mean…?"

"Extra protection. I'm on the pill."

I heave out a sigh of relief. Still naked, I sit down next to her. "Thank God."

She lets out a nervous laugh. "The good news is we don't have to use condoms anymore."

"I always use condoms."

"Why? If we're both clean, and I— Oh." She presses her lips together.

"Finish what you were going to say, Skye."

She inhales and lets out a stream of breath slowly. "I'm not the only woman you're sleeping with, am I?"

"This week you are."

The words are true, but I know how they must sound to her. Though I desire Skye more than I have any other woman, I'm not ready to say that she's the only one. I'm not sure there is a "one" for me. I have specific tastes, and I don't expect a woman to put up with me forever. I'm not wired that way anyway.

But this…

I never forget the condom. I treat my sex life the way I treat my business life.

A sexually transmitted disease or an unwanted pregnancy would intrude on my lifestyle, so I minimize the chances of either of them occurring, just as I minimize the chances of any chink in my business armor as well.

Silence for a few more seconds. Then—

I turn to her. "That's never happened to me before."

"What do you mean?"

"I've never forgotten to put on a condom."

I'm still naked. I should get dressed. But I'm finding it difficult to move. What does forgetting the condom imply?

Already I know the answer to my own question, even

though I can't let myself begin to contemplate it. To do so would entail admitting something I'm not ready to admit.

Except I don't need an admission, because I already know.

It's inside me, a part of me—something I can no longer deny.

Yes, I desire Skye more than I have any other woman. Yes, I find her a challenge. Yes, I want her to give up her control to me, to submit to me.

All that is true.

But there's more. So much more that I didn't plan on.

"Did you enjoy it?" Skye asks.

Is she kidding? I can't help a huff. "Not using a condom? Hell yeah. You felt amazing."

"Then why use them?"

"It's hard to explain." Not that hard to explain, actually. I don't take unnecessary chances.

But if I look further inside myself, I see the ultimate truth.

It's a barrier.

A barrier between my partner and me. I don't want to get too close, so I don't.

"Try."

"I'm not sure. It's kind of a…" I close my eyes. I can't lie to her, yet I'm not ready to tell her the truth. A few seconds later, I open them and meet her gaze. "We've done enough talking for one night. I owe you a climax."

Surely that will get her off this topic.

But I'm wrong.

"I don't want you to sleep with anyone else while you're sleeping with me."

Not an issue. Rarely do I have a sexual relationship with more than one woman at a time.

"I told you. You're the only one I'm sleeping with this

week. I haven't fucked anyone else since I started fucking you."

"Good," she says. "Keep it that way."

"Skye—"

"If I'm your"—air quotes—"'girlfriend,' I deserve to be the only one in your bed."

I stare at her. She's asking for something no other woman has ever had the guts to ask from me. I've always been up front with women about my expectations.

I can't help but admire her in this moment. She's making a demand—a demand that, for all she knows, could signify the end of whatever this is between us.

The problem? I don't want it to end. I haven't gotten what I want from her. Perhaps, when she finally submits to me, I'll have had enough of her and will be willing to let her go.

God, even the thought seems foreign.

What have I gotten into?

I've never made a guarantee like the one she's asking for. Even though my MO is to be sexually involved with only one woman at a time, I've never made that promise.

I already know, though, what my answer is.

"Okay."

Her eyebrows shoot up.

"You're surprised," I say.

"A little."

"What kind of man do you think I am, Skye?"

"That's just it, Braden. I don't *know* what kind of man you are. You refuse to talk about anything personal. You're intelligent, obviously. You're an excellent businessperson. You do some charity work. But that's all I know other than what magazines report."

"You know I love oysters."

"For God's sake, Braden."

I sigh. "You know as much as anyone else does. Isn't that

enough?"

"No, it's not, especially if I'm"—air quotes again—"your *'girlfriend.'*"

She's not wrong. What bothers me more, though, is that I want to open up to her. To show her who I truly am.

"Fuck," I say through clenched teeth.

I grab her breast and thumb her nipple over two layers of fabric. I lean into her and can't stop the words from flowing off my tongue.

"You want to know about me?" I rasp into her ear. "Here's all you need. Since I laid eyes on you, I haven't been able to think about anyone else. Your mouth, your tits, your curious and controlling nature—everything about you beguiles me. Since I first fucked you, all I can think about is fucking you again. You're all I think about"—I bite her earlobe—"and it...*perplexes* me. Not much perplexes me, Skye. You're like a narcotic. I hunger for you." I inhale. "God, I love how you smell—like apples and sex. You taste even better. You want to be the only one in my bed? You don't even have to ask. You're the only woman I want right now. The *only* one."

A low growl vibrates from her throat.

I scrape my teeth along the outer edge of her ear. "Now, let me give you that climax."

Chapter Thirty-Three

I lift her tank top over her head and throw it on the floor. Then I unhook her bra and discard it as her breasts fall against her chest. I cup them, knead them, and then I bury my nose between them, kissing them and thumbing her nipples.

My admission to Skye has every cell in my body humming, every thought in my mind turned to mush.

All I do is feel.

How much I want her…

How much I desire her…

How much I need her control…

How much I…

I nibble the tops of her breasts and then finally take a nipple between my lips and suck. She inhales sharply.

"So beautiful," I say against her flesh.

"Braden, please…"

"Please what, baby?"

"I…I want to come."

She has no idea that I want that climax as much as she does. "You will." I bite a nipple.

"Oh!"

"You like that?"

"Yes. God, yes."

"Good. I could suck and bite your tits all day." No lie there. And yes, she likes pleasure-pain. Good. Very good. I nibble on her other nipple and then raise my head again. "On the other hand, that paradise between your legs is even more beautiful." I slide down her body, grasping her sweats, and glide them over her hips and legs.

I spread her legs. "God, yes. So beautiful."

All of Skye is beautiful, but I swear, when she's naked, her legs spread, her pussy glistening for me—that's when she's at her most beautiful.

"I'm going to make you come, Skye," I say, my voice low and husky. "I'm going to make you come so many times that you'll be begging me to stop."

"No," she says, "I'll never beg you to stop."

"You will." I stroke my tongue over her clit.

She quivers beneath me. I tug on her flesh and then close my lips over her clit.

"You taste so good, baby," I say, lapping at her rich cream. "I'll never get enough. But this isn't about me." I glide a finger into her pussy.

That's it. All it takes.

She shatters around my finger, squeezing me with those sumptuous walls.

Damn. It's nearly as good as coming myself. In its way, it's even better. Because that thing going on inside me—where I feel what she feels—breaks me into pieces along with her.

And I want more.

I add another finger, urging her on and then sucking on her clit.

Two orgasms and then three.

I'm exploding along with her, each climax more intense

than the last.

She's a woman who only recently experienced a climax. This will be too much for her. Too much. Pleasure equals pain equals pleasure.

But she takes it.

She takes it all.

"Tell me to stop, Skye," I say, my voice more like a growl. "Tell me it's too much. Too much... Too much..."

Except it's not too much. Not too much for me and not too much for her. This is savage. Primal.

Fucking magnificent.

I pull climax after climax out of her. Any other woman would be begging by now—begging for a release from the pleasure-pain.

Skye is so far from any other woman.

She wins this round—though I'll never admit it to her—because I can't wait any longer to ram my cock into her pussy.

I can't help a soft chuckle. "You *are* obstinate. Fuck. I have to be inside you."

Then I'm in her. Her pussy walls are still spasming. I fuck her hard and quick, grinding over her clit so her climaxes continue.

"Braden!" she cries out.

"That's it, baby. Keep coming. Keep coming. You're so hot. That's it. That's it. Fuck!"

I slam into her.

She's still spasming as I release, and we come in tandem, her pussy clenching around me with each spurt of my seed into her. Perspiration glistens on her forehead, and her eyes are heavy-lidded.

She's fucking amazing.

I stay on top of her, our bodies still joined, for a few timeless moments.

And for those few moments, I feel an utter completeness

that is foreign to me.

I withdraw and roll onto my back. She snuggles against my shoulder and kisses my flesh.

"That was amazing," she says.

I don't look at her. "You didn't beg."

The words aren't harsh, though in my mind she's been disobedient. I'm not angry with her. I'm freaking amazed by her sheer will.

"No, I didn't."

"Any other woman would have begged me to stop. I know a woman's body. I know that many orgasms are a toll, pleasure morphing to almost pain. But you didn't beg me to stop." I shake my head, groaning. "I'll say it again. You're my Everest, Skye."

She giggles. "I think you've already climbed me."

I open my eyes and prop my head in my hand to meet her gaze. "This isn't funny."

"I didn't say it was."

"You laughed."

"I was making a joke. About climbing on top of me?" She smiles.

Except this isn't funny. Not at all. She's beautiful, wonderful—an amazing and brilliant woman. And damn, I've never met anyone like her. She makes me smile, laugh. She brings me to my fucking knees.

And I'm loving every minute of it.

Which disturbs me more than a little.

"I get what I want, Skye. Always. No matter how long it takes."

She swallows.

"You gave in to me once. I want it again."

"And in return?"

"You get me. You're Braden Black's girlfriend."

She bites her lower lip. "I think I'm already Braden

Black's girlfriend. Instagram doesn't lie, after all."

She's being funny again, or trying to be, but I'm not laughing.

And I know I'll do whatever it takes to get what I want from her.

"All right," I say. "What else do you want?"

She answers quickly. "To be the only one. If you become interested in someone else, you have to tell me, and that will be the end. And I don't want you to use condoms with me."

I stay quiet for a few seconds, as if I have to think it over. Truth? I don't have to think at all.

"Done."

I close my eyes then, as thoughts explode through me.

How is this happening?

How have I fallen so far from who I thought I was?

I don't mind being exclusive, but never have I made such a promise to a woman.

I picture seven-year-old Skye racing through a cornfield, frightened and lost, her little heart beating against her chest.

I picture present Skye shooting photos of Addison Ames drinking coffee—paying her dues and using any opportunity to get her name known as a photographer.

I picture older Skye, still beautiful, standing in my bedroom, naked and waiting...

Fuck. It. All.

I feign sleep as Skye touches my now-flaccid dick. Her touch scorches me, and already my cock wants to respond.

Then she kisses my shoulder.

"You are *my* Everest, Braden," she whispers. "I *will* figure you out."

Chapter Thirty-Four

I rise the next morning without waking Skye and spend more time than I have staring at her sleeping body—the warm flush covering her chest and breasts, the soft sleeping smile on her beautiful lips.

I could wake her.

Fuck her.

Pull more climaxes out of her.

But I have work to do, and a new reality hits me. I want Skye more than I want to work.

Willpower, Braden. Willpower.

This is all new to me. I can't recall the last time I spent the night at a woman's place. I'm feeling an odd combination of regret and happiness.

And the regret part is pretty small.

If I didn't have an early meeting…

Oh, for God's sake. I pad into her small bathroom and turn on the shower. The water pressure is weak, but I squeeze some shampoo—raspberry-scented and oddly refreshing—into my palms and wash my hair. Then I squeeze shower gel—also raspberry, no wonder she always smells like raspberries—into her loofah and scrub myself clean. I don't have my toothbrush, but I swish some of Skye's mouthwash around. I'll brush my teeth when I get home.

I dry off, dress in yesterday's clothes, and walk back to the bed.

I grab my phone as I kiss Skye gently on her forehead.

She opens her eyes. "You took a shower?"

"Yeah. I've never used raspberry shampoo before. I like the fruity smell." I give her a half smile.

She giggles and then parts her lips and inhales, smelling my wet hair.

"I didn't want to disturb you," I continue. "You were out."

A yawn splits her face. "I can't believe I didn't wake up."

"I can."

"You can? Why?"

"Multiple orgasms will do that to you." I stare at my phone.

"What time is it?"

"Seven."

"Oh, good. I have plenty of time to get to work."

Shit. An email from the office in New York. They need me to sign a document today and attend meetings the rest of the week—among them a meeting with McCain Global regarding some property we've been trying to purchase for years. A busy several days and then the benefit for the Boston Opera Guild on Saturday. I'm a major donor. "Looks like I have to go to New York for a few days."

"Oh," she says. "Who will take care of Sasha?"

"Annika will. I'm texting her now. I'll be back Saturday morning. Saturday evening, I'd like you to accompany me to a benefit for the Boston Opera Guild."

She nods. "Sure. Okay."

I kiss her lips softly. "Wear the black dress."

• • •

Two hours later, still wearing yesterday's suit, I arrive at LaGuardia on my jet. I don't have any luggage, as I keep everything I need at my Manhattan penthouse. After a quick change into fresh clothes and a much-needed tooth brushing, I arrive at the office.

Another two hours later, all the documents are signed, and I'm at lunch with Dimitri Stamos, who heads the company satellite in Manhattan, telling him to take the meetings for the rest of the week.

He drops his jaw. "Who are you, and what have you done with Braden Black?"

I understand his confusion. I've always been the face of Black, Inc., and in the rare event that I can't make an important meeting, I send Ben.

Dimitri is a capable man, though, and he's told me on more than one occasion that he's available to ease my workload.

"You've been wanting to do more, Dimitri. Here's your opportunity."

"Well...yeah, but this isn't like you. At all."

He's right. Still, I don't owe him an explanation, so if he's waiting for one, he'll be waiting a long time.

"Suffice it to say I have confidence in you to take the meetings and do what needs to be done."

"I'm up for it. The only issue I see is the meeting with Foster McCain of McCain Global. It's taken a while to even get him to talk to us."

"You know as much about the business as I do," I say. "If you have any issues, I'll be available by phone as always."

Dimitri's brown eyes widen further. "You mean you're

not going to call in and attend via phone?"

"Not this time," I say, taking a sip of water. "You can call me if necessary, but this is what you've been asking for, Dimitri. You've more than proved your competence over the last five years. I trust you. Implicitly."

Though I keep my expression stoic, I'm surprising myself as well Dimitri. Ben has been after me for years not to micromanage so much. We hire only the best people, have an ironclad nondisclosure agreement, and in the last ten years, we've never had an employee screw us over.

That's why I'm doing this.

It's not because I can't stand being away from Skye until Saturday.

Fuck. What a damned lie!

For a man who values control, I'm losing it where Skye Manning is concerned.

"I suppose it won't do me any good to ask why you've had this change of heart, huh?" Dimitri asks.

"No," I say emphatically, "it won't."

My private life is private. I keep it out of the workplace. In fact, I keep a large facet of it out of my hometown of Boston.

My club, Black Rose Underground, is here in Manhattan.

And it's here for a very good reason.

"Good enough," Dimitri says. "I won't let you down."

"I know you won't."

We spend the rest of lunch getting Dimitri up to speed on some details for the meetings he'll be taking. He's well prepared already, which gives me even more faith in my decision.

After lunch, I call my pilot. "Change in plans," I tell him. "We're leaving this afternoon."

"Hold on. I need to check with air traffic control for a takeoff slot. What's your window?"

"I can be at the airport in an hour and a half. As soon as

possible after that."

"Got it. I'll get back to you as soon as I can."

I'm heading to my Manhattan penthouse when I get the text from the pilot.

We're ready to go at 4 p.m.

Excellent, I text back.

Assuming no delays, I'll land in Boston by five and be back at my place by six. Enough time to see Skye. I considered sending her a ticket to meet me here in Manhattan, but she wouldn't be able to get out of work with no notice.

Plus...I'm not sure she's ready for New York Braden.

In the meantime...

I slide my card through the elevator and descend to the bottom floor of the building.

The Black Rose Underground.

The club is closed during daytime hours, but I want to be here for a few minutes. I want to soak up the atmosphere, try to get my head on straight.

This place is my escape—in more ways than one.

Yes, it's where I can indulge my darkest fantasies, whatever they may be.

But it's also an escape from home. From Boston.

Don't get me wrong. I love Boston. It will always be my home base.

But I don't allow certain parts of my life in Boston.

Here, at the club, I wear a mask—albeit a metaphorical one. But in some ways, this is the only place where I'm truly myself.

I walk past the vacant bouncer's desk and into the large common area, where I flip on the lights. The club looks so different without guests, almost as if it's in some kind of dormant state, waiting to be awakened tonight with members and their fantasies.

I love this place.

More than once I've had a woman ask me why I enjoy the darker side of sex, why I enjoy taking such a dominant role.

I never answer. It helps me remain mysterious.

But the truth of the matter is that I don't know.

Or rather, I do know, but I don't like to think about the reasons.

The little boy from the food pantry, Benji, slides into my mind once again.

One little boy who shares my brother's name…and he opened a window in my mind to things I prefer to keep dormant, much like the club is dormant at this hour.

The door to the exhibition rooms and playrooms looms ahead in the distance, but I have no desire to go through it.

I'm not here to think about sex or fantasies or what I want to do to Skye in my private suite.

I'm here to escape the thoughts that have been plaguing me since the trip to the food pantry.

Except this place is offering anything but escape…

• • •

It was Benji's birthday, and Daddy was out on a bender. That's what Momma said, anyway.

"What's Daddy bending?" I asked Momma.

She didn't answer because she was busy changing Benji's diaper. My baby brother was one year old today.

My momma was beautiful. She had dark-brown hair and blue eyes, just like mine. Benji's were brown like Daddy's.

Momma bought a special cake at the bakery for Benji. It was chocolate with white icing and words in blue. Momma told me it said, "Happy Birthday, Benji."

But when Daddy got home from work, he came in and got mad about the cake.

"The kid's too young to even know it's his birthday. Why

the hell did you spend money on a cake?"

"He'll only be a year old once, Bobby."

"For Christ's sake." Daddy pulled open the screen door. "I'm out of here."

That's when Momma said he was on a bender.

I didn't cry when Daddy got mad anymore. I used to, but I was a big boy now. Almost four years old. I only cried when Momma got mad at me.

Momma only got mad at me when I was bad. I tried to be a good boy because I hated it when Momma was mad. Luckily, she didn't get mad a lot. She didn't even get mad when Daddy yelled about the cake and left.

Instead, she said she had a treat for me. She said we'd eat Benji's cake and have dessert first tonight.

Momma set Benji in his highchair and put a piece of cake on the tray. Momma and I laughed with him as he got more cake on his face than in his mouth.

And I forgot all about Daddy's bender.

• • •

I open my eyes before I realize they were closed. I'm still in the club, sitting alone at a table in the corner. A quick check of my phone shows it's time to leave for the airport.

I rise abruptly. "Enough of this self-indulgent bullshit," I say out loud. It's becoming nauseating.

I walk briskly out of the club.

Chapter Thirty-Five

Christopher is off tonight, as I thought I'd be in New York, so I take a cab home to my place, where I find my driver hanging out talking to Marilyn in the kitchen.

"Not taking advantage of your night off?" I ask him.

"Mr. B, what are you doing back?"

"Change of plans."

"You need me to work?"

"Not tonight. I may tomorrow, but I'll pay double time, since I'm reneging on your week off."

"Not a problem," Christopher says, "though I should tell you…"

"Tell me what?" I walk out of the kitchen, looking at my phone.

Christopher follows me into the living area. "Ms. Manning was here a little while ago."

That gets my attention. "Skye? Here? Why? She knows I'm supposed to be in New York."

"Yeah, she does," Christopher says. "She brought over a basket of goodies for Sasha. It's on the island in the kitchen."

"It is?" I stride back into the kitchen.

Sure enough, a gift basket from Betsy's Bark Boutique sits on the marble counter. Not sure how I missed it.

Betsy's Bark Boutique. I know that name. Betsy…I can't recall her last name. She's a friend of Addison's. They go way back, even further than Addie and I go.

"I took Sasha on a walk earlier," Christopher says from behind me.

"Great. Thanks."

"I dropped her off for an hour of play time at the doggie daycare. In fact, I should go pick her up."

"Thanks," I say again. "You don't have to hang around here on your day off. Annika can take care of Sasha."

"I don't mind. I love that little pup. If you don't need me, I'll go get her."

"Fine. See you in a bit."

Christopher leaves the kitchen, and a few minutes later, I hear the sound of the elevator door sliding open.

Now, to deal with why I came home.

Skye.

Who has apparently already been here once today. The gift basket from Betsy is filled with homemade treats and a lot of toys. Not an inexpensive gift. Why would Skye buy such a thing for Sasha? Was it an excuse to come here? If so, why? She knows I'm gone.

Marilyn finishes cleaning the oven. "I'm done here, Mr. B. But now that you're home, do you want me to make you something?"

"No. You're off this week, too, Marilyn. I don't want my sudden appearance to upset your plans."

"Perfect." She smiles. "Thank you. See you in a few days."

Again, the elevator doors slide open, the bell dings, and with Marilyn gone and Annika upstairs, I'm alone.

Back to Skye Manning.

She's the reason I cut my trip short. The reason I gave Dimitri Stamos the extra responsibility he's been asking for.

The reason I'm standing here in my penthouse, wondering how I'm going to see her tonight.

I could show up unannounced at her place again, like I did last night.

But God, that makes me look a little needy.

I'm not needy. Not at all. I just know what I want. No shame in that.

If Skye and I are going to continue down this path, she needs to know what I want as well.

I pick up my phone to call her when the intercom buzzes from downstairs. Christopher and Marilyn are gone. Annika's upstairs, and I'm not expecting anyone.

I walk to the intercom on the wall next to the elevator and push the button. "Yes?"

A pause. Then, "You... You're supposed to be in New York."

Skye. Skye's voice.

Skye is here.

"Skye? What are you doing here?"

"I dropped off some treats for Sasha, and I think I lost an earring. I just wanted to come up and look for it."

She's not that good a liar. I smile, shaking my head. She came back for some reason, though, and it's not to see me because she knows I'm out of town. Except now I'm back.

Curiosity wins me over.

"All right. I'll send the elevator down." I push the button.

A few minutes later, the elevator doors open. I stand in the entryway. Skye's hair is tumbling out of its ponytail, as if she ran over here. For some reason, it makes her look all the more delectable.

"Good evening, Skye."

"Hi." Her voice cracks.

"Thank you for the treats for Sasha. I just saw the basket in the kitchen."

"You're welcome. I got it free at a shoot, and of course I have no use for it."

So that's how she got it. She wasn't so presumptuous as to go out and purchase a gift basket for my dog. It fell into her lap. I'm both relieved and disappointed.

"Nice of you to think of her," I say.

"Why are you home so soon?"

"I was able to complete the business early."

"In one day?"

"Does that seem implausible to you?"

It should. It's damned implausible to me, and it's also untrue. I didn't complete the business. I delegated it.

She doesn't reply right away. She twiddles her fingers together and darts her gaze around the room a few times.

She's nervous.

"Braden"—she clears her throat—"I didn't lose an earring."

"Oh?" No surprise there. I can't resist a tiny smile. "Why are you here, then?"

"Because I..." She draws in a deep breath and holds it a few seconds.

"Spit it out, Skye."

A moment passes in silence before she pulls a crumpled envelope out of her purse then thrusts it at me. "To return this."

I wrinkle my forehead and take the envelope. It's from the Ames Hotel—a bid to host a past event.

"I don't know what I was thinking," she says. "I brought the stuff for Sasha, and then I went to the bathroom. I saw all the mail in the magazine rack, and I couldn't help myself. When I saw the Ames Hotel envelope, I just... You won't tell me about you and Addie, so I thought maybe..."

"Maybe you could figure it out from this?"

"I didn't even look inside. I swear it. I felt terrible about it, and that's why I came back. I was going to come back up here and replace it in the powder room so no one was the wiser. But now you're here, and I...I don't want to lie to you, Braden."

I open the envelope, withdraw the paper inside, and hand it to her. "It's a bid for an event my foundation hosted last year."

She glances at the letter. It's dated more than a year ago. A quick look at the postmark would have given her this clue.

"You see," I say. "Nothing about Addison and me."

"I'm sorry."

"Do you really think I'd leave anything important sitting in my powder room?" I ask.

"No. I..." She sighs. "I wasn't thinking at all."

Tension flows off her body. She's waiting. Waiting for my reaction.

I'm angry. I'm amused. I'm perplexed—which seems to be my normal state around Skye.

And I'm turned on, which makes no sense at all.

She won't let my past with Addison lie, and she must. I don't talk about it for many reasons, none of which I'm ready to go into with Skye. Like most of my childhood, it's better left in the past.

"I'm sorry," she finally says. "I understand if you want to..."

I cock my head. "If I want to what?"

"Not see me anymore."

I laugh. The boisterousness of it surprises even me. I cut my trip short, delegated important duties...and she thinks I'm going to refuse to see her?

Can she let me go that easily?

She seems willing.

And then this isn't funny anymore. Not in the slightest.

"What's so funny?" she demands.

I pull her against me, my lips pressing against her ear. "Nothing is funny about this."

"Then why did you—"

"You want to know why I'm home early? Because I couldn't stop thinking about *you*. I wanted you in my bed. I almost sent you a plane ticket, but I knew you wouldn't take off work with no notice. So I came home. I came home because I couldn't wait five fucking days to see you again."

She swallows. "So…you're not angry with me?"

I meet her gaze with anger bubbling through me. "I didn't say that."

She swallows again. "Then you *are* angry?"

"Of course I'm angry. Who wouldn't be?"

She stays silent.

"The question is, what do I do about it?"

Again, she has no response.

"I could end things with you, but I didn't fly two hundred miles today to punish myself."

Ending things with Skye is not an option. At least not yet.

"I could take you over my knee and give you a good spanking. It's what you deserve."

She walks backward, away from me, until her back hits the wall beside the elevator door. I close in on her.

"Your lips are parted in that sexy way," I rasp. "I want to kiss you so hard that your knees give out."

She inhales a slight gasp.

"That wouldn't punish you, though."

She stays silent and closes her eyes.

"So no kisses tonight. I'm going to spank your creamy ass, and then I'm going to take what I came all this way for. And you're going to let me."

Her bourbon eyes narrow slightly. She's thinking.

Thinking about how she can give in yet still maintain control. She wants this as much as I do. I can feel it in the pulse of her body. Already she's wet. Ready for me.

"Braden…" she whispers.

"Yes?" I lock onto her gaze with laser focus.

She inhales sharply. "Do what you need to do."

In a flash, she's in my arms, and I'm carrying her to my bedroom. I throw her on the bed and tug off her shoes, slacks, and panties. She spreads her legs, giving me full view of her arousal. Fuck. She's pink and swollen and glistening with cream.

But that pussy won't be climaxing tonight.

I close my eyes and inhale. "You smell like heaven. I'd love to taste you, Skye. Give you a hundred orgasms like last time, but that wouldn't be punishment. So I'm going to spank you. Then I'm going to fuck you hard and fast and take my own pleasure." I unbuckle my belt and unzip my fly. I yank my pants and underwear over my hips. My dick is fully erect, and a small pearl of clear liquid emerges.

I toss her over onto her stomach and bring my palm down on her ass.

"Ow!" she cries out.

Another slap. Then another. The pain I give her flows back into me via my palm and throughout my body. My cock throbs. Her ass is deliciously rosy.

"Gorgeous," I rasp. "So pink."

I slap her again and then once more.

I raise my palm for another, but my dick has other ideas. My whole body is awake with passion and desire, as the pleasure-pain I've given Skye rips through me like a tidal wave.

I flip her back over so she's lying on her back.

I push her legs forward and thrust into her.

She cries out.

I fuck her hard. I fuck her fast.

And with her legs pushed so far forward, my pubic bone doesn't nudge her clit.

Her body responds anyway, which is exactly what I want. I'm going to take her to the peak.

But I won't let her jump.

I flick my thumb over her clit just enough to get her climbing, and then I plunge deeply inside her, embedding myself in her body and taking my own pleasure.

After only a few thrusts, I release inside her, groaning, cursing her name, and it feels amazing. Fucking amazing. Just as amazing is that I came so quickly—that my need for her is that profound.

I don't feel one iota of guilt about her lack of orgasm. She deserves to be punished.

This doesn't surprise me. What does surprise me is that my release is less potent.

Less potent because Skye wasn't joining in it.

A first for me.

When I finally stop pulsing, I stay inside her for a moment, my eyes closed and my hands clamped onto her thighs.

I pull out then and open my eyes, determined not to allow my newfound revelation to change the course of the evening, the course of giving Skye the punishment she deserves.

She says nothing. Just lies there, looking beautiful but unsatisfied.

I don't particularly like leaving a woman unsatisfied. Especially Skye.

No! I will not relent.

I pull up my pants and fasten them. "Have you eaten?" I ask nonchalantly.

She's still naked from the waist down, her legs still spread, my semen seeping out of her. "Well…no. Not yet."

"Get dressed. Marilyn is off this week, so I'll order something."

Chapter Thirty-Six

I make a quick call to a Thai place I love and order dinner. I'm pouring two Wild Turkeys at my bar when Skye appears, now fully clothed, her ponytail no longer mussed.

She's beautiful, but I like her mussed. By me.

"There you are," I say. "I ordered Thai food."

She nods. "Sounds delicious."

I hand her a glass. "Wild Turkey goes great with Thai."

She smiles. "Wild Turkey goes great with everything." She takes a sip.

I take a sip as well, enjoying the subtly harsh smokiness on my tongue. I let it trickle down my throat slowly.

The silence grows in the room.

"Braden?" Skye finally says.

"Hmm?"

"I'm…really sorry about…you know."

"We don't have to talk about that." She doesn't know how much I mean the words. She did it. I punished her.

Now it's over.

I'll file it away in my mind along with those myriad other

things I don't like to think about.

The list seems to grow longer by the day.

"But we do," she says. "I don't want you to think I'm the kind of person who—"

"Skye, you did what you did. No amount of telling me what kind of person you are will change what already happened." The words come out more harshly than I mean for them to, so I continue. "Do you think I've never made a bad choice? Done something I regret?"

Offhand, about twelve scenarios come to mind, including a few on that long list of things I don't think about.

"No. I mean, I don't know."

"You don't get to the top without making mistakes along the way. I learn from every mistake, and I never make the same mistake twice. Do you see what I'm getting at?"

"Yeah. I won't do it again. I told you that already."

"I understand mistakes. I've made my share."

Call that the understatement of the world. I vow never to bring up the piece of mail she stole again.

As long as she doesn't.

I'm hoping she'll take my cue and never bring up Addison and me again, as well.

She nods and takes another sip of Wild Turkey.

Christopher brings the Thai food into the kitchen.

"Sasha's up with Annika," he tells me. "She enjoyed the doggie place."

"Thanks, Christopher. You're off the clock now. Go have some fun."

"I think I'll just go up to my room and binge watch some TV," he says, "so I'm here if you need me."

"Okay. Thanks."

He heads out of the kitchen, while I pull dishes and utensils out of cupboards and drawers. I dish out a plate of food and hand it to Skye.

"Thanks," she murmurs. She sits on one of the barstools at the granite island and winces slightly.

"Sore?" I ask, warming. She'd better be sore.

"No. Just a little tender." She takes a bite of the spicy curry.

Again, silence descends.

"Something interesting happened at work today," she finally says.

"Oh? What's that?"

"Strangest thing," she says after swallowing a bite of curry. "The social marketing VP for Susanne Cosmetics called the office today. Addie does a lot of Instagram posts for Susanne, so naturally I thought that's who the call was for. I put it right through."

"And...?"

"Turns out she wanted to talk to me."

I raise my eyebrows. "Oh? What about?"

"Get this." She takes a sip of Wild Turkey. "Remember that post you tagged me in at the MADD Gala?"

"How could I not?" I say dryly.

"Well, after I made my profile public, as you suggested, someone asked about the color of my lip stain."

"Right. I saw that." Which effectively tells her I've been looking at the picture of us on Instagram.

Fuck it. I'm interested in this woman. Why hide it? Everyone else seems to know.

"Yeah, so I answered," Skye says. "I told her it was Susanne Cherry Russet."

I nod.

"So anyway, like I said, I transferred the call straight to Addie. A few minutes later she comes out of her office with smoke coming out of her ears. I mean, she's pissed!"

I roll my eyes. "I imagine that's a normal occurrence."

"It can be, but she's full of rage now, her whole face is

red. She demands to know what's going on. I don't know what she's talking about, of course. I've been answering emails, doing other grunt work, so I figure she's mad about some new offer. You know, probably forty-five K instead of fifty or something. So I make some silly comment about lip plumper, and she goes off. Accuses me of sabotaging her, making her look like she's out of the loop, all kinds of shit that's untrue."

Addie spreading untruths? Not real shocking. But I'm getting angrier by the minute at her treatment of Skye.

"Apparently," Skye continues, "Eugenie—that's her name, the social media person from Susanne—told Addie that they've gotten hundreds of orders for the Cherry Russet lip stain because of the comment I made on your Instagram photo."

"Wow," I say. "That's pretty amazing."

"You're telling me. But then Addie flies into this serious rage. She grabs my purse and unloads it right on my desk. She grabs a tube of lipstick, which is of course the Cherry Russet lip stain. It's my go-to shade. Then she throws it on the floor, making her yappy little dog shriek."

"Her dog was in the office?"

"Yeah, she takes him on shoots for pet-related stuff."

"Okay. Go on."

"So I'm really mad now, but also curious, so I ask Addie if Eugenie called to thank me for making the comment on your post. Addie goes mental again and says Susanne wants me to do an Instagram post and promote the product."

I widen my eyes.

"So I say, 'Me? I'm no influencer.' And she flies back into her rant. Apparently now that I'm Braden Black's girlfriend, I have some kind of clout, and that Eugenie said the color was"—air quotes—"'absolutely fabulous on me.'"

She stops abruptly then and closes her mouth. She wants to say something more, but she's thought better of it.

I could press her, but I choose not to. I don't want her

pressing me on certain things.

"Are you going to call her?" I ask.

"I haven't decided yet. Addie won't like it. I'll probably lose my job."

"She hasn't fired you yet."

"No, but we had a shoot today. For the pet boutique where I got Sasha's gift basket. She needed me."

"She'll always need you."

"I'm not sure of that. Besides, the only reason Susanne wants me to do a post about the lip stain is because of you."

"So?"

"How can you be so nonchalant? I'm a nobody. No one gives a crap what kind of lip stain I wear except for the fact that apparently I'm your girlfriend now."

"So?" I say again.

She lifts her eyebrows, shaking her head slightly. "What don't you get about this?"

At the moment, what I get is that Addie reacted like an immature brat—which she is—and took it out on Skye, which pisses me off to no end. But instead of saying this, I put on my business hat.

"Here's what I get," I say. "This is an opportunity for you. Would you have this opportunity if not for me? Maybe not, but it's still an opportunity that has presented itself. Take it, Skye. You're a fool if you don't."

"A fool? How dare you—"

I gesture for her to stop. She does.

"Don't get all excited. Anyone, including me, is a fool not to take advantage of what's thrown in his lap. Do you think I haven't taken every opportunity that's come my way? I won't leave you in suspense. I have, and some of them came along simply because I was in the right place at the right time. They had nothing to do with me."

"I can't believe that."

"Why not?"

"You're a self-made man, Braden."

"For the most part, that's true. But do you truly think I never had any help along the way? That opportunities fell into my lap simply because I'm me?"

She doesn't know the half of it. File one thing in particular under that heading of "things I don't talk about."

"I've read all about you," she says.

"The media never tells the whole story." They can't, because I don't talk about the whole story, and I make sure no one else does, either.

She smiles. "Will *you*, then, Braden? Will you tell me the whole story?"

My lips twitch. Yeah, I should have seen that one coming. This is a woman who sees me coming from every direction. Damn.

"You *are* a challenge, Skye."

"You've said that many times," she says. "Has it escaped your notice that you're *also* a challenge?"

"I never said I wasn't."

"What will we do, then?"

I swallow a bite of food. "I've never backed down from a challenge."

"Neither have I."

"Then you'll do the post for Susanne Cosmetics."

She freezes, her forkful of food stopped midway between her plate and her mouth. She walked right into that one, which was wholly my intention.

"You don't play fair," she says.

"Sure I do. I'm just more experienced than you are."

"Posting about lip stain isn't exactly a challenge."

"Of course it is. It's something new. It's something you're not sure you're up for, but it fell in your lap. You can take your own pictures, Skye. Get credit for them. This is what you want."

"I want to take photos of things that move people. No one's going to be moved by me wearing Susanne lip stain."

"How do you know?"

"Because it's makeup, Braden. Who cares?"

"Your followers."

"The mobs who follow influencers aren't concerned about anything real."

"Do you know all of them?"

"Of course not, but—"

"Don't you see, Skye? You have the chance to grow a platform. To reach people. Once you reach them, you can introduce them to the kind of photos that *will* move them."

Chapter Thirty-Seven

Her mouth drops open.

Yup, got her.

Social media wields a lot of power these days. Skye should know. Social media pays her salary.

"But," I continue, "never take the first offer. I don't care how high it is, counteroffer something higher."

"What if they tell me to go jump in the lake?"

"Then they tell you to go jump in the lake."

"But then—"

"Skye, show them you know what you're worth. They're not getting just Braden Black's girlfriend with you. They're getting an ace photographer, someone who can make their product look amazing. They know that, and if they don't, they will soon."

"Wait a minute," she says. "You didn't…"

I know what she's asking. She doesn't have to say the words. It's not the first time someone thinks I made a phone call. I don't know anyone at Susanne Cosmetics. I had no idea Skye wears their makeup or that Addison does posts for them.

"Of course not. I had nothing to do with them calling you. It may surprise you to know that I don't have time to call cosmetics companies and ask them to hire my girlfriend."

She nods.

"Never be afraid to turn down the first offer. You're new at this, so they know they can lowball you."

"You really are brilliant."

"I'm no more brilliant than the next guy," I counter. "I just know what my strengths are, and I know what they're worth."

True story there.

"Braden…"

"Yeah?"

"Addison thinks you're behind all this, that you're trying to make me into an influencer and destroy her in the process."

Not a surprise. Addison Ames is such a narcissist that she thinks the whole world revolves around her. It wouldn't ever occur to her that I don't have any extra minutes in the day to give her a second thought. And when I do have an extra minute? She's about one billionth on the list of things I'd choose to think about.

I take a drink. "That's what she said?"

"Yeah."

"And you believe her?"

"No." She shakes her head vehemently. "Of course not."

I don't reply right away. I will take Skye at her word, but I can't help but wonder… Does she consider for a moment that I'm trying to sabotage Addie? Does she think I'd resort to such pettiness? Because it *is* pettiness. Addison and I have a history—a history that is mostly negative.

I drain the rest of my Wild Turkey. "Addison is a troubled woman."

"What's that supposed to mean?"

"I think you know."

"No, I really don't."

"Don't you? You've been working with her for more than a year. Isn't it clear that she has to be the center of attention? And when she's not, she sprouts claws?"

"I see your point," she says. "Can you tell me more about her?"

I pour myself another Wild Turkey. "Nice try."

"I don't understand. Why won't you talk about your time with Addison? You were both young. Surely it couldn't have been *that* horrible."

"'Horrible' is too tame a word."

Try scandalous. Terrifying. Shocking.

Try the one thing in my adult life that truly scared me.

She swallows. "How was she in bed?"

I stay silent. I can't answer that question. First, Skye doesn't actually want to know. No woman who ever asks that question of a man about another woman truly wants the answer, no matter what it is.

Second, I won't go back to that place. Not for anything or anyone. Even Skye Manning. Even with that pleading look in her beautiful eyes, her lips parted in that way that makes me heart gallop.

"Tell me, Braden. Please."

"Why do you care?"

"I just...do."

"For God's sake, Skye. We were kids. Neither one of us knew what the hell we were doing."

"So you *did* take her virginity."

"Who said that?"

She doesn't answer.

That question didn't appear in her mind out of thin air. Someone planted it there. Addie? All these years later, she's going to violate my confidence? Or someone else? Which means Skye's been making queries she shouldn't be.

I advance toward her. "Why does any of this matter to you? Do you want to know if she was better in bed than you are?"

No response.

"Do you want to know about *all* my previous lovers? There are a lot of them, and I won't apologize for anything I did in the past."

She trembles. "I'm not asking you to."

"Then exactly what *are* you asking, Skye?"

"I…don't know."

"I'll tell you what you're asking. You want to know how you compare to Addie, to everyone I've slept with."

Rather, she *thinks* she wants to know, but she actually doesn't. I take a long drink of my bourbon and get ready to give her all she'll get out of me tonight, including an admission of gratitude to one woman in my history.

"I'll tell you only this. I've never cut a business trip short for any woman. Never…until now."

I move forward until only inches separate us, but I don't touch her. "You challenge me. You perplex me. And damn it, Skye, you fucking *infuriate* me. You want to know how I feel about Addison Ames? Honestly?"

She nods shakily.

"I'm grateful."

"G-Grateful? Why?"

"If it weren't for her, I wouldn't know *you*."

"Braden, I—"

"Shut the fuck up." I slam my lips down onto hers.

She opens instantly and accepts my tongue. I denied her a kiss earlier, and I meant to deny her the rest of this night.

But damn it… The sheer challenge of this woman. Her beauty and her candor. Her utter audacity.

She spreads her legs, straddles my thigh, and grinds

against me.

Fuck. I kiss her harder, letting her seek friction against me, but only for a moment. I'm not yet ready to let her climax.

After a few moments, before she gets too far toward her goal, I break the kiss, turn her around against the kitchen island, and brush her slacks and panties down her hips.

"Braden... Christopher. And Annika."

"This is my house, not theirs."

"But..."

"Quiet!" I roar, fumbling with my belt buckle. I unzip my pants, free my rock-hard cock.

Then my dick is inside her, pressing like a steam engine between her closed thighs and into her tight channel. God, she feels perfect. Wet and wonderful and perfect.

She cries out.

I grab her hands and place them flat on the marble countertop. "Don't move," I command.

I thrust into her again and again.

I've chosen this angle on purpose. She won't get the friction she needs on her clit. Yes, I'm still denying her an orgasm, at least for this moment. Still punishing her, but this time, it's not for stealing a piece of mail.

It's for getting inside me. Taking me to a place I never wanted to go. I cut a fucking trip short for this woman. She's trying to become a part of me, whether it's conscious or subconscious on her part.

Doesn't matter. She's doing it.

And I'm angry. Angry that she means so much to me in so short a time. Angry that she makes me want things I have no business wanting.

Angry that she's still fighting me. Still determined to keep her control.

Even now, I feel her pushing, trying to move forward against the marble countertop. Trying to touch her clit to the surface.

"I feel you searching," I growl against her neck, willing her to sense the rage inside me. "Don't, Skye."

"But I need—"

"Don't!" I smack the cheek of her ass and then hold on to it, gripping her tight, keeping her still as I fuck her harder, lose myself in her tight little body. "I told you to keep quiet. You'll get your orgasm, but on my terms."

She tenses, and I feel her brace herself against the counter, brace herself against my thrusts.

"God, you're tight. Feels so good." I bite her neck lightly and then suck at it. "Mine. Mine. Mine."

Mine.

The word surprises me.

But in the same moment, it doesn't.

I'm claiming her. Claiming control over her body, her orgasms. I may not have the control I crave over all of her, but I can at least control her climax.

I release her ass cheek as I pull out of her pussy.

She gasps, looking over her shoulder. "You didn't—"

"All in good time. I needed to be inside you for a minute. Now I need something else."

"What?"

"Did you forget you're not supposed to be talking?" I slap her ass, and then I reach past her ass cheeks and I tap her clit.

Again. And again. Until it's no longer a tap but a soft smack.

I'm giving her just enough with each slap to push her slightly toward the peak.

Until— "Ah!" she cries out.

Yes, she's climbing, but she won't reach the top yet. I slide my tongue between her legs and lick the juices coating her thighs. Then I glide forward, caressing her slick folds and then her clit. I swirl my tongue around it.

She melts against the granite, and finally, I feel her willingness to let me control her orgasm.

Which makes me want her climax as much as she does.

But it will be all the sweeter if we both wait.

The intensity of the emotion coiling inside me surprises me, threatens to overwhelm me. I could so easily slide a finger inside her, pluck at her G-spot, and send her spiraling outward, force her to endure climax after climax.

But not yet.

I probe her pussy and her ass with my tongue, keeping her right at the tip of the peak, but not letting her jump.

I love the control. But even more, I love that she's letting me have it. Her intense flavor, her responsiveness, her very essence consumes me.

All of me.

My cock is aching and throbbing, but I'll wait for my release.

I'll wait, because Skye is so delicious, so lovely, so warm and sweet under my touch.

Yes, yes, yes.

It's time.

I slide a finger inside her while I lick her asshole. She moans her pleasure.

"Skye," I say, my voice low as I thrust my fingers into her and massage that velvety place inside while, with my other hand, I find her clit. "Come. Now."

Chapter Thirty-Eight

She bursts.

Garbled words float from her mouth to my ears. She clamps her hands against the edge of the marble countertop. Her pussy tightens, loosens, tightens, loosens—all on my finger, and I'm so in tune to her pleasure that I swear to God, I feel like she's coming on my cock.

"Braden!" she cries out. "Yes, Braden, Braden!"

I continue my chant. "Come. Now. Come. Now."

I pull another climax out of her and then another. She's limp against the granite countertop.

"That's right," I say. "Keep coming. Give me another one."

Each times she clamps around my fingers, I want to give her more. I want to take her to the heavens, to paradise. I want her to know, in her soul, that only I can give her what she's feeling at this moment.

"Give me more, baby. More."

Again she responds to my command. Again. And again. Oh, yes. There's a submissive inside this woman just dying to burst out. How many orgasms will she give me? Who will tire first? Will she?

Or will I?

I know I won't. It's become a competition.

A competition I will win. Hands down.

"Keep going," I urge. "Again."

She braces herself once more against the counter, still coming all over my hand. My whole wrist is wet with her juice. It dribbles down my forearm, wafts to my nose, and I inhale her potent perfume.

"One more, Skye."

"Can't," she grits out.

"You can."

"No. Please. I can't. Stop."

Point. And. Match.

In a flash, I replace my fingers with my cock, ramming into her. I thrust and thrust and thrust, my groans a hum of vibration around the bubble of lust encircling us.

I fuck her hard and fast, again and again, until I plunge deeply into her. "God! Skye!"

I come quickly and urgently, giving everything to her with that last thrust. My whole body throbs in time with my cock. My blood boils. My flesh prickles.

All the while, her hands stay glued to the countertop.

I remain embedded in her, reveling in the euphoria floating around us like an invisible dome.

And I think, for a split second, that I never want to be without her in my life. Damn.

After a few minutes, I pull out and zip and snap my pants.

Still, she doesn't move.

"You may move now," I say. "Christopher will drive you home."

She stays in position for a few seconds before she turns to face me, her pants and underwear still around her knees.

"You said you'd never kick me out of your home again."

"That's true. I did." I walk out of the kitchen but look over my shoulder. "You're welcome to stay as long as you like. I left my business meetings to get back here, so I have a lot to do. I'll be in my office working."

Skye pulls up her undies and pants, while I mourn the loss of her naked pussy. I want Skye here. I would love to wake up next to her again.

But I need to maintain control as much as she does. Much more, actually. And with Skye…my control is hanging precariously by a thin thread.

I text Christopher quickly, thankful he decided to stay in tonight.

Are you available? Skye needs a ride home.

Be down in a minute.

Great. Thanks.

And that's that.

I ignore the part of me that wants her to stay.

I ignore the part of me that wants to throw her over my shoulder, take her to my bed, and make love to her all night long.

I ignore the part of me that wants to say those words—words I've never said to a woman, words I never thought I'd even consider saying.

I ignore all of it, because if I don't, I'll be walking straight into a whirlwind I'm not even close to ready for.

Then I head into my home office, leaving Skye to wait for Christopher.

Chapter Thirty-Nine

I'm restless the remainder of the night. I didn't lie to Skye when I said I had work to do. I always have work to do. But it wasn't because of cutting my trip short. I delegated that work, and the team in Manhattan will get the job done. If Foster McCain is a problem, I'll go back, but I have full faith in Dimitri to handle it.

I fire up the computer and sit down to go over tomorrow's agenda when my phone buzzes.

It's my brother.

"Yeah?" I say into the phone.

"Good evening to you, too," Ben says.

"Sorry. It's late. What's up?"

"It's nine thirty, Braden. You're always up until midnight, and you rise at six a.m."

"Yeah, yeah, yeah. Sorry." I shouldn't be short with Ben. None of this is his fault. It's not like he waved some wizard's wand and hurled Skye Manning into my life to throw it into chaos.

"So hey," he says, "I just got a call from Stamos in

Manhattan."

"And...?"

"Well, once I went outside and convinced myself that pigs weren't flying and glaciers weren't rising from hell freezing over—"

"Ha-ha. I assume he told you I came home."

"Yeah, and he wanted to check with me and make sure it was really what you wanted. To which I replied, 'How the fuck should I know? This is the first I'm hearing of it.'"

"Sorry, bro. I didn't mean to leave you out of the loop."

"So you're finally delegating, huh? What's the deal, Bray?"

"And you're opposed to this why?"

"I didn't say I was opposed. Hell, I'm the one who's been after you for years to quit micromanaging everything. But there's got to be a reason."

"Not necessarily."

"Give me a break. For you to do a full one-eighty like this, there's a reason, and I'm guessing she's got one hell of a magic pussy."

Anger slides along the back of my neck. My brother's not saying anything off-brand, but it irks me that he's right.

But it's not Skye's pussy—though she has a pretty spectacular one. It's not her sexy lips or her great rack. It's not her gorgeous brown eyes. It's not her talent or her intelligence. It's not anything specific about her.

It's more about me and my reaction *to* her. My feelings for her—how she's crawled under my skin, challenging my body and my mind.

"It's Addison Ames's assistant, isn't it?" Ben says.

"She has a name," I say. "It's Skye."

"Interesting that you're not denying it."

Why bother? My brother knows me as well as anyone. No one knows the real Braden Black. I'm not even sure I do sometimes. But Ben knows me pretty well. We've been brothers for thirty-three years, and he was with me the night the whole Addison Ames thing started.

"No," I say succinctly. "I'm not denying it."

"Then you should know I had dinner with Apple tonight."

"For fuck's sake. Didn't you just fuck her a few days ago?"

"Dinner, Bray. We had dinner tonight. We didn't fuck. The only reason I bring it up is because she ran off at the mouth about you and Addie's assistant—"

"Skye," I say. "Her name is Skye."

"Christ, okay. Skye. Anyway, apparently Addie's really freaked out now. Thinks Skye's after her job or something."

"That's not true."

"Are you sure? How well do you know this woman, Braden?"

Not as well as I'd like to.

Damn.

"Well enough," I say. "She wants to be a photographer. What do you see in Apple anyway? That black hair of hers is freaky."

"What can I say?" Ben laughs. "She's hot. And she's a good person. She's not her sister."

No, she's not. I need to remember that. Back when all the shit was going down between Addie and me, Ben and Apple were on my side.

"Look," Ben says. "I think it's great if you've found someone you care about. Really. And if she's the reason you're taking a step back and doing some delegating that's long overdue, I'm all for it. There's just one thing that concerns me."

"Yeah? What's that?"

"You barely know her."

He's not wrong. "You're right."

"Wow. Should I check the sky again? Will I see flying

swine?"

I chuckle at that one. "I know what I'm doing, Ben."

"Will you take her to the club soon?"

"When she's ready."

"I'm happy for you," Ben says.

"What for?"

"Sounds like you're falling in love."

God, those words… "I'm *not* falling in love. Like you said, I barely know her."

"That doesn't always matter. There's no timetable for love."

I scoff. "Like you'd know."

He laughs. "I suppose you got me on that one. All right. I just wanted to check in. Since you're not in Manhattan, I'll see you at the office in the morning."

"I'll be there." I end the call and throw my phone on the desk.

My own words haunt me.

I'm not *falling in love. Like you said, I barely know her.*

It's not the words so much as the fact that, as I replay them in my mind, their cadence like a snare drum, they seem…*off* to me.

Off as in I'm not sure I truly mean them.

Then I whisk the thought from my mind and do what I do best when I don't want to think about something.

I work.

Chapter Forty

I work far into the night and finally hit the sheets at four a.m. I allow myself an extra hour of sleep in the morning, rising at seven instead of six.

I don't have any appointments anyway. As far as the office knows, I'm still in New York.

Once I arrive at work and let Claire know I'm available if anyone needs me, I head into my office.

A few hours later, Claire leaves for an early lunch, so my calls come straight to me from Reception. When the phone buzzes, I hit the speaker button. "Yes?"

"Mr. Black, I have Skye Manning on the line."

My heart does a little flip-flop just at her name. What the hell is wrong with me? I've purposefully kept my mind Skye-free since my call from Ben last night.

"Sure," I say. "Put her on." A click. Then, "Good morning, Skye."

"Hi, Braden."

My breath hitches just hearing her voice.

Fuck.

"I'm sorry to bother you at work, but I got the contract with Susanne Cosmetics, and I was wondering if you knew a good, reasonably priced lawyer who could review it for me."

"Email it to me. I'll review it."

"But you're not—"

"An attorney? True, but I've reviewed my share of contracts. I also have four attorneys here in the office who can help me with the legalese if necessary."

"Braden, I didn't call you to give *you* work. I'm perfectly willing to pay an attorney."

"I have the best attorneys here at corporate."

"None of which I can afford, I'm sure."

"Did I say you had to pay?"

"No, but—"

"Forward it to me. I'll be in touch. Goodbye."

Yeah, I was short with her. I have to take a step back.

For God's sake, I cut a business trip short for this woman. I agreed to "date" her. I'm letting her call me her boyfriend.

I cannot and will not let my infatuation with Skye Manning affect my work.

As for her contract? It will take me ten minutes to review and pronounce sufficient. There's no need for her to pay for an attorney, not when I'm perfectly capable of reading the document and offering advice.

I check my phone. It's noon, so I order lunch to be brought in.

Just as it arrives, Claire returns. She walks in carrying the containers. "I'll get this set up for you."

"Thanks," I mumble, my nose in my phone.

Claire sets a bare spot on my desk with a ceramic plate and stainless steel utensils. I hate eating out of takeout containers with plastic flatware. The damned forks always break. Ben says it's because I spear my food like I'm spearing a fish. Whatever. I'm worth a billion dollars, and I'm not going to use plastic utensils. Yeah, I said it.

Claire's phone buzzes, and she looks up.

"Don't worry," I tell her. "Finish up in here. It's lunchtime. Whoever it is can call back."

She raises her eyebrows at me.

Man, I am going soft.

She finishes setting up while my phone buzzes. "Yes," I say.

"Mr. Black, Skye Manning is here to see you," says the floor receptionist.

"Oh?" There goes that flip-flop of my heart again. Damn. "Sure, send her back."

"All right, thank you," she says.

I turn to Claire. "There's a young woman on her way here. It's okay to let her come into my office."

"Sure, no problem, Mr. B." Claire exits.

About a moment later, a knock at my door—a harsh knock.

"Come in."

Skye opens the door and stands before me, wearing her trademark skinny jeans, this time with a black silk camisole and patent-leather pumps.

My cock responds to her mere presence.

"Skye," I say.

"I brought the contract." She pulls it out of her purse. "I thought maybe we could look at it together."

"That couldn't have waited until tonight?"

"We didn't make any plans, and I thought—"

"You'd interrupt me at work?"

"You're not working. You're eating."

"I'm always working, Skye. Close the door, please."

She shuts it quietly, walks forward, and hands me the contract.

"Leave it on the desk. Have you eaten?"

She sets the document on the corner of the desk. "No."

"Would you like half of mine?"

"No, that's okay."

"So you want to sit here and watch me eat?"

"Well...I guess."

I stand, gather my containers of food, and move them to the table across the room. I walk back to my desk and push the call button on my phone. "Claire, could you bring in another plate, please?"

A few seconds later, Claire knocks at the door, enters, and sets another plate and utensils on the table.

"Thanks, Claire."

She nods and leaves the office, closing the door behind her.

"Sit down and help yourself," I say to Skye. "They always deliver enough for two or more people."

"I didn't come here to—"

"Eat, Skye. You'll need energy for what I have planned for you this afternoon."

"I—"

"You barge into my office with a contract you could have easily emailed me, looking sexy with your red lips parted. You think I'm not going to fuck you after that?"

"I... I didn't mean—"

"You promised me your control, Skye, yet you hold on to it in any way you can. Don't think I don't know why you showed up here. It was in complete defiance. I told you to email the contract, so you did what you do. You got around my instructions."

"You told me to *forward* the contract, Braden. You didn't say to email it. So I forwarded it. In person."

"You knew exactly what I meant."

And I did mean it. This morning, I was determined to distance myself and my growing emotions from the woman standing before me.

Now, she's here. Looking tantalizing and making me want her.

So much for distance.

If she thinks I'm *not* going to fuck her after this little stunt? She can think again.

"So I got around your instructions. Just like how last night, you got around our agreement never to kick me out of your place. You said I was welcome to stay, but you made it very clear you were done with me for the evening."

At least she's not arguing. She knows well when to push and when not to push. Smart woman. I can't stop my lips from trembling a bit. I almost want to chuckle, except this isn't funny.

"I never promised to give up my control *outside* the bedroom, Braden."

"That's true," I say, "but you're forgetting one very important detail."

She whips her hands to her hips. "What's that?"

"Any place can be a bedroom."

Chapter Forty-One

I'm busy thinking about the dozens of ways I can fuck Skye over my desk when another knock sounds on the door.

"Come in," I say.

In walks Claire, her forehead wrinkled. "The *Babbler* just came out online. I've ordered copies but figured you'd want to see this now, so I printed it. Let me know how you want to handle it." She hands me a paper and then leaves, closing the door.

I scan the paper. Fuck.

Braden Black Dating Kansas Native and Budding Influencer

Boston's own billionaire Braden Black of Black, Inc. was seen nuzzling a new love interest at the recent MADD charity event. She is Skye Manning, a self-professed farm girl and aspiring photographer who works for mega-influencer Addison Ames. "She's smitten," a source close to Manning says. "I've never seen her so infatuated."

Black, known for his womanizing ways, hasn't dated anyone seriously since his short relationship with model

Aretha Doyle ended last year. "I wish him all the best," says Doyle. "He and I remain close friends."

Black and Manning met at Ames's office recently and have been inseparable since. They've dined together in public several times, and Black will escort her to the Boston Opera Guild Gala this Saturday evening at the Ames Hotel Downtown.

Aspiring photographer Manning is reportedly thrilled by the attention. Several of Ames's clients have reached out to her personally, asking for Instagram posts. As she's familiar with the business, she's poised to become the next sweetheart of Instagram. "She's over the moon," the source says. "Not only is she on the arm of Braden Black, but she's getting the attention she craves for her work."

Black's office had no comment.

I have no clue what to say to Skye, so I opt for nothing. I simply hand her the paper.

She blinks a few times. "What the heck?"

"Did you think this would stay quiet for long?" I ask.

"But I didn't tell her anything."

"Do you think that matters?"

"Why do you keep asking me questions?"

"Let me put it to you this way. Neither of us said a thing. We didn't have to. Read the article."

She glances down.

"Nuzzling?" she says.

"To lean against," I say.

She rolls her eyes. "I know what it means, Braden. Jesus. We weren't nuzzling."

"Just read."

She gulps. "Braden, I never said any of this."

"I know."

"And I have no idea who this purported source is."

I nod.

"How can they lie like that?"

"Easy," I say. "They found a '*source*' who's borderline credible and got them to say what they want. Happens to me all the time."

"Not this time. You had no comment. It makes me look like I'm chasing you."

I twist my lips to keep from smiling. "And you're not?"

"Braden! I'm being serious. I've had *one* call from Susanne Cosmetics, not several calls. This isn't right. And how do they know we're going to the opera gala?"

I chuckle. "Do you really think I announce where I'm going and who I'm going with?"

"Someone knows. Christopher? Annika?"

"I trust my staff implicitly."

"Then who?"

"A *source*, most likely."

She looks around nervously, darting her gaze to each corner of the office.

"You're getting carried away," I say.

"What do you mean?"

"I know what you're thinking. The same thing I thought the first time this happened to me. You're wondering who's watching you. Who's listening to you. Who among your circle of friends could have sold you out. The answer? No one."

"Then how—"

"I already told you. They find a source who doesn't want to be named. Surely you've read tabloids before."

"Actually, I haven't," she says.

"Do yourself a favor, then. Don't ever start reading them. It will slowly invade your mind, and it's not worth it. No one gives the *Babbler* any credence."

"Then why did Claire bring it straight to you?"

"I have to keep up with what the rags are saying about me. Doesn't mean I give it any value whatsoever."

"Then why—"

"If anything is said that could affect business, I have to be aware and file the necessary defamation lawsuits."

"Well, I want to know who this source is."

"Journalists don't have to reveal their sources."

"This isn't journalism, Braden. It's gossip. Fabricated gossip."

"Potato, po-tah-to, as far as the courts are concerned. Besides, look at the facts. We *are* dating. We *did* sit together at the MADD event. We *are* going to the Opera Guild Gala. And we've pretty much been inseparable since we met."

"Except they make me sound like a lovesick schoolgirl who's after Addie's job. She's going to have a field day with this."

"Maybe she won't see it," I say.

Skye laughs, and I can't tell whether it's real or forced. Probably a combination of both.

"Addie won't see it? The woman thrives on attention. She googles her name all the time. How will she *not* see it?"

I don't reply.

"I'm nothing like Addison," she says indignantly.

"If you were anything like Addison, do you think I'd have the slightest interest in you?"

"Honestly? I don't know, Braden, because you won't tell me what happened between you two."

"Skye, you do try my patience." I stand, pull her out of the chair, and into my body.

She parts her lips.

"Fuck, you're so sexy."

That's all I say. What I don't say is that the article in the *Babbler* doesn't upset me nearly as much as it should. What I also don't say is how, twelve hours ago, I vowed to distance myself from this woman because I was afraid I might be falling in love.

So much for distance.

I kiss her. Hard.

Everything else vanishes. The engagements Claire just put on my calendar. The article in the *Babbler*. Skye's contract and how she manipulated her way into my office.

It's all gone.

Only our kiss exists.

Only my lips sliding against hers, my tongue probing between them, the groans coming from her throat, my erection pushing into her belly.

I break the kiss and inhale deeply. "God, what you do to me." I whip my tie off my neck and finger the fabric.

She gasps sharply.

Good. She knows what I'm thinking.

"Silk isn't the best for binding," I say. "The knots are sometimes too tight, which can be a problem if I need to untie you quickly."

She lifts her eyebrows, raising them in challenge.

Too late for that.

I'm binding her with this silk tie, and I'm doing it now.

"However, it's all I have at the moment." I unbutton my shirt and remove it. I stand in a white tank. "Take off your clothes, Skye."

Chapter Forty-Two

She eyes the door.

"No, it's not locked," I say.

She parts her lips, and God, it takes every ounce of my resolve not to rip the offending garments off her. She's nervous, and for good reason. She's thinking someone—anyone—could walk in. Though I'm tempted to let her wonder—

"No one will interrupt us. They know the penalty for entering without knocking." I finger the soft silk of my tie. "I've never bound your wrists before."

She shakes her head.

"Are you ready?"

She nods.

"Take off your clothes, Skye," I say again.

She trembles as she obeys, and with each item she peels off her body, I get to see more and more of her soft flesh—that soft flesh that drives me wild, makes me want to kiss her and spank her and, God help me, feel things I have no business feeling.

Finally, she stands, naked, her clothes folded neatly over the back of a chair.

"Now hold your wrists out," I say. "Together."

She does, and I wrap my tie tightly around them and secure it with a knot.

She gapes at me. I don't need to ask if she's ever been bound by anyone else. I already know the answer. It's written in her eyes. They're full of an intoxicating combination of trepidation and desire.

Her wrists are bound. She can still walk, still touch, but she doesn't, even though I haven't given her any orders to the contrary.

"You look beautiful, Skye."

She smiles, her gorgeous lips trembling.

"Bound for my pleasure," I say.

Naked. Skye naked in my office, her wrists secured with my necktie. I'm about to fuck her here, leave her mark in this room.

"Walk to the window, Skye, and face it. Hands above your head."

She obeys, pressing her bare breasts against the glass, her bound wrists resting on the pane above her.

I unbuckle my belt, unzip my zipper. My cock springs out, hard and ready.

I stand behind her and push into her. Then I grasp her bound wrists, raise them, and hold them clamped against the window. "Don't move," I whisper against her ear.

In one quick thrust, I'm inside her. I clench my teeth, letting the walls of her pussy suck around me. Fucking paradise.

She cries out.

"That's it, baby," I say. "Take it. Take all of me." I pull out and then push back in.

Her cheek and breasts are crushed against the glass.

What a lovely picture she must make, her tits smashed—if only she were visible to outside viewers. The idea makes me hot. I keep my hand clamped onto her bound wrists, rendering her immobile.

With my other hand, I grip her hip as I fuck her. "Good girl. Don't move. Let me take what's mine."

It's a hard and primal fuck. No kisses to her neck, no nibbles on her ear. Just a raw taking. What I need at this moment. She barged into my office with a contract she could have emailed. Interrupted my day. I remember this as I fuck her against my window.

"That's it." I pump faster. "Yeah, baby, just like that."

I glide my hand from her hip and touch her clit gently. She gasps.

Then I pull on it...not so gently.

She explodes.

Quick as lightning, I withdraw and spin her to face me. I lift her, her ass pressing against the glass window.

"Put your arms around my neck," I command.

She looks down at the binding, her lips parted and eyebrows raised.

"Do it!" I grit out.

She lifts both arms and rings them around my neck. She's suspended now, flat against the window, her arms bound and around me. I spread her legs as wide as they'll go, my arms under her thighs like a makeshift swing. I'm holding all her weight, pushing her up and against the glass.

I charge into her, thrusting and thrusting.

"Fuck," I groan. "Feels so good."

"God, yes," she says. "Please."

I know what she's after. She wants me to touch her clit. She wants another orgasm. I'm happy to give it to her, but I'll do it my own way.

I lean into her, our chests touching, and rock my cock

gently back and forth into her. It's a deliciously erotic sensation for both of us, and little by little, she's getting the clitoral stimulation she needs.

I rock and I rock and I rock, her tight pussy gripping my cock with each push and my pubic bone gently caressing her clit, until—

"Braden! I'm coming!"

"That's it, baby." I pull back slightly and plunge deep. I withdraw and then thrust.

A fuck. A good, hard fuck.

The orgasm rolls through her as her body releases. And I feel each contraction of her walls. Every. Single. One.

She shouts. She screams. She's forgotten that Claire and others sit right outside this room.

Good. Very good. I don't care, so why should she? She's giving up control, and it spurs me on.

I shove my cock into her one last time, pulling another climax from her as I give in to my own.

Together we soar through the window and over the skyscrapers of Boston. I come hard—as hard as I ever have, maybe harder.

By fucking Skye Manning in my office against my window, her wrists bound in silk.

I'm not in the club. I haven't bound her body, spanked her, flogged her—none of those things I thought were required for me to come so hard.

All I need is her.

Skye.

Giving her control to me.

I gaze out the window as I relish the high from my orgasm. The colors are so much more vivid. Downtown isn't gray and brown. It's silver and gold and bronze, the sun casting luminous rays over the buildings and down onto the cars and passersby below.

Then I look at beautiful Skye, her eyes closed, a contented smile on those beautiful lips. She's still euphoric. Still in that dreamy haze.

When she finally opens her eyes, I withdraw, panting.

She doesn't move.

Good. I told her not to.

Finally, I maneuver her so I can loosen the knot and remove my tie from her wrists. Silk can chafe, and I don't want that. "Okay?"

She nods.

"Tell me."

"Yes. I'm okay."

"Good."

"Braden?"

"Hmm?"

"That was…amazing."

I nod. "It was."

"I mean, *really* amazing. Anyone could have seen us."

I smile. Sort of. A half smile. A devious smile.

"What?" she asks.

"The windows are tinted on the outside, just like my apartment. We can see out, but no one can see in."

"Oh." She frowns slightly.

Is she disappointed? Did the idea that anyone could look up and see us turn her on?

Maybe she'll be ready for the club sooner rather than later.

"Did you like being bound?" I ask.

"I'm…not sure."

"You're not sure? You said yourself it was amazing."

"I meant the sex."

"Your wrists being bound was part of the sex."

"It was everything, though. Being in your office. The unlocked door. The window."

I gaze intently into her brown eyes still clouded in climactic bliss. "You like to be watched."

"No, not really. It was more—"

"You just admitted it. You never cease to amaze me, Skye."

"I guess I never thought about it. It was knowing anyone could walk in. The suspense. It was…"

"Erotic. Erotic and a little frightening because you were taking a risk. Did you like being tied up?" I ask again.

Her already flushed cheeks redden further. "Yes. And being tied up with *your* tie," she says.

Good. Very good. Maybe it's time to entice her with what could come. "Would it surprise you to know I'd like to bind all four of your limbs, have you splayed out, naked, for me to do whatever I want?"

She quivers, and her nipples react by hardening.

She doesn't want to like the idea, but a part of her does. That part of her that wants to lose control.

"Skye?"

"No," she says, trembling.

"Good," I say, "because I want to do all that to you and more. Have you ever been fucked anally, Skye?"

She gulps. "No."

"Do you remember the instrument I stroked you with while you were blindfolded?"

"Yeah. It felt cool against me."

"Did you enjoy it?"

"Yes."

"Do you know what it was?"

"How could I? I was blindfolded."

I resist a smile. "It was an anal plug."

"What's that?"

"A tool. To prepare you for anal sex."

"Braden, I—"

"Don't worry. We won't go there yet. Not until you're ready."

She shudders slightly. Anal sex scares her a bit. Not a bad thing. She'll be well prepared when we finally go there.

"Go ahead and get dressed," I say, "and we'll go over your contract."

Chapter Forty-Three

The contract is straightforward and fair. "I'd sign," I tell Skye.

"You don't want to check with an attorney?"

"If it means that much to you, I can run it by someone in legal, but this is small potatoes compared to the stuff I review. Everything is spelled out clearly—your obligations and theirs."

She nods. "Okay. I trust your judgment, Braden. Thank you."

"I'm happy to help."

"Crap," she says. "I've got to get back to the office."

"You didn't eat anything."

"No time. Thanks so much, and again… I'm sor—"

"Stop apologizing, Skye. You're not sorry you barged in here, and we both know it."

Her lips curve into a smile that lights up her warm eyes. She kisses me on the cheek. "Bye, Braden."

After she leaves, my hand wanders to the cheek she kissed.

Odd. It was sweet and chaste. I'm not getting hard from

it.

Yet in a way, it means more to me than the fuck we just shared.

. . .

I spend most of the afternoon in meetings with Ben. Since I returned from New York early, he asked me to sit in, and I was glad to do so. It put my focus back where it should be—on work.

Instead of Skye Manning.

By five, I'm back in my own office. I breathe in. The scent of lust and sex is still thick in the air. Could be my imagination, but whatever it is conjures up images of Skye, her back against my window while I'm frantically pumping into her.

Absently, I pick up my phone and pull up Instagram.

Front and center is a new post from Skye. She looks beautiful and vivacious. She's laughing about something, and her lips have never looked sexier. In a photo, that is. They're much sexier in person.

Love my Susanne Cherry Russet lip stain. It's my go-to for every occasion. Perfect for a casual afternoon! @ susannecosmetics #sponsored #lips #lipgloss #kissproof #youknowyouwantsome @beantheredonethat

She works quickly. Clearly she signed the contract electronically and has already begun posting. Pride wells in me. Sure, Instagramming is far from her true calling, but it will get her noticed as someone other than Addie's assistant.

And if I have it my way, she'll be able to quit her current job. The farther away she is from Addison Ames, the better.

Already, she has a ton of comments.

Gorgeous on you! #orderingnow Love the color!

You look so happy!

Totally getting this for my wife.

I scroll through several more until one catches my eye.

@realaddisonames #fuckyou

Angry prickles crawl up my spine.

In an instant, another comment blares at me, pulsing along with my heartbeat.

@realaddisonames #youllneverbeme

I scoff aloud. She got that right. Skye Manning is already eons above Addison Ames in dignity, intelligence, and honesty.

Addison Ames should hope to be Skye Manning.

Of course, she's too narcissistic to ever see the irony.

I'm tempted to intervene, but when I refresh my feed, the offending comments have disappeared. Skye obviously saw them and deleted them without responding. The woman has class.

And so do I.

I won't intervene. I never do.

Except that one time when I was in a pissy mood and that damned coffee post got to me.

I can hardly regret that, though, even though it was impulsive and immature.

It led me to Skye.

I can't resist leaving Skye a comment of my own.

@bradenblackinc You're gorgeous. See you tonight.

I attend to a few more emails, including one from Dimitri about the meeting with Foster McCain tomorrow. As he suspected, McCain only wants to deal with me. Dimitri will try to smooth things over. If he can't, he'll call me tonight.

I sigh. This isn't unexpected. But until I hear otherwise, I'm going to enjoy my evening with Skye. I head out of the office by six. Normally I go to the gym after work, but tonight, I'm heading to Skye's. We didn't make any formal plans, but my comment made it clear I want to see her.

She'll be home by the time I get there.

I take the elevator down, stride through the lobby, and find Christopher waiting.

"The gym?" he says.

"Skye's place," I tell him.

"You got it."

A half hour later, after braving rush-hour traffic, we arrive.

"You want me to wait?" Christopher asks.

"Yes, please." I exit the vehicle and walk into Skye's building.

When I reach her door, I knock.

No response.

I knock harder.

Again, no response.

Odd. Did she have to work late?

I text her.

Where are you?

Esteban's. Having a drink with Tessa.

I'm at your place. Why aren't you here?

Nothing for a minute. Then the little dots begin to move.

Because I'm at Esteban's having a drink with Tessa.

The fuck? That prickly anger seizes my neck and squeezes. She knew I wanted to see her tonight. If she didn't want to see me, she should have let me know.

Then again, we didn't make any actual plans. Is it possible she didn't see my comment? No, she saw it. She had to. This is her first sponsored post. She's no doubt monitoring the comments with an eagle eye.

She should have known I'd be coming by.

I can stew about it and get angrier, which in turn will make her angry when I confront her, or I can simply go see her.

I choose the grown-up route.

Be there in fifteen.

I head back down and get in the car. "Looks like we're going to Esteban's," I tell Christopher.

Once we arrive, I stroll in, excitement at seeing Skye making me feel a lot younger than I am. It's wild, how she affects me. I mumble to the hostess that I'm meeting a friend who's already here and whisk past without waiting for her reply, nearly bumping into Tessa Logan.

"Oh! Hi, Braden," she says. "Skye said you'd be joining her."

"Are you leaving?" I ask.

"Yeah, I just came in for a drink. I left Skye some money for the bill."

"I'll take care of it. She'll return your money."

"You don't have—"

"I insist," I say quickly. "Please excuse me."

I don't mean to be rude, but all I can think of is getting to Skye. I arrive at the table and find Skye counting bills and looking over the check.

I sit down at the table and take the check from her. "I've got it."

"You don't have to. They left money."

"I saw Tessa on the way out," I say. "I told her you'd be returning her money."

"What about Betsy's money?"

"Who's Betsy?"

"Betsy... Huh. I don't know her last name. Anyway, she owns the Bark Boutique where I got Sasha's gift basket."

Right. That Betsy. The one who has history with Addie. Was Skye pressing Betsy for information about Addie and me?

I don't know how much Betsy knows, but I won't worry about that at the moment.

"You can return her money, too," I say.

"That's generous of you, but you don't have to—"

"I know I don't have to, Skye. I want to. This is pennies to me."

She smiles. "Okay, then. I'll let you, because I'm now officially unemployed."

Damn. Those comments from Addie on Skye's post siren back into my mind. I'll bet Addie fired Skye.

Good riddance.

I shake my head. "Why am I not surprised?"

"I don't know. I still have no idea what went on between you and Addison."

Yeah, she was definitely asking Betsy about us, and now I know Betsy knows little to nothing. I throw a credit card on top of the bill. "Nice try. Still not going there."

The server arrives and grabs the bill and credit card. "Can I get you anything, Mr. Black?"

"Yes, a Wild Turkey, one ice cube, and a menu please. Ms. Manning and I will be dining."

"You want to eat here?" she asks.

"Why not?"

"It's not exactly fine dining."

"So? You seem to forget I come from South Boston. I grew up on beans and stew."

"Boston baked beans?" she asks, smiling.

"One and the same."

"No chains like this when I was growing up, but we had some great little mom-and-pop restaurants in the nearby small towns. Not fine dining, but delicious food where everyone knew everyone else. We had this amazing Mexican restaurant run by a couple who'd emigrated twenty years previously. The best Mexican food ever. The stuff here can't compare."

"Esteban's is yuppy Mexican food," I say. "But it's still decent."

"True."

The server returns with the menus. She glances over hers.

"Eat hearty, Skye," I say. "You're going to burn a lot of calories tonight."

Chapter Forty-Four

As soon as we enter my penthouse, I attack her next to the elevator, kissing her hard and deep.

Then my phone buzzes.

Fuck.

Probably Dimitri, which means I'm going to New York. Fuck.

I break the kiss.

"Ignore it," she whispers.

So tempting.

"I can't. I'm sorry. I'm expecting an important call."

"At nine thirty?"

I don't answer, just pull my phone out. "Black," I say, walking toward the living room.

Skye follows me, but a few seconds later, I walk away from her and into my office, closing the door. I don't need her distracting me right now.

"So...?"

"No dice," Dimitri says. "I did my best. I answered every fucking question he had with as much knowledge as anyone could possibly possess, but he's one of those sticklers who thinks his shit don't stink. He won't talk to anyone but the big boss."

"It's okay, Dimitri. Thanks for trying."

"If it's any consolation, everyone else is good with going through me. Foster McCain's the only problem."

"Don't worry about it. This is the first time McCain's even agreed to a meeting. I should have stayed in New York."

The truth of my own words hits me like an anvil to the head.

I should have stayed in New York. I knew how important this meeting was, and I also knew McCain might be a problem.

But I let my personal life interfere with business.

I made the wrong choice, though I can't quite bring myself to regret it.

"Sorry," Dimitri says. "Here I've been buzzing in your ear for more responsibility, and you give me what I want, but I can't get this deal done."

"It's okay. You deserve the responsibility, Dimitri. Don't worry about McCain. I'll be at the meeting tomorrow."

"It's at eight a.m.," he says.

"I know. I'll be there."

Now, to tell Skye. I shove the phone into my pants pocket and leave the office but then make a detour to my bedroom. I head to the mahogany wardrobe, open it, and then pull open one of the drawers.

I grab a silver chain and smile.

I'm getting hard just thinking about what this will do to Skye. I adjust my groin and then walk back out to the living area where I find Skye sitting on the sofa.

"I'm sorry," I say. "I have to fly back to New York."

"Right now?"

"Yeah. I shouldn't have left early. My bad."

"Oh." She frowns, and for a moment, I imagine giving my

entire fortune never to see her looking sad again.

God, I need to get a grip.

I stalk toward her. "I seem to make questionable decisions because of you, Skye."

She says nothing. Just shivers.

"I want you to think about something while I'm gone."

She shivers. "What?"

I push the silver chain into her hands. "About wearing this to the gala on Saturday."

She wraps it around her neck and secures it like a lariat necklace. "All right. It will go nicely with the black dress."

I laugh. One of those serious laughs that just erupts before I can stop it.

She smiles. "What's so funny?"

"It's not a necklace."

She reddens and then removes it from her neck and holds it out to me. "What is it, then?"

"Those things on each end are nipple clamps, Skye."

Her jaw drops as she examines the baubles on each end. They resemble tiny clothespins with a screw-on device like old-fashioned clip-on earrings.

I've been imagining Skye in nipple clamps since I first noticed her amazing tits.

"I control how tight the clamp is," I say. "And when I give the chain between them a good yank… Well, you can imagine."

She hands the chain back to me and clears her throat. "I'll…think about it."

I lower my eyelids slightly, my whole body heating. "Think about it a *lot*, Skye."

She nods.

"I'm sorry about tonight. Christopher will drive you home."

"When will you be back?"

"Saturday afternoon, as originally planned. I'll pick you up at your place for the gala at six p.m. sharp. I'll bring the chain and put it on for you."

She nods. "Braden?"

"Yes?"

"I... I'll miss you."

Her words warm me and go straight to my cock. I smile. "I'll miss you, too, Skye. More than you know."

Chapter Forty-Five

I text Ben, and he meets me at the airport at one a.m. If Foster McCain wants to meet with me, Ben and I will go together. The big guns.

After we reach cruising altitude for our short flight, Ben and I each have a bourbon.

"You shouldn't have left Manhattan, bro," he says to me.

"Tell me something I don't know." I take a sip, let the smokiness sit on my tongue, and imagine Skye's pussy juice instead of the alcohol in my mouth.

"Think you're ready to admit it?"

I swallow. "That I shouldn't have left New York? I think I just did."

"Not that." Ben takes a sip and swallows. "That you're falling for this woman."

"I don't fall for women, Ben."

"That's called denial, bro." He takes another sip. "You know, there's a lot better bourbons out there than this stuff."

"It's hardly rotgut."

"Did I say it was? The Blacks can afford the best. Why do

you love this stuff so much?"

"Because it's damned good."

"I'll give you the flavor, but it's a little harsh going down."

"It reminds me of those days on the construction site when we were in our early twenties. How we worked our asses off and had a Wild Turkey at Clem's after a long day."

"Except for that one day," Ben says, "when we went to a certain party."

"For fuck's sake. Why do you insist on bringing that up? You know I don't talk about it."

"I know. But I talked to Apple again tonight."

"Seriously? Is she your new girlfriend? The yin to your yang or whatever?'

"What?"

"Isn't she into all that Zen shit?"

"Some, I guess. She's definitely not your typical hotel heiress. But that's not why I brought her up. She only called to tell me Addie had fired Skye."

I take another sip. "I figured as much."

"Skye told you?"

"Not in those words. She just said she was now unemployed. She's getting some outside work, but Skye isn't the type to leave a sure thing until she's got another steady income."

"Addie's really pissed off about some cosmetics deal."

I nod. "I know. Skye's better off away from Addie and her toxicity." Addie's comments on Skye's post race back into my mind. Just thinking about them gets anger rustling through me.

"I won't argue with you there," Ben says. "You ever going to level with her? About Addie?"

"Why should I? It's in the past."

"Yeah, but it's got a lot to—"

"Stop right there," I say, using my best big-brother voice.

It still works sometimes, believe it or not. "I don't talk about it. I don't think about it. Some things are better left buried. We worked hard to make sure it would never surface."

"We did."

"So I don't need you spouting off about honesty and trust and all that other bullshit. Skye and I aren't in a relationship, so those things have no bearing. Case closed."

The big-brother voice works.

Ben drops it.

But all I can think about during the rest of the flight are my own words.

Skye and I aren't in a relationship.

They're certainly true, as far as she knows. I made it clear we could date but there would be no relationship.

In my heart, though?

I want more than Skye's control.

I want more than Skye's submission.

I want more than Skye's humor, brilliance, and beauty.

I want more than Skye's energy.

I want her love.

• • •

I got all of an hour of shut-eye before the meeting with Foster McCain, a surly Irishman who actually came to us eight years ago offering to take our initial products into Europe. At that time we had better offers, so we declined, but McCain got a deal with three companies in China to manufacture knockoffs of our goggles, Black, Inc.'s flagship product. We sued—nearly depleting our coffers—and won, but at that point, McCain had made a shit ton of money in bitcoin and didn't care anyway. Now he's the Warren Buffet of the UK, and he's started his own Berkshire Hathaway competitor, McCain Global.

In short, I don't like him.

Neither does Ben.

Neither does Dimitri.

But we like his money. After we won our lawsuit, McCain took the high road and got out of the knockoff business. He used his bitcoin fortune for good instead of evil, and now McCain Global owns some prime property in the UK that we want to get our hands on. We're willing to pay top dollar, but we need to get it yesterday.

Dimitri, Ben, and Dimitri's right-hand woman, Lizzie McCullough—we hope Lizzie's Irish surname will win us some points—sit in the smallest of our seven conference rooms.

My idea. McCain may come with an assistant, but we have four people at the table. Ben, Dimitri, and I are big guys, and Lizzie's near six feet herself.

Hence the smallest room.

We want to own it, and the four of us in a smaller room make a more imposing presence than we would in one of the larger spaces.

Plus we're at the Black, Inc. office. Home-field advantage.

Surprisingly, McCain arrives alone.

We all stand and shake hands, and one of the assistants serves coffee and tea.

Once we sit, Dimitri hands out the prospectus detailing our offer.

McCain pushes it away. "I'm not selling. For any price."

I stand. "Then I guess you came a long way for nothing, Foster. Greta will see you out."

Ben and Dimitri stand then.

But McCain doesn't move.

He's waiting for us to sweeten the pot. He'll be waiting a long time.

Finally, he pulls the prospectus back and opens it.

"Does this mean you've changed your mind?" Ben asks.

"It means I'll hear you out."

Dimitri begins the presentation.

And I sit back, the same satisfied grin on my face that I see on my brother's.

He'll sell.

He wouldn't have come if he didn't have that intention, especially after putting us off for two years.

Dimitri's presentation is flawless. He could have handled it without me with his eyes closed.

But there's only one problem.

He's not Braden Black.

* * *

"You have a gift, Brady," Momma said to me after Benji had fallen asleep.

"A present? Where is it?"

She smiled at me and swept my hair—I always needed a haircut—off my forehead and then kissed it.

"I'm not talking about the kind of gift you unwrap," she said. "I'm talking about something God gave you. Something you were born with."

I was born with a gift? Why hadn't I ever seen it? I didn't understand.

"It's confidence," Momma said.

"What's con-fee-dance?" I asked.

"It's something that will take you far," she said.

"All the way to the other side of the world? Like to China?"

She laughed. "Maybe. Who knows? But I don't mean far away. I mean far in life. You'll do great things. I know it."

"How do you know it?" I asked Momma.

"I see it in you already. You're only seven years old, but you're the leader of all your friends. Of your brother. They

look up to you because they see your confidence, and they want it, too."

I still didn't know what Momma was talking about, but I liked hearing her voice. And since it was bedtime, she wasn't wearing her scarf, so I could see her pretty face.

"One day, you're going to be a great man, Brady."

"Why, Momma? Why will I be a great man?"

She kissed my forehead again. "Because you're Braden Black."

Chapter Forty-Six

Ben, Dimitri, Lizzie, and I celebrate with a gourmet lunch at Gabriel LeGrand. Afterward, before the next meeting, I take a walk through the Diamond District between Fifth and Sixth Avenues. I love the old New York feel of the area.

"Hey, boss!" A hawker calls out to me. "You buying?"

I walk by.

As many cops as hawks hang out in the district—probably the last old block in all of New York City. As much as technology has done for my business and for me, I can't help but wonder if we're missing out on old-world culture.

Old-world culture is abundant in the Diamond District.

I'm not looking for anything in particular. I don't wear jewelry myself, other than a watch, and I've never purchased a piece for a woman—other than the pieces my Boston jeweler designs for my staff members for the holidays. I ignore the hawks and stop in front of a shop called Gray & Davis. A diamond choker draws my gaze.

It's beautiful in its simplicity.

I imagine placing it around Skye's creamy neck—

collaring her.

God, collaring her.

I've never collared a woman, other than on a scene-by-scene basis. If I take a woman into my club, she's under my protection, so I collar her. But it's a temporary collar for the club only, so that others will know not to approach her.

Before I can think better of it, I walk into the store.

A clerk accosts me within a second. "What can I help you find, sir?"

"There's a diamond choker in the window. I'd like to see it, please."

"Of course." The clerk unlocks the bars protecting the pieces in the glass showcase, withdraws the choker, and hands it to me. "The piece is from the nineteen twenties. It's set in white gold and has just over seven carats of VSS-clarity round-cut diamonds."

"It's heavier than I expected," I say.

"Yes, it is. They don't make pieces like this anymore."

"How much is it?"

"Fifty thousand dollars, sir."

A lot of money for a woman who may very well never consent to being collared.

But already I know this gorgeous choker belongs to Skye. Whether it becomes a collar or not, it's already hers.

"I'll take it."

He lifts his eyebrows. "Just like that?"

"You expect me to haggle?"

"Most people do."

"Well, I'm in a hurry." My gaze falls on a black pearl choker in one of the inside display cases.

Skye's neck was made for a choker, and this one won't be a collar.

"How much is that one?" I ask. "The black pearl."

"Those are premium cultured pearls from Japan, hand-knotted with a platinum clasp."

"Right. How much?"

"Three thousand five hundred."

"Would it make you feel better if I asked you to throw that in with the diamond purchase?"

"I can take two hundred off the pearls, sir."

"Sold." I pull out my wallet.

· · ·

I leave the Diamond District with my purchases, ready to head back to my Manhattan office, when an idea strikes me. I don't want to wait to give Skye the pearl choker. I want her to have it today. No service will get it to her that quickly, so I click a photo of the piece and place a call to my Boston jeweler.

"Donald," I say into the phone, "Braden Black."

"Hello, Mr. Black. What can I do for you?"

"I'm texting you a photo of a black pearl choker. Take a look at it. Do you have something similar in stock?"

I wait a few minutes while he checks the photo.

"I have a lovely one from Akimoto Designs. The pearls are slightly smaller, but it's a fifteen-inch choker much like your photo."

"Excellent. Charge it to me, and I want it delivered this afternoon in plain brown paper. Put a handwritten note in an envelope on the package. Got it?"

"Yes, of course. What would you like the note to say?"

I ponder his question for a few seconds. "I'll text it to you. That way you have it in writing."

"Good enough. And the address?"

"It's going to Skye Manning. I'll text the particulars."

"Very good, Mr. Black. Thank you for your business."

"You're welcome. Thanks, Donald."

I end the call and quickly text him Skye's address.

I sigh. For the note.

I start a text. Erase it and start another.

Fuck it. Why not just get straight to the point?

This will go beautifully with your black dress. Wear your hair up and paint your lips red. Bloodred. I'll pick you up at six.

As I walk out of the district, a tiny masquerade shop catches my eye. In the display case is a striking black mask, satin with black feathers and a large crystal jewel fanning out from one side.

It was made for Skye. I don't know when she'll have the chance to wear it, but within two seconds, I'm in the store making the purchase. The salesperson wraps it for me and then nods to a display of plain masks.

"You get one of those for free with your purchase."

"Oh?" I take a quick look. They're simple masks in various colors. No embellishments, just a covering for the eyes.

I have no plans to take Skye to a masquerade, but if I do, I'll need a mask as well. I choose the black one.

An hour later, my phone dings with a text. From Skye.

I love the pearls, Braden. Thank you so much.

You're welcome, I text back succinctly.

But there's so much more I want to say.

• • •

I'm in and out of meetings for the next twenty-four hours. Finally free, and eating takeout at my New York residence, my phone buzzes.

It's a Boston number, but one I don't recognize.

"Black," I say.

"Hi...uh...Braden?"

"Yes? Who's this."

"Tessa Logan. Skye's friend."

My heart punches my sternum. "Is Skye all right?"

"Oh, yeah. She's fine."

I sigh in relief. "Good," I say, hoping I sound nonchalant. "How did you get this number, Tessa?"

"Well…I kind of kiped Skye's phone for a minute, found it, and memorized it."

"Oh?"

"Yeah. I have one of those minds for numbers. You know?"

Not really, but I don't say so. I'm not sure what to make of Tessa calling me. "Is there something I can do for you?"

"Actually, there is. Skye and I went to the local pet shelter tonight. I adopted a dog. Anyway, Skye saw this little puppy. She was so sweet and lonely, and she adored Skye and Skye adored her. But you know Skye's place doesn't allow pets. Skye was just beside herself about the whole thing. She asked me to adopt the puppy, but I had already picked out a dog. That's why we were there, to pick her up."

"I see."

"I told her to call you, but she wouldn't."

"Why?"

"Well…I thought…if you could adopt the puppy and keep her until Skye has a better place, maybe…"

"Tessa—"

"She was nearly in tears when we left."

Crying? Skye was crying? My heart becomes a cannonball in my chest.

I say nothing.

"Are you there?" Tessa finally asks.

"I'm here."

"I guess it was pretty out of line to call you," she says. "Skye was just so sad to leave that poor puppy there. She can't be more than about ten weeks old, probably missing her mother something awful."

"Give me the information," I say.

"Are you going to get her? Skye will be so happy!"

"I'll figure something out. The information, Tessa."

"Right. She's puppy number 347. A Heeler mix. Black with white markings."

"You remember her number?"

"I have a way with numbers," she says again.

"I'm glad you do," I tell her. "I'll call my driver in Boston and have him pick up the pup. Don't tell Skye, though. I want to surprise her."

"Braden, thank you!" Tessa gushes. "If there's anything I can ever do for you, please, I'll do it."

I chuckle slightly. "I can't think of anything at the moment. Thank you for letting me know about the puppy, Tessa."

"You're welcome. And thank you. Skye's the luckiest woman ever. Bye."

I text the information to Christopher quickly, hoping it's not too late.

An hour and a half later, I get a text back from him.

Congratulations. It's a girl.

Chapter Forty-Seven

I return to my Boston penthouse early in the afternoon on Saturday.

I've purposefully thrown myself into my work the last two days in Manhattan, purposefully not called or texted Skye. Purposefully stayed off Instagram.

I needed a clear head to finish up the business with Foster McCain, and while I was in Manhattan, I took care of some other loose ends as well.

Try as I might, though, my thoughts never fully strayed from Skye.

She'll most likely be angry that I haven't been in contact with her. Why shouldn't she be?

Normally, when I'm seeing a woman, I don't mix business with pleasure. I don't think about her at all while I'm working. Only when we're together. So naturally, I don't call and text often when we're not together. I'm determined not to do things differently with Skye, which is why I haven't communicated with her since her text about the pearl choker.

The difference, though?

I've wanted to.

Every time I look at my phone, I think about giving her a quick call or sending her a quick text. Even just checking Instagram.

Every time I check email—which is a lot—I think about writing to her, just to see how she's doing.

I stayed strong, though. I did not.

Skye's puppy is adorable and already a terrific playmate for Sasha. She'll keep Annika and Christopher on their toes. I spend a few minutes playing with her and letting her lick my face before I head to my bedroom to shower.

My date with Skye for the gala tonight is still on, and I'll be there at six as promised.

Once I'm clad in one of my tailored tuxes and in the car with Christopher at the wheel and a bouquet of bloodred roses and the plain black eye mask from New York sitting next to me, the nipple clamps securely in my pocket, I finally succumb. I'll check Instagram. That will tell me what Skye's been up to. I click on her profile.

She's been busy. The first post is a selfie of her pretty face sans makeup and shiny with sweat after a yoga class.

Who loves yoga? I do! Check out the relaxing atmosphere at Wildflower Yoga. #yoga #treatyourself #youknowyouwanto

I smile. She looks so fresh and happy. The post shows a real person, not a fake Addison Ames clone in a posed post.

Skye is going to be good at this. Really good. Better than she can even imagine at this point.

The next post is Skye at a bakery in front of a display of baguettes. Her smile is addictive.

Need bread? Check out Le Grand Pain! Best baguettes around! (And if you need a special cake for your bachelor/bachelorette function, LGP can hook you up!) @LeGrandPain #sponsored #bakery #bread #baguettes #getyourglutenon #breadisgoodfood #soiscake

I smile at the hashtags. She's on fire.

A new post pops up just then.

Damn. Skye, in the dress. The dress I had made. The dress I will most likely destroy again. Her makeup is flawless and her lovely hair is swept up into a messy bun that showcases that gorgeous neck of hers.

She's not wearing the choker.

I grit my teeth. Did she forget?

Wearing my Cherry Russet lip stain by @susannecosmetics again. My go-to color is perfect for everything from a day at home to a formal evening! #sponsored #lips #kissme #formal #littleblackdress

The color is lovely on her sexy lips, but did she forget I asked for bloodred?

A not-so-subtle reminder of who's in charge may be warranted.

Christopher pulls the car up to Skye's building. I grab the roses, secure the mask over my eyes—to give myself a little mystery—and head up to her place.

I try to eliminate the pounding of my heart as I secure the mask in place and knock on her door.

She opens the door.

Her jaw drops.

Though I'm tempted to drop my own jaw, I lock it firmly in place.

It's not easy, though.

Skye looks devastatingly beautiful. The dress and the hairstyle I've already seen in the post, but she's one hundred times better in person. Her long, lean legs are bare, and her pretty feet—toes painted red—are strapped into silver sandals.

I'm in a black tux. The plain mask covers my eyes, and in my arms I hold the bouquet of roses.

Bloodred roses.

They match her lips perfectly.

She changed her lip color.

She didn't forget.

The black pearl choker—even more gorgeous than the one I purchased in the Diamond District—sits perfectly on her neck.

She didn't forget.

No need for my not-so-subtle reminder of who's in charge after all. I'm a little disappointed, truth be told, but no matter. Later, I'll make it abundantly clear who's in control here.

I walk in swiftly, closing the door behind me.

Already, I own this room.

Already, she feels it. I see it in her eyes, in the quick shudder she tries—but fails—to suppress.

I move closer to her, lean toward her, my lips ready to take hers—

Only a millimeter away, and I stop.

Hardest damned thing I've ever done.

"I won't," I say gruffly. "I won't ruin those perfect lips. Not yet."

She sighs. "Please."

"Not yet," I say again.

She trembles before me.

My cock responds.

How easy it would be to grab her, haul her the few steps to her bed, say, "Fuck the gala," and fuck her instead.

I ache with how much I've missed her, how much strength it took for me not to constantly check in with her. Then Tessa's phone call about the puppy, about how Skye was crying.

Crying. My Skye. And I wasn't there to comfort her.

As if reading my mind, she says, "I missed you. Why didn't you call?"

"I was busy," I say.

"You couldn't find two minutes?"

I rip the mask off my eyes, grab her cheeks, and blurt out words before I can stop them. "Baby, if I'd called, I wouldn't have been able to stop myself from getting on a plane and flying back to you."

She inhales swiftly.

"I couldn't do that. I did it once, and I nearly lost a deal because of it. I had to take care of business."

So easy.

So easy to kiss those lips…

But clearer heads must prevail. I'm expected at the gala, and I promised Skye a night out.

"Christopher's waiting," I say. "Let's go."

She grabs the bag sitting next to the door.

"What's that?" I ask.

"Oh." Her cheeks redden. "You said for me to bring over some clothes and stuff."

"And you assume we'll be going to my place?"

"Yes," she says boldly.

"You assume correctly." I stare at her, the nipple clamps burning in my pocket. I need to put them on her now, before we leave. "Remove the top of your dress."

She slips one strap over her shoulder, slowly. I suck in a breath. She slides the other strap over her shoulder and urges the fabric downward. The only thing standing between her breasts and me is a strapless bra.

We stand there, gazes locked, until— "Fuck it." I crush my lips to hers.

Her lips are already parted, and I thrust my tongue between them. Fucking bra. Between those gorgeous tits and my fingers. I unclasp it deftly and toss it to the floor. Then I cup her breasts, thumbing her hard nipples as I deepen the kiss. Our mouths are one, giving, taking, licking, kissing. She reaches downward, toward my crotch, and grasps the bulge beneath my slacks.

Fuck the gala. Fuck the gala. Fuck the gala.

I groan into her, a low, melodic hum like the beginning of a rolling clap of thunder.

She arches, grinds into my thigh, still holding my clothed erection—

I break the kiss and inhale sharply. "Damn, Skye."

So easy. So easy to lift her in my arms, carry her to the bed. Pound her into next week.

But all my plans for tonight. I can't do them here.

And the gala…

I'm expected there…

And the nipple clamps.

I pull the chain from my pocket. "Your tits are so beautiful, your nipples so hard. God, I want to suck and bite them until you can't stand it."

"Go ahead," she says boldly.

Every ounce of strength I possess is required not to do as she asks.

"Later. For now…" I position one of the clamps around a nipple.

She jerks.

"Easy," I say. "This won't hurt."

"It won't?"

"Not unless you want it to."

I tighten the tiny screw slowly, squeezing her nipple, all the while a phantom hand tightens around my cock.

"Good?"

She nods, her lips parted.

"You look incredible right now," I say. "So fucking sexy."

My words are just words. "So fucking sexy" doesn't begin to describe Skye's newly bejeweled nipple. Once I clamp the other, just a flick of the chain will send her reeling.

I'll control her sensations all evening.

Fuck. This isn't anything I haven't done before, but my

level of excitement is a hundred times higher.

I adjust the second clamp around her other nipple. "Beautiful. So beautiful. Are you ready, Skye?"

"Ready for what?" Her words come out on a sigh.

"For this." I yank on the chain between the clamps.

"Oh!" Her chest and the tops of her breasts redden, her nipples protruding as the clamps bind them.

She reaches toward my bulge, and again, all my willpower is required to brush her hand away, which I do reluctantly.

"Time to go, baby."

"Braden…"

"I know. This will keep you on edge tonight. Right on edge and under my control. You aren't to touch that chain, Skye."

"But it's on me. How can I not?"

"Because you won't. If you do, I'll know."

"But how can you—"

"I will know. Trust me." I pull her dress upward. "I want you to go without your bra tonight."

"But the clamps will show."

"No, they won't. Your nipples will show, which is hot. They'll be hard all night and will jut out farther than the clamps themselves. No one will be the wiser."

"But—"

"And I'll be able to subtly pull on your chain whenever I want."

She gulps. "That will…"

"Drive you wild. I know. That's the point." I lean down and bite the shell of her ear. "Then maybe you'll know how completely out of control I get just thinking about you."

She nearly stumbles. Nice. I've got her in a haze. An edgy haze. Exactly where I want her. I steady her, and damn, just gripping her makes my cock take more notice.

"Go now. Fix your bloodred lips."

She nods and walks to the bathroom.

I head into her kitchen and open cupboards until I find a vase for the roses I brought. I set the resulting bouquet on her small table.

When she returns, she gazes at them. "Thank you," she says, "for the flowers."

"You're welcome. Are you ready?"

She nods.

Good.

She's ready.

So am I.

For a night neither of us will ever forget.

Chapter Forty-Eight

"Mr. Black," Byron Daniels, one of the opera board members, says, shaking my hand, "we're so glad you're here. I'll escort you to your table personally. Who's this lovely lady with you?"

"Skye Manning," I say. "Skye, this is Byron Daniels, a member of the opera board."

Skye smiles radiantly, though her lips tremble just a touch. "It's nice to meet you."

"My pleasure, Ms. Manning. If you'll follow me, please."

Our table is the best in the house, right up front, and it's a table for two, as opposed to the others that seat eight or ten. A chilled bottle of Dom Pérignon and a platter of berries sit waiting.

"They think we like this better than Wild Turkey," I whisper to Skye after we're seated.

She giggles. A server attends to us quickly, opening the bottle and pouring two flutes. He hands one to Skye and then the other to me.

I take mine and clink my glass to hers. "To control," I say, casting my gaze down to her breasts.

I'll be controlling her all evening via the nipple clamps.

I'm looking forward to it more than she knows.

"To control," she echoes and takes a sip of the champagne.

It's crisp and dry, and though I don't drink sparkling wine often, Dom Pérignon is in its own class. The bubbles effervesce against my tongue and seem to explode as they crawl down my throat.

The room is already full of guests. I don't attempt to speak to anyone. People seek me out, come to me, schmooze me. Takes me back to the early days of the company when I was the one doing the schmoozing. I sucked at it. Ben was the schmoozer. He still is. My brother could sell a life estate to a dying man.

Peter Reardon and Garrett Ramirez sit a few tables away from us. When Peter looks Skye's way, I dart him a glare. He looks away quickly. My architectural planning committee hasn't made the contract decision public yet, so Reardon and his father may think they still stand a chance.

They don't.

"Braden!" George Stanford, chair of the opera board, approaches our table.

I rise and shake his hand.

"We can't thank you enough for your generosity," he says.

"I'm glad to do it." I nod to Skye. "George, meet my girlfriend, Skye Manning."

My girlfriend. I'm not unaware of how strange the term sounds coming from a thirty-five-year-old businessman. I'm not sure I've ever used the word before.

George holds his hand out to a still-seated Skye. "A pleasure, Ms. Manning."

"Please, call me Skye."

He nods and turns back to me. "We had a great response this year. The gala is sold out. The first time that's happened in fifteen years."

"Interest in opera must be growing in Boston."

"It is, especially among the younger crowd. I think young people are finally tired of the same old hip-hop and are willing to give the classics a try."

"It's probably also because you've added some contemporary opera to your season the past couple of years," I say, smiling.

George laughs. "Yes, that was a great idea you had, Braden. Seems to have paid off handsomely." He turns to Skye. "Tell me about yourself, Skye."

She jerks and meets George's gaze. I can't help a slight smile. She wasn't listening to our conversation. She was busy people watching. It's what she does. A photographer thing, I'd guess.

"I'm a photographer," she says.

"Interesting. What kind of photography?"

"Mostly social media at the moment, but my dream is to photograph for *National Geographic* someday."

"Interesting," he says again and turns back to me. "How did you two meet?"

Loaded question. I'm hardly going to tell the chairman of the opera board that I sent a snide Instagram comment to Skye's employer.

"Skye used to work for Addison Ames," I say.

"Oh, I see. Used to?"

"Yes." I take a sip of champagne. "She's on her own now, doing her own social media influencing as a way to get her photography seen."

"Social media." George shakes his head. "Call me old-school, but I don't get it."

George is at least twenty years older than I am. "The opera guild has an Instagram account," I say.

"I'm sure we do, but I've never seen it." He laughs. "Good to talk to you, Braden. I'll see you onstage after dinner."

I nod as George goes on to the next table.

Skye takes a sip of champagne as she continues to look around the room. A moment later, she touches my arm gently. "Excuse me for a moment."

I nod.

She leaves our table and walks around the room, darting her gaze here and there, until she disappears near the entrance. I soon see why when I look at her phone. A post pops up on my Instagram feed—a selfie of Skye in front of the banner at the entrance to the ballroom.

At the Boston Opera Guild Gala! #operaguild #formalball #supportthearts

Comments follow almost instantaneously.

Love your lips! What color are you using?

Just as instantaneously, she replies.

Night on the Town lip stain by Susanne. Perfect for an elegant evening!

I catch sight of her reentering the ballroom. Instead of returning to our table, though, she heads to the table where Peter Reardon and Garrett Ramirez are seated.

Icy rage curls at the back of my neck. What the fuck is she doing?

I play it cool, though, as several guests are approaching me. I say hello and shake hands, still watching Skye out of the corner of my eye.

Peter and Garrett both stand. At least they're being gentlemen. Or playing the part, anyway. Nope. Take that back. They're both staring at her tits now.

Those tits, over which I have control.

Fuck. I ought to waltz right over there and give Skye a good yank on the chain. Remind her who she's with.

Not that I think Reardon or Ramirez are competition, but still… They're staring at my woman's tits.

My woman's tits.

God, I'm fucked in the head. She's not my woman. I'm not falling in love.

This is nothing but what it is—two adults who are attracted to each other having a good time.

Except I had to mentally remove her from my mind while I was in New York…and I wasn't even wholly successful.

Damn it. Those tits are mine. Those lips are mine. Those legs are mine.

That woman is mine.

Once the guests are done schmoozing me and leave, I glare at Peter and Garrett. After a minute of what I hope is casual conversation, Skye looks toward our table.

She smiles.

I don't.

Peter and Garrett both sit down.

Do not sit down at that table, Skye.

She doesn't, thank God. Another moment later, she makes her way back to our table. I excuse myself from the newcomers who have swarmed around me and take her aside, walking her swiftly out of the ballroom and to a secluded hallway.

"What was that?"

"I was talking to Peter and Garrett. They're the only two people here I know."

"You know a lot of people. I've introduced you to everyone I've talked to."

"That doesn't mean I *know* them."

"You know them as well as you know Peter Reardon."

"Not really. Peter and I have danced. We've had a drink."

I grip her shoulder, not hard but in a way that makes her know I'm serious. "For God's sake, Skye. Are you trying to drive me to distraction?"

She wiggles against my hold. "I'm trying to have a good time here."

"Being with me isn't a good time?"

"That's not what I mean, and you know it. I just—"

I grab the chain beneath her silky dress and yank.

"Oh!"

"Don't forget who you came with," I say.

"I haven't forgotten. I—"

I yank the chain again, this time slightly harder.

I swear to God, everything she feels on her nipples I feel quadrupled in my cock.

"Dinner is being served now. We're going to go back to the table, eat, and then we're leaving."

"But it's a ball. Aren't we going to dance?"

"No," I say. "We're leaving after they thank me for my generous donation, which will happen right after dinner."

"But—"

"No buts, Skye. You've already driven me out of my mind tonight. It's time for me to return the favor."

Chapter Forty-Nine

I take Skye's arm and escort her back into the ballroom.

The crowds have dispersed a bit as people take their seats for dinner. Servers bring out plates covered in silver domes.

We're nearly back to the table when someone steps in front of us.

"Don't you two look stunning?"

Addison Ames, dressed to the nines, of course, in what couldn't have cost less than about ten grand. Only she would have the nerve to speak to us after firing Skye. I won't be drawn into her drama, and I won't allow Skye to be, either.

"Nice to see you," I say shortly.

"And you, as always," she says curtly and then tugs on Skye's other arm and whispers in her ear.

Skye reddens slightly but stays calm and mature. I have no idea what Addie said to her, but this isn't the time or place to rehash it.

I whisk her quickly to our table, where we sit down.

Servers place plates in front of us almost immediately. "Don't let her get to you," I say.

Skye nods, and though she tries to hide it, I feel her demeanor change.

She places her napkin in her lap, picks up her fork, but then sets it back down. She's upset, and I want to help. I need to help.

And I also can't stop thinking about that chain beneath her dress that's begging for a yank.

"Braden," she says.

"Yeah?"

"She's trying to ruin me."

I lift my eyebrows, anger surging through me. Addie has upset Skye once again, and I won't have it.

"What has she done?" I ask.

"It's a long story."

"I've got time."

All the time in the world when it comes to Skye.

She sighs. "The day you went back to New York, I got an email from this place called New England Adventures."

"The hot-air balloon place?"

"Yeah, that's the one. Have you ever ridden in a hot-air balloon?"

I shake my head. "No. Not yet, anyway. I'd like to try it sometime."

"You'll be doing it without me," she says. "The idea scares the shit out of me."

I smile and trail a finger over her sexy forearm.

And think about those nipple clamps.

"Anyway," she continues, "they wanted me to go up in one of their balloons and take some photos and then do some posts. They had this great name for the campaign already. 'Skye takes to the sky.' I figured I'm new at this influencing thing, so I can't really say no to opportunities, right?"

"Right," I say. "Good to know you listen to me."

"God, Braden, why wouldn't I listen? You're an expert at

business. Look what you've done."

I nod. Yes, I did it. With Ben's help. With…some other help that I don't like to think about.

Skye continues, "So I called the person who emailed me, Tammy Monroe, to get some further clarification. I tell her how scared I am of plummeting to my death from a balloon, and she assures me how safe it is, how it's controlled by the FAA and all. She offers me a test ride for free, and if it's not my thing, I can bow out. So I agree to go on a balloon ride the next day."

"How was it?"

"It wasn't," she says.

I lift my eyebrows again.

"I mean it didn't happen. But I'm getting ahead of myself. We talked about payment, and I followed your advice. I didn't take the first offer, except that I actually did, because she explained they were a small operation and couldn't offer the kind of money Susanne could."

"Okay," I say. "You asked. That's what's important."

"So I agreed. I agreed because I'm new at this and I want my name out there."

I nod. "I can't fault your logic."

"So it's all decided. Tammy emails me the contract, and I sign it electronically and send it back. Then—seriously, like, a minute later—I get an email back from her canceling the balloon ride for the next day. She said they didn't have availability after all. Still, I expect her to send the countersigned contract later."

"Why didn't she send it with the email?"

"Well, I'm getting to that. I get in Instagram to check my first Susanne post, and it's doing really well. That makes me think of Addie, so I head to her profile out of curiosity."

"You haven't blocked her?"

"No. Why would I do that?"

"I saw the nasty comments she made on your first Susanne post."

"Did you? I deleted them as soon as I saw them." She smiles coyly. "Are you checking up on me?"

I'm a grown man. I don't embarrass easily. But at this moment, my cheeks are warming. "Just curious," I say. "About your new venture. I figured you'd block her."

"I thought about it pretty seriously," she says, "but I ultimately decided not to for a couple of reasons."

"Which are…?"

"Well, she's a major influencer, so I can learn a lot from how she does things."

"And the real reason?" I ask.

She smiles. "You're too much. How do you know what I'm thinking?"

"Ancient secret," I say. Except it's no secret at all. Much of Skye reminds me of myself.

"The real reason," she says, "is twofold. I don't want to be the immature person who can't deal with anyone who disagrees with me. That's Addie, not me. And I also want to keep an eye on her."

"Well done," I say.

"I have a good teacher."

She smiles again, and damn, that chain is calling me.

"So," she continues, "I get on her profile, and you'll never guess what I find."

Except I've already guessed. "Don't tell me. A balloon ride."

"Yup. Her post is all about how she's going up in a balloon with New England Adventures tomorrow. She even used a hashtag #takingtothesky, which sounds an awful lot like the name of the campaign Tammy pitched to me."

"So you think Addison somehow got wind of the offer and went to this Tammy?"

"How can I not think that? I haven't received the countersigned contract yet, and it's been three days. They canceled the balloon flight on me with the excuse they didn't have availability, but apparently they have availability to take Addison Ames up that same day?" She shakes her head. "I don't know how she found out, but she did. And here's the thing, Braden. They could only pay me two thousand dollars. Addie won't even think about posting for less than twenty grand."

"It's possible they offered her more," I say, though I doubt my own words.

"I don't think so. They're a small operation. Addie must have agreed to do it for two. Just to get me."

I flatten my lips into a line as a spark of anger ignites in my veins.

I don't ever think I've been angrier with Addison Ames that I am in this moment, and I've been ready to blow my top at her many times before.

I agree with Skye. This has Addie's stench all over it.

"I'll take care of it," I say.

"No! That's not what I meant. I don't want you to get involved. This is *my* problem."

"All it'll take is a quick call to your balloon place."

"Please. No. That's not why I told you."

"Then why *did* you tell me?"

She doesn't reply, just parts her lips in the way that drives me wild.

"Skye, when you tell me about a problem, I find a solution. It's what I do."

"I'm not asking for a solution. Please. I'll handle this myself."

"Are you sure?"

"Definitely sure. Let's just have dinner."

I won't push her. Not on how she chooses to handle her

career. To handle Addie.

I'll be doing enough pushing in the bedroom.

The salmon *en croute* with asparagus and walnut sauce is delicious, but Skye hardly touches hers.

"Don't let Addie ruin the evening for you," I tell her.

"I'm not. I won't. Addie doesn't control me."

"Good girl," I say, adding to myself, *Only* I *control you.*

"Do you want some more champagne?" I nod toward the bottle sitting in ice.

She smiles. "You know what I'd really like?"

"Wild Turkey?"

"Yes. Please."

I head to the bar. No one waylays me this time, as everyone's busy eating dinner. I bring back two bourbons.

Skye takes a sip, but her mood is still subdued.

Again, I don't press. She eventually eats about half her food.

Dessert is served, and then George takes center stage.

"Thank you all for being here tonight," he says. "I'm happy to report that we've surpassed our expected donations for the evening thanks to our generous benefactor, who has doubled all our receipts. Please give a hand to Boston's own Braden Black."

I stand to thunderous applause. I've learned to take the appreciation and applause gracefully and sit down after several seconds when it begins to wane.

George continues speaking, and I turn to Skye. "Time to go."

"Now? While he's talking?"

"Yes. Now. Before I tear that dress off you right here."

Chapter Fifty

I insisted that Christopher take a rare night off and I ordered a limo.

"Where's Christopher?" Skye asks when we're secure in the limo.

"He has the night off."

"Oh."

"You didn't really think I could wait until we got to my place to have you, did you?"

She gulps. "I...didn't think about it."

I move toward her, softly brush her straps off her shoulders, baring her breasts, and then give the chain between them a good yank.

She cries out.

"That's right. I've been thinking about those nipple clamps all night, Skye. Every time I looked at you. Every time someone *else* looked at you."

"No one looked at me," she says.

"Not blatantly, no. They wouldn't dare. But they looked, baby, and every time they did, I thought about what I'd do to you tonight in this limo. What I, and no one else, would be doing to you."

"What are you going to do?" she asks.

I yank the chain again. "I'm going to drive you as wild as you've driven me all evening." I crush my mouth to hers.

She opens instantly as I continue to pull on the chain in tandem with the thrusts of my tongue.

With one swift movement, I have her on my lap, her dress around her waist and her clamped nipples in full view. We kiss and we kiss and we kiss as the rhythm of my yanks on the chain becomes discordant and nonsensical. I'm enthralled. Intoxicated. Wild with passion as I tantalize her nipples. Finally, I pull my mouth away from hers, her lips swollen and parted just so.

"God, those tits." I lift her skirt and rip her panties off her. Then, holding her to the side, I unbuckle my belt, slide my pants and boxer briefs over my hips, all with my one free hand. My cock juts out, hard. "Have to have you now." I grip her hips and push her down onto my erection.

I've been aching all night for this—this homecoming, this joining of our bodies, this shoving of my cock into her heat. Every time I looked at her—those lips parted, those nipples hard, those brown eyes so warm and intense. She sits on me, all pink and creamy, and just once—just this once—I'll give her the control she craves.

"Ride me, Skye," I say huskily.

She begins to fuck me hard and fast. I don't care that the driver is right behind the wall. She doesn't seem to care, either. She moans, gasps, cries out my name, all the while knowing the chauffeur can hear us.

My fingers never leave the chain between her breasts, and I pull on it in the same discordant way as she fucks me. Her nipples are sticking out farther than I've ever seen them, and they're red from pinching.

Fuck. I made them red. Gorgeous red.

Her boobs bounce as she fucks me harder and harder.

"Damn. Those tits," I say again, yanking on the chain.

Then I grip her hips, taking over the thrusting. This is *my* rhythm now, and as I take over, I twist the chain between her nipples tight, parachuting her into an intense climax.

A moment later, I'm releasing, slamming her down onto me. With every spurt, I grow closer and closer to that place inside me. That place I never go.

That place I never thought I'd want to share with another person.

I'm no longer perplexed. No longer disturbed.

I'm fucking in love.

In love with Skye Manning.

And scared out of my wits.

When we both finally come down from our high, I can't move.

I embrace her, holding her close—something I've done very seldom.

I think about how she's consumed my thoughts since we met, how I left New York early for her and then had to stop myself from doing it again.

How I walked through the Diamond District and couldn't resist buying gifts for her.

How I wanted to pummel everyone who looked at her tonight—which was every man, and quite a few women—at the gala.

How I couldn't bear the thought of her heartbreak over the little puppy at the shelter.

I smile against her hair.

"We'll be home soon," I say. "I have a surprise for you."

Chapter Fifty-One

The limo arrives, and the driver opens the door for us.

I thank him and we walk into my building. I call the elevator.

Skye says nothing as we ascend. Nothing as the door opens.

Nothing as—

"Oh my God!" She clamps her hand over her mouth.

Sasha runs toward us, and she has a friend.

The puppy from the shelter. Skye grabs her and holds her, and the tiny dog peppers Skye's face with puppy kisses.

Joy. Pure joy in the smile on her lips, in her dancing brown eyes. And on my end? I don't think I've ever been happier in my life to see Skye so happy. I'm feeling pure joy, too.

And damn, it's been a long time.

"You like her?" I ask.

"I love her! I adore her. How did you know?"

"Tessa called me."

"But...you know I can't keep her. My apartment doesn't—"

I place two fingers over her lips. "I know. She'll live here with Sasha and me until you get a new place."

Or until you move in with me.

The thought doesn't even surprise me. It scares the hell out of me, but it doesn't surprise me.

My feelings are what they are. Not much time has passed since Skye and I met, but I was drawn to her as soon as I laid eyes on her, and everything I learn about her makes me want her more.

Yes, she can be impulsive.

Yes, she has a need to take charge.

But she's also kind and loving and focused and determined.

She's young, and she has much to learn about life.

But I want to help her. Help her grow in all ways.

"Thank you!" she squeals. "Thank you so much."

The puppy squirms out of her arms and jumps to the floor, chasing Sasha.

"Annika is paper training her," I say. "And she'll go out with Sasha on walks with Christopher and me. She'll be house trained in no time."

"She's three months old," she says. "It won't exactly be no time."

"I've had dogs all my life"—well, all my adult life, anyway—"I know what I'm in for."

Skye smiles. "She seems so happy now. Yesterday at the shelter she sat in a corner and didn't interact with her littermates. She gave me such a sad look that said, 'Please take me home.' I was distraught when I couldn't. And then Tessa…" Tears well in her eyes. "I can't thank you enough, Braden. Truly. This is the nicest thing anyone has ever done for me."

I smile.

A really big smile.

I can't help it. It's the joy. The fucking joy on Skye's face, in her eyes. I rescued a puppy for her. I swear I'll rescue the whole damned shelter if it keeps that joy in her eyes.

"Do you have a name for her?" I ask.

"Penny. I named her at the shelter."

"Oh? Tessa didn't tell me."

"Because I didn't tell *her*. I kept it to myself. I didn't think I'd ever see this baby again." She picks Penny up once more and snuggles her against her cheek. "I love her so much."

Again, I'm smiling.

As beautiful as Skye is, I've never seen her look more beautiful than she does at this moment.

I take Penny from her and usher her and Sasha out of the room and up the stairs.

"Braden," Skye says.

I finger a few strands of her hair. "Hmm?"

"Take me to bed. Please."

Chapter Fifty-Two

I don't hesitate. I sweep her into my arms and march to the bedroom. The lights from the harbor illuminate the dark wood and bedding.

She meets my gaze, her own eyes smoldering.

"I'm yours," she says. "Do whatever you want to me."

My heart races. "That's a tall order, Skye. Are you sure?"

"Absolutely sure."

I lift my gaze to the contraption above the bed. "Anything?"

She nods, trembling. "What is that thing?"

"It's no longer functional. It was a harness, where I could suspend a partner, but I found that sort of play wasn't particularly enjoyable for me."

"Oh? What about your partner?"

"Depended on the partner."

Aretha enjoyed it, which is why I had the contraption installed. Some consider suspension play edge play. It creates a heightened sense of vulnerability and inescapability in the person suspended, and like all forms of bondage, it becomes mental as well as physical. I've found that I don't like my partner to be quite so helpless. Partial suspension is another story altogether. I have no problem with that, but full suspension, if not handled with exacting care, can be dangerous.

I never want my partner in danger. I'm fine with her not having control, but with full suspension, I risk giving up some control over her safety as well.

Not on my watch.

"Why is it still there, then?" Skye asks.

"I just haven't gotten around to having it removed yet."

"Why not?"

"Because I met a woman who invades my mind every fucking second." I set her on the bed. "And all I can think about is all the dark and dirty things I want to do to her."

She swallows.

"Did you like it when I bound your wrists?" I ask.

She nods.

"How about these?" I tug the chain between the clamps, my cock responding as much as her nipples. "Do you like these?"

She nods again, inhaling swiftly.

"Say yes, Skye."

"Yes. I like them. A lot."

"Did you like it when I covered your eyes?"

"Yes, Braden."

"What else would you like me to do to you, Skye?"

She sucks in a breath. "Whatever you want."

I raise my eyebrows. She's learning more quickly than I anticipated.

She just gave me the perfect answer.

This sexual lifestyle that I enjoy is about what I want. My partner has the ability to say no, in which case I won't get what I want. But I choose what we do and how we do it. And if we're in sync—and I believe Skye and I are well on the way to synchrony—what I want will be what she wants.

I sit down on the bed next to her and finger the notches on the rungs of the headboard. "Do you know what these are?"

"No."

"I had this headboard specially designed. I have bindings that secure here and here, and same on the footboard. They'll hold you in place, all four of your limbs, render you completely helpless, Skye. What if I want to do that to you? Tie you up spread-eagle and then have my way with you?"

She doesn't hesitate at all. "Then I want you to."

I stand, walk to my highboy, open a drawer, and pull out a riding crop. The leather is cool against my palm. Already my cock is straining. I hold it in Skye's view. "What if I want to use this all over your body while you're tied up?"

"I want you to do it."

Fuck. Already I feel the crop coming down on her pink flesh, the burning pain it will inflict, the hot pleasure it will morph into.

I set the crop down and pick up the stainless steel butt plug. "This is the anal plug I used on your body while you were blindfolded. What if I want to put this in your ass and then fuck you?"

She clears her throat. "I want you to."

Excellent. She's not ready for anal yet, so I won't go there tonight. But her response shows me she's serious about letting me control her in the bedroom.

I set down the plug, pick up a spider gag, and hold it, already imagining it strapped around her head, forcing those beautiful lips open. "This is a spider gag, Skye. Do you know what it's for?"

"No." Her voice is breathy.

"It holds your mouth open so I can fuck it. What if I want

to use this tonight?"

"Then I want you to."

I narrow my gaze slightly. I don't want to take her further than she's truly ready to go. "Are you sure?"

"Braden," she says, "let me be clear. I'm giving myself to you. I'm giving you the control you so desperately want. If you want to put a collar on me and lead me around on a leash like Sasha or Penny, do it. I'm yours."

God, my cock is throbbing as I walk toward the bed. "For good this time? I get your control in this room?"

"Yes, Braden. I yield to you. I give up control."

I groan, push her onto her back, lie on top of her, and dry-thrust my cock against her. "See how hard I am for you? See what you do to me? All these things I love to do, all these toys—I don't even need them with you. All I need is your lush little body, your gorgeous parted lips, those luscious tits. Your control. But mostly I just need *you*, Skye. I can fuck you all damned night."

She opens as I slide my lips against hers, push my tongue into her mouth. We're still fully clothed, but I feel as though we're already making love, our bodies already joined in that most intimate way. I deepen the kiss.

Emotion coils through me, beginning deep in my core and flashing outward.

I'm in love with her.

I'm in love with Skye.

How did this happen? How did she break through my barriers so quickly? So easily?

I break the kiss, gasp sharply, and give the chain between her breasts a hard yank. She arches her back. Then I grasp the fabric of her dress and rip it, tearing it from her body. So satisfying to rip the fabric, to bring her beautiful body into full view in such a powerful and animalistic way.

"Braden!"

"I already told you. I'll have this dress remade as many times as it takes."

Her nipples are red and hard from the nipple clamps that still grip them. Fuck, she's hot. I could unclamp them, suck them, bite them…

But as much as I want to, I have other plans.

Only her black panties remain, and I'll leave them on for now. A strip of black lace and nipple clamps—the only clothing she needs at the moment.

"Grip the rungs of the headboard, Skye," I say, my voice low and dark.

I'm ready—so ready—to show her how I can please her in the dark. Not just the dark of night but the darker side of our sexuality and passion.

She doesn't hesitate to obey. She grips the wood firmly.

"Don't let go," I command.

"I won't."

I rise, walk back to the highboy, choose a piece of rope, and return to the bed.

I show her the rope. "Nylon doesn't cause rope burns."

She nods as I deftly tie her wrists in place, using the notches on the rungs. She pulls against her restraints, most likely an involuntary move. Very common. But her pulling has no effect. She's secure in my bindings.

I walk back to the highboy, grab a silk blindfold. When I return to the bed, I place the blindfold around Skye's eyes.

"Do you remember the last time I took your sight?"

"Yes."

"That was to heighten your other senses. But that's not why I'm doing it this time."

She doesn't respond.

"This time, I'm taking it because I can. Because you're giving it to me."

"Yes."

"You can't move your arms. You can't see. What else should I take from you?"

"Whatever you want, Braden."

I yank the chain between her breasts once more. She arches into the sensation, her feet flat on the bed as her hips rise. She pulls against the restraints again, and this time it's not voluntary.

She wants to touch me.

I allow my lips to curve into a smile I know she can't see.

Oh, I want to touch her as well, but more than anything, I want her control. I want her to bend to my will.

We'll both reap the rewards when she does.

I undress quickly and quietly, laying my tuxedo jacket and pants on a chair, my shoes and socks on the floor. My erection is ready and willing, and though I want more than anything to shove it into Skye's pussy, I steel myself.

First, the riding crop.

I walk to the wardrobe to retrieve it.

Again, the leather is cool against my palm as I grasp the handle.

It is now an extension of my arm—of me—and what it feels, I will feel.

What it does to Skye, I will do to Skye.

I head to the bar in the corner of my bedroom, grab the ice tongs, and place a few cubes on a small plate.

Slowly, I return to the bed.

Skye lies, her wrists bound above her head, secured to the headboard with my nylon rope. Her gorgeous brown eyes covered. Her body supine and at my mercy.

And her lips.

Those gorgeous bloodred lips are parted just a bit—that look that captured me the first time I saw her.

Her flesh, rosy and taut, so very—

Whip!

I bring the crop down on her breasts, jiggling the chain and clamps.

She jerks, and her breasts redden.

I bring the crop down on her again and then again.

As she reddens further, the warmth of her body caresses me.

Another lash. Another.

The sting of the crop travels through the leather as if it's an electric current sending an intense sensation through me.

"The tops of your breasts are rosy pink, Skye. So beautiful. Do you want me to do it again?"

"Yes, please. Whatever you want."

I bring the crop down once more and then again. She gasps and then sighs. Gasps and then sighs. Gasps—

"Oh!"

Fuck. I can't take it anymore. I pull one nipple clamp off, freeing her nipple. Then the other. Then I suck. Take that engorged nipple between my lips and suck hard. Her nipples will be sore tomorrow, but that's okay, because every time she feels the prick of pain, she'll know I was there.

She'll know those nipples belong to me.

I continue sucking. One nipple and then the other. I lick the pebbled flesh, nip at the hard nubs. She writhes beneath me, pulling at her restraints, moaning, arching.

In a flash, I grab one of the ice cubes from the nightstand and touch it to a nipple.

"Oh!"

Her areola shrinks up tight.

Nice. Very nice. So beautiful.

I trail the ice cube around both nipples and then over the tops of her breasts. She shudders, and the chill of her skin floats up to me, making goose bumps rise on my forearms.

I trail down her flat belly, letting the warmth of her skin melt the ice into a tiny river that pools in her belly button.

Again I imagine a piercing there—a barbell I can tug on with my fingers, my teeth.

I continue the path of ice down her vulva.

When I touch it briefly to her clit, she jerks and arches.

"Braden!" she cries.

"Baby," I say, my voice more of a raw growl. "We've only just begun."

Chapter Fifty-Three

I slip the ice cube inside her then, and she lifts her hips. I let her embrace the chill for a moment, until I can't take it any longer. I spread her legs and dive between them, replacing the ice with my hot tongue.

I devour her pussy, licking and sucking, moving upward to her clit but then leaving it before she can reach the precipice.

The ultimate tease. I'm good at it, and in the end, I know it's better for the woman if she waits.

I eat her and eat her, sucking the cream from her hot pussy, letting it sweeten my tongue and slide down my throat. God, I could lick her forever and never tire of the soft texture of her folds, the tangy taste of her juices, the way she grinds into my face.

But all things must end, and now I have something to say to her—something that may surprise her.

I leave her pussy then, and she whimpers.

I move forward, brushing my chest against her breasts, my cock aching for her heat. I kiss her chest, her neck, and then her earlobe.

"I know your secret, Skye."

"Wh-What secret?"

"You only come when you give up control."

Her eyebrows shoot up, away from the black silk.

"That surprises you?" I say softly.

She says nothing.

I'm not surprised this is news to her. She probably also doesn't realize that I know she never climaxed before me. I've been with a lot of women. I know the signals.

And I also know how to recognize a potential submissive. I recognized one that day in Addison's office, when Skye dropped the contents of her purse.

"I've given you climax after climax," I continue, "but only when you yield to me. You told me tonight that your fight is over. That I have your control."

"Y-Yes," she says.

"Do you know what that means to me?"

"N-No."

"It means you're mine, Skye. In this bedroom—in the *dark*—you're mine."

"Yours," she echoes. "Yours in the dark."

Her words feel like salvation, and the truth of them spears into my heart with warmth and love.

Then I thrust my cock into her.

She arches into the invasion.

"So much more I want to do to you," I say against her cheek. "So much more. And now that I have your control, I will. But for now, I want to fuck you like this, while you can't touch me, can't see me. Your tits are so beautiful, your nipples red from the clamps and your chest pink from my crop. Colors I gave you, Skye. Colors that prove you're mine here in the dark."

"Yours," she says again as she wraps her legs over my hips.

Thrust. Thrust. Thrust.

Such completeness. The sexual act has never felt more acute, more intense, more excruciatingly mind-blowing.

It's the emotion.

Emotion I've never felt.

Emotion I never thought I could feel.

Emotion I never had the desire to feel.

It's all part of this passion, this pleasure.

It's drugging, mind-numbing, like a kaleidoscope of color and sound.

My balls slap against her, and the smacking sounds drive me further toward the brink.

She's ready, too.

I feel her right on the edge with me.

But she won't come.

Not yet.

Not until—

"Come, Skye. Come for me."

She explodes around me, her pussy walls hugging my thrusting cock, pushing me further, further, further… "That's it, baby. Show me. Show me how you come for me."

"Braden!" she shouts. "My God, Braden! So good! I can't. I can't… Braden!"

She's coming and coming, and though she's arching and grinding into me, she's no longer pulling at the restraints.

She's accepted my control over her.

Accepted her place in this bedroom.

And my God…I've never been so ready for release in my life.

I give her one last thrust and release.

I give to her my body.

And with it…

I give to her my heart.

Chapter Fifty-Four

"You're beautiful," I say, stroking her cheek. "You have an amazing 'just-fucked' look."

I remove the blindfold and release her wrists.

She rubs them.

"Okay?" I ask.

She nods. "Probably more instinct than anything. You took good care of me."

"I always will."

She smiles, wraps her arms around me, and kisses my lips lightly.

I love her.

I truly love her.

I may not be ready to say it aloud, but I will. Soon.

She gazes beyond me then, out the windows to the illuminated Boston Harbor, a contemplative look on her face.

"What are you thinking?" I ask.

"How perfect this all is."

"Can't argue with you there."

"Yes, the sex was amazing and perfect, but I mean

everything else, too. The way the light from the harbor is shining in here. How it could perfectly capture…"

"What?"

"I want to do a post from here. Standing in front of the window."

I cock my head slightly. A post here? At my place? My private life is private. I've never posted anything from my home. Kay Brown will jump on this.

"You don't like the idea."

"I haven't heard the idea in its entirety, Skye. Go on."

"My three posts for the first contract were casual, formal, and dramatic. I've done the casual and formal. And I'm thinking…this would be perfect for dramatic. You say I have a 'just-fucked' look. What if I wrapped myself in a sheet, wore the lip stain, and stood in front of this window? I can adjust the lighting so it will work beautifully. I can't think of anything more dramatic."

I edge into a smile. "It's brilliant." Kay Brown be damned.

"Will you let me do it, then? Will you?" Her eyes dance.

"I will. You just can't post that you're at my place."

"I wouldn't do that," she says. "Our private life is private."

"Don't be surprised if the *Babbler* does some kind of exposé."

"Good point. I'll wear a robe instead of a sheet."

"God, no, Skye. Wear the sheet. You'll sell so much lip stain that Eugene what's her name won't know what hit her."

She heads into the bathroom with her purse and then emerges with her lips painted Cherry Russet. I watch in amazement as she sets up the shot. She tests different angles with her phone, makes adjustments to the camera. A few minutes later, she hands her phone to me and pushes me to a point on the floor.

"Stand right here. I want a profile shot against the harbor. Make sure you get a good shot of my lips."

She takes her place at the window, and though I'm mesmerized by her beauty, I instantly know what will make her lips stand out even more.

"Wait," I say.

"For what?"

"You'll see." I walk to my closet and find the box containing the black mask I purchased in New York. Talk about dramatic. "Wear this."

"A mask?"

She may be the expert on photography, but I'm the expert on Skye Manning's beauty. "Trust me. Go to the bathroom and put it on. See what you think."

She nods and traipses into the bathroom, securing the sheet around her.

She returns transformed. As beautiful as ever, but those lips—those sexy lips that are going to make Susanne lip stain fly off every shelf in America—are front and center.

She returns to the window where I wait, still holding her phone.

"You look breathtaking," I say.

"Remember, it's the lip stain I'm selling."

How can I forget? The mask makes the lips stand out like crimson on snow. "I'll take several," I tell her.

"We'll get a good one." She adjusts her stance at the window.

"Smile," I say. Then, "No, don't. Part your lips in that sexy way."

She chuckles and then moves her mouth.

"Perfect." I shoot several photos and regard the screen.

Skye can't take a bad photo. She's too beautiful. They're all stunning, but it's the second one that floors me. She's focused on nothing in particular, as if she's contemplating something almost ethereal.

"The second one, Skye. Use the second one."

She takes the phone from me and peruses the photos. Then she nods, taps into her phone, and then tosses it to me.

Cherry Russet lip stain by @susannecosmetics. Perfect for all life's moments. #sponsored

No other hashtags. She's a genius.

I walk toward her and wrap my arms around her. We look out at the beauty of the harbor, the moon shining down and casting silver sparkles on the boats below.

"I have more in store for you," I whisper, "now that I control you in the dark. Will you follow me, Skye? Trust me to give you all kinds of pleasure?"

"I will."

I kiss her forehead. "I can't believe what I'm about to say."

She pulls away slightly and meets my gaze.

"What?" she asks.

"Maybe we can give this relationship thing a try."

She smiles then, and of all the smiles I've ever seen on Skye's face, this one is the most radiant.

She parts those lips—

"I love you, Braden."

The words.

The words I've been feeling in my heart but was going to wait to say.

She said them.

Skye said them.

My heart fills with everything I never knew I wanted. She loves me. I love her and she loves me. We have a lot more to learn about each other, a lot more to experience together.

But in this moment—

"I love you, too, Skye."

Chapter Fifty-Five

After a beautiful weekend together—a lot of time in the park playing with Sasha and Penny—I take Skye home, actually drive her in one of my cars rather than have Christopher drive us, on Monday morning before I head into the office.

"I'd like to see you tonight," I tell her.

"I'd love that, Braden."

"Are you ready to discover more about yourself in the dark?"

"Very ready."

I kiss her lips. "See you tonight, then. I'll text you the details." I kiss her again. "I love you, Skye."

"I love you, too."

• • •

I text her a few hours later.

Be ready tonight. I'm going to take you where you've never gone before.

She replies instantly. *Can't wait!*

Neither can I. Will she be ready for what I have in mind?

I rub my arms against a chill. Nerves? Damn. Braden Black doesn't get nervous. Of course, Braden Black also doesn't do relationships. Braden Black doesn't fall in love.

Things change, apparently.

Things change where Skye Manning is involved.

A smile edges onto my lips.

I'm in love. Truly in love, and while I'm ecstatic about it, I'm also looking at tonight with a certain amount of trepidation.

I don't want to drive Skye away by going too quickly too soon. I want tonight to bring us closer, so I must tread carefully.

I must think about things I'm not used to thinking about.

And it dawns on me...

Being in love is about giving up a little of my control.

I'll make sure it's damned little.

After an afternoon of grueling meetings, I make a few calls. Plans. For tonight.

I text Skye again.

Everything's ready for tonight. Are you?

Acknowledgments

My stories are normally written from both the hero's and heroine's points of view. *Follow Me Darkly* and its sequels, *Follow Me Under* and *Follow Me Always*, are written from Skye's point of view only. When *Follow Me Darkly* was published, readers began clamoring for Braden's side of the story...and *Darkly* was born!

Thanks to everyone at Entangled for allowing me to write *Darkly* for my readers. Liz Pelletier had to get through edits in record time, and Stacy Abrams was even quicker with copy edits. Thanks also to Bree Archer for the incredible cover art featuring Braden's favorite bourbon, Wild Turkey. Thank you, Jessica Turner and Riki Cleveland, for getting the word out, and thanks also to Curtis, Greta, Meredith, and everyone else at Entangled for jumping on this project. I'm so happy to have all of you in my corner!

And thank you most of all to my readers. Without you, none of this would be possible. You wanted Braden, so here he is!

About the Author

#1 New York Times, #1 USA Today, and #1 Wall Street Journal bestselling author Helen Hardt's passion for the written word began with the books her mother read to her at bedtime. She wrote her first story at age six and hasn't stopped since. In addition to being an award-winning author of romantic fiction, she's a mother, an attorney, a black belt in Taekwondo, a grammar geek, an appreciator of fine red wine, and a lover of Ben and Jerry's ice cream. She writes from her home in Colorado, where she lives with her family. Helen loves to hear from readers.

Don't miss the Follow Me series…

FOLLOW ME DARKLY

FOLLOW ME UNDER

FOLLOW ME ALWAYS

Discover more sexy romances...

Sin and Ink
a *Sweetest Taboo* novel by Naima Simone

Being in lust with my dead brother's wife guarantees that one day I'll be the devil's bitch. But Eden Gordon works with me, so it's getting harder to stay away. I promised my family—and him—I would, though. My days as an MMA champion are behind me. But whenever I see her, "Hard Knox" becomes more than just the name of my tattoo shop. Surrendering to the forbidden might be worth losing everything...

Montana Mavericks
an omnibus by Rebecca Zanetti

Against the Wall: The last thing city girl Sophie Smith expects when arriving in Montana to oversee her latest project is to be yanked atop a stallion by a cowboy. And not just any cowboy—Jake Lodge, the lawyer opposing her company's project. But Sophie has banked everything on its success. She can't fail, no matter how tempting Jake may be.

Under the Covers: Juliet Montgomery fled to Montana to escape her not-so-law-abiding family, but when someone back home finds her in the small town near the Kooskia reserve, sexy sheriff Quinn Lodge must push aside his own demons—and try to contain his explosive attraction to Juliet—to keep her safe.

Rising Assets: Melanie Jacoby's chances for having a family are shrinking with every passing day. Her only comfort is her best friend, sexy cowboy Colton Freeze, but when a heated argument between them turns into an even hotter kiss, the boundaries of their friendship are blurred. But will their new friends-with-sexy-benefits arrangement destroy everything they once shared?

Made in United States
North Haven, CT
09 February 2022

15946908R00193